Halfnote's Song

A tale of the glass singers of Albermarle

By Lynette Hill

To Ruth

For Everything
Thank you

Acknowledgements

The author would like to thank:

- Dan Webb for his wonderful cover art and illustrations;
- John Jarrold for his insightful editing and suggestions;
- Sara Brook, Sara Jane Errington, Jenn Fay and Mary Tanzer, among many others, for their unflagging encouragement and support;
- The Cat Vacuuming Society Writers Group in Arlington, Virginia (USA) for their insights into the character of Octavia;
- And the Milton Keynes Art Centre (UK) for space to write.

Finally, the author would like to thank the Smithsonian Institution of Washington D.C. for holding a most amazing festival in 2002 celebrating the traditional arts of the people who live along the fabled Silk Road. This is where the author first encountered the phenomenon of Tibetan throat singing and became inspired to write this book.

Copyright

Table of Contents

The physicians have fled
The right price
Mama has the sickness

Octavia makes a promise
What thieves know
An argument renewed

It's not your fight
Caring for Mother
What have you done?

A new hope
Finding out what doesn't work
Is patience really a virtue?

It's time
Another idea
Discord

Defining health
Out of time
Getting ready

An unjust attack
How many dead?
Assignments

Robbie's voice
Purification
Lies

Right. Best to just stay busy then.
Verre House secrets
Back into your hole, rats!

No return
The mirror calls
Inside the looking glass

Hidden

Halfnote, youngest girl apprentice in Verre House of Glass Singers, knew very well she wasn't supposed to see Octavia's test. Only those who had already passed the singer's test – glass singers and masters of a glassmaking house – could attend. That meant, as strange as it seemed, that Mama stood among the crowd of witnesses and Grandma did not. It also meant that Halfnote should be in the kitchen with the other Verre House apprentices helping cook Alma prepare for Octavia's victory celebration.

But I have to be here.

The thought of Alma and the other apprentices hard at work in the kitchen gave her a guilty pang. She tugged nervously on the end of one tight braid. What if Alma sent someone to look for her?

I'll just make sure they don't find me.

Halfnote pressed her lips together firmly in the way that she knew Octavia did when she made up her mind about something. And no one would dare to disturb Octavia's test. Not even Alma.

Nevertheless, Halfnote kept very still in her hiding place under the black marble stairs. She'd made a spot for herself between some worn out bellows and an old supply cart with a broken wheel. From here, she could stay hidden and still see the making platform.

Octavia stood ready – back straight, hands clasped – on the platform, also built out of black marble. The freshly scrubbed hard stone still showed signs of the wear left by its use by generations of glass singers.

A leather work scarf, meant as protection against errant sparks, covered Octavia's carefully braided black hair.

Bright sunlight from three clear glass windows set into the rounded ceiling filtered down onto the raised forming dais just behind Octavia.

She doesn't even look worried. Halfnote felt her own jittery stomach clench. *Of course Octavia isn't nervous.*

But how could she not be? Octavia had to pass this test to become a glass singer. If she failed, Octavia would have to find another trade.

Of course she won't fail. Octavia never failed at anything.

Octavia took a breath and considered the wrinkles around the knuckles of her tightly clasped hands. She felt the indrawn air pressing out against the wall of her lungs.

Balance … she told herself, slowly pushing the air out again. *Harmony. I have completed these tasks a thousand times. I only need to stay calm and do what I already know how to do.*

Would the test never begin?

Halfnote took a breath and peered out at the twenty or so witnesses lined around one side of the former cavern that now held Verre House's main creation room. By sheer chance, or the designs of dragons, depending on who told the story, the walls of this rounded, underground space naturally caught and amplified sounds voiced from the center of the forming dais. Halfnote knew no other glass house could boast such a wonder.

By looking carefully through the forest of legs in front of her hiding place she could just find Mama at the front of the crowd of witnesses, near the cluster of Verre House staff. For once Mama wore her light brown hair in the tight braids of a glass worker instead of her usual decorative shells and loose Khelani bun. Tiny motes of light flashed off the clear crystal of Mama's dragon's head charm, sign that she was a singer in the Guild of Glass Singers.

The strangest thing, to Halfnote, was Mama's clothing.

For the first time that she could remember, Mama wore the full red and green robes of a Verre House singer. Mama earned her robes, and her dragon's head, in those hard–to–imagine years that Halfnote could only think of as *before.*

Before you were born, Mama would say with a smile as she began some story. Or, even more impossible to consider, *before I met your father ...*

As Halfnote watched, Mama's river green eyes sought out and found Octavia's black eyes. Octavia flinched and looked away. A thrill of nerves scurried up Halfnote's back. The nest of crow's feet around Mama's eyes deepened. Mama's mouth twisted into an expression both proud and concerned. Halfnote crinkled her own eyes in dismay.

Could ever confident Octavia truly feel afraid on this most important of days?

Octavia's test

Grandpa, resplendent as always in the full red and gold robes that declared him Grand Master of Verre House, stepped forward into the center of the room. He gave a polite bow to the trio of solemn-faced judges who stood to one side. They responded in kind. Besides the colorful robes of their respective houses, Grandpa and each of the judges wore the heavy gold charms that declared them grand masters. The senior judge, a white haired woman bent with age, gestured with one shaking hand. The witnesses fell silent. Grandpa, his coal black eyes bright with pride, smiled at Octavia, as did Mama and most of the audience. So did Halfnote. She forgot for the moment that she couldn't, or at least, shouldn't, be seen. Octavia swallowed and nodded.

"The test begins."

Grandpa's practiced bass tones reverberated off the rounded walls as he stepped quickly back out of the way.

"The test begins ... begins ... begins ..."

Octavia built up the fire under the cooling bath, bringing the coals to a steady, moderate burn. She wanted warm water, not hot.

It must be just cool enough that the glass solidified instantly when it dropped into the bath. If the water was too hot, the creation would remain liquid and lose its shape. Too cool and the piece would shatter on impact.

Octavia's test drop – a single, molten tear – hit the water and formed a perfect ball. Despite the strict rule of silence during a test, Halfnote heard the slightest hum of a group exhalation. Octavia had easily passed the first challenge.

Octavia sighed as well. The tightness in her shoulders eased ever so slightly. Sweat dripped from the edges of her leather hair covering. The sweat darkened the back of her cream-colored work dress; made new for the occasion, of course, and of a shade that naturally set off Octavia's raven hair and eyes. Halfnote felt her own shoulders relax a bit.

Octavia filled the granite melting box with yellow sand: one, two, three scoops and an extra sprinkle for luck. She worked the foot bellows until fierce flames surrounded the granite container evenly on all sides.

Halfnote didn't have to see the sand to know what happened next. The yellow grains of sand would sit there as the air around the melting box grew hotter. Suddenly, just as an inattentive maker might grow bored and look away, golden liquid would bubble up and swallow the dry grains from below. Soon even the last stubborn bits in the middle vanished into liquid.

Octavia started to sway and hum. The sand's transformation was complete. Halfnote bit her lip in anticipation as Octavia produced a deep, toneless vibrato from the center of her diaphragm.

Octavia's clear soprano, caught and magnified by the swirling grooves in the forming chamber's spiral granite columns, swelled until the vibrations shook the dust free from the floor. Halfnote clapped both hands over her mouth and nose to keep from sneezing. Any unexpected sound at this point would be disastrous.

The forming process began.

Breathing in a deep, rhythmic fashion, Octavia focused her tones on the molten glass. Carefully, ever so carefully, she wrapped the sound of her voice around the swirling ball of liquid. By the response of the vibrations holding that globe Octavia could tell its weight and size. By subtly changing pitch and frequency Octavia could shrink or expand the ball, or even divide it into pieces.

Time all but stopped. Halfnote watched the sphere coalesce. She shifted impatiently, knowing Octavia wouldn't settle for anything less than a perfect globe. Sometimes she wished Octavia could stand a little less perfection.

The pitch of Octavia's song rose and the whirling, glowing ball rose with it. Carried by rhythmic pulses of voice the ball moved up from the melting box to hover in the center of the forming chamber, directly above the cooling bath.

Octavia's song changed again, its vibrations intensifying. The hot and swirling ball elongated as she quickened her rhythm. Now the pulsing movement of sound began to push the liquid glass into the creation's basic shape.

Most apprentices chose a fairly simple object for their test – a many-petaled stalk of lavender or aconite, with the leaves and petals easily spinning out from the center; or an ornate, twisting representation of a dragon, again with the exterior decorations spinning out from the fast-moving center.

As usual, however, Octavia wanted to impress. Halfnote knew Octavia's plans. The two sisters had discussed little else in the preceding weeks.

Octavia intended to create not one dragon, but three.

She meant to make a sculpture of Mother Piasa from a central clockwise swirl. At the same time she planned to create Mother Piasa's two surviving children. And, just to show she could, she would make them simultaneously, with a counter clockwise swirl.

"But that's master's work," Halfnote gasped when Octavia first told her.

"I know," Octavia smiled. "That's the point."

That afternoon they had been assigned to do Verre House's monthly mending. They settled comfortably on to one of the double beds in the apprentice girls' room to talk and sew. Halfnote replaced buttons and straightened sagging hems while Octavia tackled ripped sleeves, burnt cuffs and more complicated issues.

"Grandfather doesn't think I can do the counter clockwise swirl." She glared at her needle and thread as if they had somehow insulted her as well. "I want to add color, too. Just a hint of green on the edges but he won't let me."

"Why not? I've seen you do it lots of times."

The sound of a throat clearing made them both jump. Halfnote looked up to see Grandma, still dressed in a simple blue house dress, standing in the doorway. Her long, thick hair was freshly dyed a bright red. It had been curled and wrapped in protective cotton cloths in preparation for her evening performance at Albermarle's Grand Dragon Theater.

"The craft exam is meant only as a test of basic skills, dear heart." Grandma's elaborate curls bounced as she spoke. "A simple melody clearly sung will pass. A complicated chorus performed poorly will not. We all know you have great talent. Why make things more difficult for yourself?"

Octavia's lips thinned and her nostrils flared but she didn't say anything. Halfnote wondered if it might be a good time to drop a button and crawl under the bed to retrieve it.

Grandma considered the girls a moment longer with the river

green eyes she'd bequeathed to Mama and sighed.

"Anyway, hurry up with the mending. Once it's finished you're needed in the smaller making room."

"I'm still doing the counter clockwise swirl," Octavia muttered into her sewing, but only when she knew for certain that Grandma couldn't hear her.

With this image in mind, Halfnote simply smiled when, under the quickening vibrations of Octavia's song, two smaller balls separated from the central sphere of molten glass. Some of the witnesses looked worried. They thought Octavia was losing control.

She'll show them. The making energy set her thick braids to trembling.

Halfnote's smile broadened as Octavia began a double vibrato. The main pulse of her voice shaped the central sphere while the counter pulse carefully slowed and separated the courses of the two smaller balls. Slowly, carefully, the three whirling pieces lengthened into their final shapes. Halfnote heard the in-drawing of breath around the room as Octavia's plan became apparent to everyone else. Octavia's voice deepened triumphantly as she added the final touches to all three pieces. Not just a rendering of Mother Piasa and her children, but a very detailed creation including perked ears, hooked tails, individual scales, grasping claws.

She's done it. Halfnote barely suppressed a cheer.

The glass screams

I've done it, Octavia thought. Arms extended, she drew in the deep breath necessary for her notes of completion.

A shrill screaming filled the room.

What?

What? Halfnote jumped, banging her head painfully against the thick stone above.

The glass is screaming. But why?

Halfnote stuffed her hands into her mouth to keep from crying out as she watched Octavia, white with shock, falter.

For the space of three thudding heartbeats every piece of finished glass in Verre House cried out in shrill, teeth-rattling tones.

Octavia's song and liquid creations all but collapsed. Halfnote watched in terror and amazement as somehow, by sheer force of will, Octavia smoothed out both. Then, as suddenly as it began, the screaming stopped. Octavia's black eyes darted toward Grandpa.

He looked as shocked as everyone else.

What's my key? Octavia thought desperately, and then found it in the echo of her own tones.

She sang out emphatically, pushing the tones from the very base of her diaphragm. Somehow she managed to restore the smooth current of the making energy before her pieces collapsed. Octavia drew a deep breath and forced herself to focus only on her voice and the three bits of molten glass floating before her.

Deliberate interference isn't allowed, is it? Octavia took another calming breath and shoved those thoughts away.

It doesn't matter. Hold the maintaining tones. Hold the note. Hold the note until the image is clear in your mind again. Hold the image clear in your mind and it can't help but come out in the music. That's what Grandfather says.

Just on the periphery of her vision, Octavia saw the astonished witnesses, Mother among them, staring around for an explanation. She forced her concentration back to her creations. She held her forming notes until all seemed ready, then took a breath to begin completion.

The glass screamed again.

Octavia, slightly less surprised this time, returned to her holding tones.

This can't be part of the test. That's the warning cry. But warning of what? Is something wrong with my piece? How can that be? This is just a craft test.

Hold, Octavia told herself as the glasses screamed a third time. *There is a pattern.* The glass cried for three beats then held for five before screaming again.

But what does it mean?

Hold the note. Stay on pitch. I've worked too hard to let this stop me. Whatever the problem is, it will have to wait. I know what I'm going to do. The image is clear in my mind.

The witnesses muttered to each other despite the rules. Mother, her face pale, clutched the arm of the woman standing next to her. Grandfather stepped into the center of the room. Octavia's heart skipped a beat when she realized that he intended to stop the test. She refused to acknowledge him. The glass screamed again. A completed piece of glassware shattered.

Octavia changed pitch and waited. The glass screamed. She began the completion tones. She worked much more quickly than she ever practiced but her images took and held their shapes: Mother dragon and her two surviving children in intricate detail.

Mother Piasa help me now. Falafel, first teacher, I call to you!

She held her pitch as the finished glass screamed again. Jagged spikes rippled across her unfinished images in response. Octavia waited out the scream and moved into a smoothing tone, quickly polishing her images.

She had planned a more intricate representation, complete with a tiny, bearded Father Bartholomew in Mother Piasa's claw but her control was slipping. She couldn't wait. One thudding heartbeat, two beats, she barked the command of completion. Her works dropped into the cooling bath just as the glass screamed again.

I'm done.

Octavia dropped her arms. She was now a glass singer. Or not. The judges would decide.

But why did the glass scream?

Halfnote completely forgot that she wasn't supposed to be in the room. She scrambled out from under the stairs and ran to embrace Octavia.

Mama and Grandpa quickly joined them. Octavia accepted their tight hugs. Martin, his bald head gleaming in the sunlight streaming down from the sunports, carefully netted the three dragons and placed them on the display table for the judges to inspect. The room, momentarily abuzz with excited voices, fell silent. Even the glass stopped shrieking.

The senior judge stepped forward. Everyone took a breath of anticipation.

"These pieces are wonderful," the judge said. "Absolutely perfect. Master Verre, your granddaughter is truly a credit to you." The judge started to say more but the loud cheers of the witnesses drowned her out. Everyone rushed forward to congratulate Octavia. Grandpa gave Octavia another hug and whisked Halfnote out from under the sudden crush of adults.

"Now let's go see what all the noise is about," he said.

Looking for trouble

Grandpa snagged a pair of spyglasses from a closet. He led a delighted Halfnote up the outside stairs to the balcony that bordered the four-story glassworks' slate roof. Halfnote loved every moment she spent up here. The glassworks, built into and on top of several caverns at the top of Viridian Mountain, rose above every other building in the city of Albermarle. It stood higher even than the Council Hall.

Only the mountain's summit – a rocky promontory called Piasa's Perch after the dragon mother – stood higher. A footpath zigzagged up the side of the granite rock.

At night astronomers climbed it to take their readings with telescopes made by Verre House. During the day the city's signal corps stood on the perch and used mirrors to send and receive messages from towns all across the plains below.

Of course Verre House made the signal mirrors as well.

From the balcony, it seemed as if she could see to the ocean itself; certainly all the way south across the farms and pastures and woods of the neighboring kingdom of Aethelstan. The trip by river to the great port of Tulum could take three months or more on her parents' raft. East lay the low hills and vineyards of Malmesbury. North and west the view ran smack into the tooth–like Gauri Sankar. This range of impassable mountains stood so tall that most never lost their white caps, not even in summer.

Halfnote took a deep breath, enjoying the tang of pine trees and the scent of cooking. She was mildly surprised to find it not quite mid-afternoon. Octavia's test had begun promptly at one, just after the mid-day meal.

Grandma often brought the apprentices here for lessons.

"Sit quietly," Grandma would tell them, "and *listen.*"

"Listen to what?" Halfnote asked that first afternoon.

"Everything." Grandma smiled. "Just relax. Take a deep breath and let it out. How does it sound? Feel the sun and the breeze on your face. Can you hear them? Breathe again and listen to each sound around you. How many different noises can you hear? What do they tell you?"

Now Halfnote automatically closed her eyes and opened her ears. Of the great waterfall at the city's western edge she could hear little more than a faint hiss. Closer by, iron shod hooves clop-clop-clopped up the steep cobblestone road just beyond Verre House's outer wall. The rattling and creaking of a conveyance followed.

Carriage or cart, Grandma would have asked. Carriage, Halfnote decided.

Wheels on carts usually gave off a deeper squeal against road stones because of the greater weight of their loads.

The horse snorted and huffed in response to the driver's calls and whistles. Nearby children played, their high–pitched voices echoing off stone walls. Families of thrushes nesting in the cliff face gossiped and chirruped incessantly. Locusts thrummed, rising to a great crescendo. The sound faded and then expanded.

A shadow crossed Halfnote's upturned face and the shrill chorus fell silent. She opened her eyes in time to see an enormous river eagle glide across the sky. The brown raptor hung a moment above Albermarle's red and green slate rooftops, then folded its wings and dropped like a stone toward Lake Kerguelen. Near to the shoreline the eagle caught a rising air current and, stretching out its wings, floated effortlessly upwards again.

The wind, a relief after the heat of the making room, teased Halfnote's tight braids and even dared to fluff Grandpa's gray braids and neatly trimmed gray beard.

Halfnote automatically looked past the jumble of rooftops and walled gardens to the banks of the deep running Khelana River. Papa said this river sprang from the mouth of an ice dragon who lived in the far north. The great current of water tumbled rough and cold through rocky highlands before racing past sprawling Albemarle and flinging itself over the precipice into Lake Kerguelen three thousand feet below. From there, perhaps stunned by its fall, the river meandered demurely through the southern plains of Aethelstan to the great seaport of Tulum.

Halfnote closed her eyes and took in a big gulp of air, hoping to catch the distinctive scent of the river that had once been her home. She did enjoy her life in the glassworks with Grandma and Grandpa and Octavia, but she also missed the scents and rhythms of life on the Khelana River.

Halfnote wondered if Octavia missed the river. Mama always said that Octavia's talent as a glass singer had been obvious from her first cry. Octavia's apprenticeship began two years before her own birth. Halfnote could not bring to mind any image of her sister on the Khelana. She never actually considered joining Octavia at Verre House until … well, until the day that she actually did. Now cousin Mischa and year-old Cadie traveled with Mama and Papa.

Grandpa's cough brought Halfnote back to the present. She smiled up at him. He handed her a spyglass – her favorite.

If you spun the etched copper casing quickly enough it looked as if a hunter chased a wolf that stalked a deer that startled a pheasant that flew after the hunter …

"Halfnote, I know you'll be careful with that."

Grandpa peered through his own spyglass across the southern fields and hills. She flushed and focused on the upper river. The wooden rafts of Khelani traders and the circular leather-skinned boats of the mountain miners called Gorani dotted the deceptively serene surface like so many water flies. Bright banners declared the clan loyalty of each raft. Halfnote picked out three banners for Clan Breydon but the rafts were too far away to identify the occupants.

"What do you see? Anything unusual?"

"No, Gr … I mean, Master Verre. Everything looks fine."

"Yes, it does," Grandpa murmured. He frowned and leaned against the parapet to consider the wide southern horizon. "There's no smoke in the forest, no disturbance in any town, no building storm. The river traffic moves about as calmly as it ever does."

But what does it mean?

"Does it always mean something bad, when the glass screams?" Halfnote asked.

Footsteps clattered up the stairs. Octavia, still in her sweat-stained making dress, hurried toward them. Her once tight black braids, now free of their leather fire ward, hung limp and undone about her shoulders.

"Master Verre," she demanded, "Why did the glasses scream? Was it me? Was it something I did in the test?"

"Octavia …"

"Was it because I disobeyed you and used the counter clockwise swirl?"

"Of course not," Grandpa said in a calming tone. He put a reassuring hand on Octavia's shoulder but she pulled away from him. Halfnote looked for a discreet way to squirm free, but she was trapped between them and the balcony.

"Are you sure?" Octavia's hands, rock still during the test, trembled visibly. A muscle in her sweat-covered cheek twitched, then twitched again.

"Quite sure. The cry of the glass is always a warning of imminent disaster. Your test was surely a great triumph and certainly no catastrophe," he added with a smile.

Octavia refused to be consoled. "Why during my test?"

"Because that simply happened to be the moment when the spirit of the glass became aware of the danger."

"But ..."

"You should not take it personally, Octavia. I am certain it is simply coincidence. This is the fourth time I have heard the warning cry. The first two times the glasses warned of forest fire. The glasses screamed in the middle of the night that first time. They cried out, as near as we could tell later, at the moment when a lightning bolt struck a tree and so gave birth to the blaze; the second time the glasses cried their warning as the flames neared the city boundaries.

"The third time," Grandpa hesitated and glanced at Halfnote, "the third time you heard it yourself. The glasses heralded the great floods two years ago. As you know, they cried out early in the morning as the rains began upriver. The flooding did not actually occur until late that night. Whatever the trouble, I am quite certain that even with your considerable talent you are not its spark."

Octavia glared at Grandpa suspiciously.

"You don't have to laugh at me," she said. "You told me to make something simple and I made something complex instead. But how will anyone know what I can do if I don't show them? Even Halfnote can make a flower and she's only just begun. I'm good, Grandfather, I'm really, really good. I just want people to see that. Why do you hold me back?"

Something unreadable flashed across Grandpa's face.

"Octavia, you have amazing talent. I am incredibly proud of you. It is true that I wanted you to do something simple for the test. I feared you would seek to fly too high and fail by daring too much. There is so much more that I want to teach you. To lose you now to simple pride ..." Grandpa took a deep breath and shook his head.

"Clearly I underestimated your abilities. Obviously we must find you some greater challenge." He smiled again.

Halfnote knew that expression. She always liked it when Grandpa sent it in her direction.

"You have certainly set a precedent for yourself, Octavia. Everyone will watch you now. They'll expect great things."

"They should. I won't let you down."

"I know you won't."

Octavia's eyes narrowed.

"Perhaps," Grandpa added gently, "one day you'll even learn to trust me. Now, enough. Clean up and rest so you can enjoy your celebration tonight. You've earned it."

Octavia peered intently into Grandpa's face for a moment as if searching for something. Then she whirled and clattered down the stairs just as junior master Geoffrey pounded up them. Halfnote stepped quickly away from the balcony's edge before Geoffrey could trap her there as well.

Geoffrey with his dark, heavy eyebrows and bushy hair always looked angry to Halfnote. He carried the muscular shoulders she normally expected to see on a blacksmith. Lorraine, Verre House's other junior master and Geoffrey's diminutive wife, hurried up behind him. Lorraine smiled sympathetically after Octavia as they passed on the stairs.

"See anything?" Geoffrey panted to Grandpa.

Grandpa shook his head. "Did you send a messenger to the Council Hall?"

"Yes, Master Verre."

"And the river wardens and foresters," Lorraine added.

"Good. Check all of our supplies, especially the food and medicines. And the cistern and well, of course. Make sure the fire buckets are full. Top off everything. And post two apprentices up here to watch for anything unusual."

"Halloo up there," a cheerful voice called from the street, the way one Khelani rafter might greet another.

"Papa!" Halfnote cried out joyfully. She rushed over to the banister and waved energetically.

In the middle of the cobblestone road by the ivy–covered wall stood Papa and gangly cousin Mischa. Both stood with their long legs widespread, knees flexed, balancing as if they still stood on a bobbing river raft. Mischa held year-old Cadie comfortably in the crook of one muscular arm. They waved cheerfully back. Papa's white teeth flashed in a wide grin of greeting. Instead of the river traders' usual knee-length breeches and bare feet, today they wore townsman's trousers, woolen shirts and leather boots. Halfnote winced in sympathy for Mischa. He hated shoes, even in town.

"Is the test over already?"

"Yes, Papa. And Octavia was wonderful. Her pieces were perfect, the judge said so, even though the glass screamed and …"

"The glass screamed?" Papa said, his brown eyes suddenly intent. "What …"

"Come inside," Grandpa called down. He leaned over the parapet beside Halfnote. "Ring the bell for Alma and come in. We don't want to bore the whole neighborhood with our gossip." The lines around his coal-black eyes tightened as he looked down at Papa and Mischa.

Halfnote wondered why her stomach always seemed to hurt when Papa and Grandpa got together. She glanced nervously at Papa, but he stood already at the gate, ringing the visitor's bell. The clear, high-pitched ping cut easily through the other noises of the area. Alma, Verre House's portly cook, bustled out of the kitchen door and across the front garden to open the gate. Her leather slippers scuffed noisily across the tiny rocks of the gravel path.

Halfnote turned to go but Grandpa called her back.

"You know Octavia isn't the only one who set a precedent for herself today."

"What do you mean, Master Verre?" Halfnote's shoulders hunched and her head dropped.

"You are aware that you should not have seen the test. We did warn you as we do every apprentice."

"Yes, Master Verre."

"You have created trouble for yourself by attending. The masters who examine you will use a different method, now, when your turn comes. Your test will be much harder."

Halfnote's eyebrows quirked up in surprise at this thought. Of course she knew that she would also be tested, but that moment seemed too far in the future to consider.

"Yes, Master Verre." She couldn't think of anything else to say. But how could it be more difficult? Could the masters make the glasses scream again?

They stood for a moment in awkward silence, then Grandpa's eyes warmed up. He patted her on the shoulder.

"Come on. We're needed inside."

They found junior master Lorraine waiting for them by the stairs. Blonde Lorraine, barely taller than Halfnote, smiled a greeting but then her expression turned serious.

"Master Verre." Lorraine tucked a stray hair back behind one ear. "I don't understand. The glasses screamed. It's a warning, yes, but of what? What's going to happen?"

Grandpa shook his head, his eyes grim. "I don't know."

Could it be dragons?

That night all of Albermarle turned out to honor Octavia's success; and to sample Alma's well-celebrated pastries and meat pies. At least that's how it seemed to an elated Octavia as brightly dressed guests filled the reception hall. The test had been both harder and easier than she expected. And when the glass screamed ...

Octavia took a breath and greeted the first arrivals as calmly as she could. Controlling the energies of the glass now seemed easy compared to her current struggle to simply rein in her excitement.

It was all she could do to keep her features in an expression of appropriate modesty as master after master, accompanied by the makers of their respective houses, came by to congratulate her. Each paused to admire her twisting, roaring dragons and to press a purse of coins or other small gift into her hands. After all, this party traditionally marked the moment that a young maker began saving up to open his or her own workshop.

I did it. I really did it. And with the counter clockwise swirl.

Triumph created its own music in Octavia's mind, louder even than the lively dance tunes performed by the hired orchestra.

Next she would become a master of the trade. And then ... mistress of Verre House? How would it feel to stand here as Octavia Breydon, Grand Mistress of Verre House? How would it feel to see her work displayed in the tall glass cabinets that lined the long, wide reception hall?

Hundreds of pieces sparkled under the brilliant light of the three-hundred-lamp chandeliers created by her great-great-grandparents. Multi-tiered tree-shaped candelabra taller even than most Gorani mountaineers added to the room's radiance. Lorraine had helped Grandfather make two of those.

Floor to ceiling mirrors on two walls caught and reflected all of this illumination back into the hall. Large glass cases showed off distillery equipment for physicians and brewers, dragon-shaped lamps and candle holders, the distinctive lenses used in telescopes and other samples of all the best of Verre House's creations. What could she create that would stand out in the midst of all these beautiful pieces?

Naturally, all of the glass masters and singers within a day's travel attended. Most of these arrived right at the appointed hour, Octavia noted. Masters of guilds most closely aligned to the glass singers on the city's council arrived next. These included the porters, apothecaries, physicians, cooks, astronomers, musicians, brewers, and Grandmother's own guild, the actors.

Intermixed with them came members of Clan Breydon and the other Khelani river trading clans close to Octavia's parents. Local farmers and winemakers, river wardens and forest rangers and other prominent persons from Albermarle and its environs attended as well.

Masters and makers from the guilds belonging to the Metal Workers League in Kerguelen trickled in last, as expected. But they did turn up and, somewhat to Octavia's surprise, in force.

Some of Octavia's elation ebbed as she noticed all of the guild masters and some of the others slipping into her grandfather's office as soon as they could discreetly do so. Perhaps they weren't here just to congratulate her. The other attendees filled the hall with the usual loud talk and laughter, but even the orchestra's cheerful tunes couldn't quite drown out a strong undercurrent of worry.

"They don't know what caused it? How can they not know? Of course they know. They just aren't telling us. Don't want to cause a panic, I suppose, but don't they know that not telling us just makes everyone more nervous?"

The heavy-set speaker wore a brilliant green dress, her grey hair worn in loose curls that fell below her shoulders.

She murmured in the ear of an equally large man as they made their way up to the front of the reception line. The man wore a sleeveless high-necked blue tunic over tight brown leggings. Both wore about their necks thick gold chains holding heavy gold time pieces to show their rank as masters of the clock makers' guild.

"Octavia, darling, wonderful pieces, really, what an accomplishment." The woman bustled up to present Octavia with a small but heavy leather purse. "We all knew you had great talent, but, oh my goodness. And to finish in spite of the warning... We'll know to expect great things from you, young lady. You've really outdone yourself ..."

Octavia did her best to pretend she hadn't heard the woman's earlier comments. She curtseyed and thanked the clock makers for their gifts. Could anyone really believe that Grandfather would lie about something as important as the warning of the glasses?

Halfnote carried a tray of raspberry and cream tarts. She managed to stay near her mother while offering these to the guests. Mama, as usual when visiting, was dressed in an attractive compromise between river and town fashion.

Tonight she wore a sheer, embroidered trader blouse over a green guild-style dress with a low-cut bodice and full skirts. Glass beads sparkled among her tight glass singer braids. She also still wore the clear glass dragon's head charm on a filigreed silver necklace that signed her as a singer of glass. Halfnote struggled with the strangeness of it all while Mama traded cheerful greetings and gossip with old friends.

Grandpa took Cadie to show off around the room. Halfnote couldn't help but notice, however, how often Mama's river green eyes turned to the closed door that led to the office. Papa and Grandma had vanished through those doors earlier, followed by a great many others. Every now and then another person would knock quietly and speak softly to someone just inside before entering.

"Mama," Halfnote asked during a lull in the adults' conversation. "Are you scared about the glass screaming?"

"I'm concerned." Mama took a raspberry tart from the tray. Mama always smiled with her eyes first, Halfnote realized, just the way that Grandma did.

"Does it mean that the river is going to flood again?"

"No." Mama frowned a little. "That wasn't the flood warning. Or the fire cry. It sounded like the warning for pestilence or infestation, but the note at the end indicated something else."

Mama spoke quietly. Even so everyone around them fell silent as if *listening*.

"Go on, Sweetie." Mama gave Halfnote a little nudge toward the kitchen. "You need to refill your tray. We don't want the guests going hungry."

A brown-haired woman in the blue and green party dress of a town resident leaned conspiratorially towards Mama. "Some say it was not a warning but the cry of the dragons; could they be returning to us after all these years?"

Halfnote's eyes widened. What would it mean, if the dragons came back to Albermarle? She offered her last tarts to some brewers and listened intently for the answer, but a burst of applause for the orchestra drowned out Mama's response.

An iron worker demands answers

As the reception line began to falter, gangling cousin Mischa – looking very grown up in new knee-length breeches and the stiff, embroidered ceremonial shirt of the Khelani – slipped up beside Octavia. He held a kitchen stool in one hand and a pastry filled plate in the other.

"Seat?" he offered politely. When she refused he plunked it down and settled himself on it.

"Pastry?"

"No. Thank you, Mischa."

"You sure? Everyone says you haven't eaten today."

"That's not true. I had soup for lunch."

"You had Alma's stomach-soothing peppermint tea, you mean. That's what she said."

"Well, I can't very well greet guests with cream dripping off my lip, now can I?"

"What? Oh, sorry," Mischa wiped his mouth clean with the back of his hand as a thin, very pale man in black robes studded with white glass stars came up to greet Octavia. "Who was that?" Mischa asked after the pale man left.

"His name is Hipparchus. Did you see the silver spyglass he wore? That shows that he's an astronomer. We create the lenses for their spyglasses and telescopes."

"A master?"

"A journeyman. You can tell the person's rank by the color of the necklace and charm that they wear – silver for makers or journeyers, gold for masters."

"A journey… you mean he travels, like a river trader?"

"No," Octavia laughed. "He's like a maker, only their guild doesn't make anything so they call their makers journeyers."

Mischa frowned, and then shrugged. "Still sounds like a traveler to me. Doesn't it bother you that I travel with your parents and you don't?"

"What?" Octavia gave him a startled glance. "No. Of course not. Why would it?"

"I mean," Mischa looked down and scuffled his feet. "You don't really like living here, do you? It's so cold. Even in the middle of summer. Everything's made of stone. It's just so different from the river. How can you stand it?"

Octavia stared in astonishment at her cousin. "I love it here. I can't imagine any other life."

Mischa goggled back at her. "Don't you miss living on the Khelana River?"

"No, not at all. I mean, it's nice ..."

"Nice?" Mischa stared at her, clearly aghast. "Nice? Compared to this stone prison?"

"It's not a prison," she said hotly, and then gave him a wry smile. "It sounds like we're both where we belong."

"But don't you miss your parents?"

"Hardly. They're here nearly every other day. You of all people should know that."

"Yeah, but ..."

"Mischa." Octavia put a hand on his shoulder. "It's all right. It really is. I am so very glad that we were able to make a place for you after … after the flood. You are a part of our family. Father always did want a son, you know."

Mischa frowned and opened his mouth to ask another question but someone began shouting.

"Verre!" A heavily muscled man with wavy auburn hair stumped out of the back room, his face dark with fury. Other masters, all members of the Metal Workers League, hurried after him. Some looked equally angry, others worried. The shouting man reached Octavia and then turned abruptly on his heel to look back at the crowd now staring at him.

"Verre! Where do you hide?"

"Now, now, Falchion," a balding master barrel maker called in a placating tone. "This is Octavia's celebration. Leave your arguments aside for once."

Falchion ignored him. "Verre!" he shouted again.

"Does he mean to fight?" Mischa asked, standing up.

"No, he just likes to make trouble," Octavia sighed. "He's Falchion, the head of the iron mongers guild and the Metal Workers League. You know that the metal workers and glass singers don't, um, get along very well, don't you?"

"*That's* Falchion?" Mischa put down his plate. "I should have known. He must have forgotten that Clan Breydon would be here too. Hasn't that iron fool made enough trouble for himself with the Khelani already?"

And, indeed, most of the river traders present were moving through the crowd toward the shouter and his entourage. Not just Clan Breydon, Octavia realized with a mixture of gratitude and alarm. Every upper river clan was well represented at her party and so were most of the clans from the Kerguelen area as well. Several of the city guard, although technically off–duty, began to move forward as well, presumably to try and stop any trouble.

"Oh, no you don't." Octavia grabbed Mischa's arm and pulled him back before he could join the other Khelani. "I won't have you fighting at my celebration."

Grandfather, with baby Cadie napping on his shoulder, also made his way toward Falchion. He paused a moment to greet this person and another, drawing snorts and giggles from onlookers as he slowly moved through the crowd.

Octavia thought, as members of Clan Breydon reached the iron monger first, that perhaps Grandfather took a little too long. Still, the grand master of Verre House managed to smoothly insert himself between the Khelani, angry on Octavia's behalf, and Falchion and his entourage before the two sides came to blows.

"Grand Master Falchion." Grandfather's murmur carried easily across the room, "How good of you to attend our little celebration."

"You know why I'm here," Falchion bellowed. Unlike Grandfather he had to shout to make himself heard over the buzz of the crowd. "You say the glasses cried a warning. What is it? What is it all about? Quit your posturing and tell us what's going to happen."

"Alas, we do not know. As you heard with the other …"

"I am not here for secret meetings and back room reassurances. You are the keeper of the glasses and they have spoken. I demand that you tell us what they say."

But even as Grandfather started to reply Falchion waved away his unspoken words with a dismissive gesture.

"This is a complete fraud, I say," he shouted to the crowd. His face turned even redder. "A fraud and deceit perpetrated on the people of Albermarle and Kerguelen. I won't be a party to it.

"The glass singers say there's a warning, but a warning of what? They can't tell us. They say we take precautions, but how do we prepare for a catastrophe when we don't even know what it is?

"It's all a lie, I say, a deceit and deception, meant to further the sorcerous glass singers' influence on the council. You may fool those already in your pocket, Verre, but you don't fool me. Or these others with sense enough to see through your lies."

Falchion strode out of the hall, brushing hard against Octavia's display table as he did so. Mischa grabbed the table to keep the pile of purses and other gifts from spilling. Only his abandoned pastry plate fell. It hit the floor with a clunk.

"Wow," Mischa said. "The plate didn't break."

"Of course not," Octavia said. "It's Verre House glass."

A young woman with the same auburn hair and strong chin as the ironmonger paused beside Octavia. She wore the tiny gold hammer of a jewelry master.

"I am so very sorry," she murmured even as she pressed a large purse into Octavia's hands. "Please don't let this stupid tiff ruin your party. Your pieces are amazing. We're really quite impressed."

She hurried out the door after the other metal workers.

"Who was that?" Mischa asked, eyes wide in surprise.

"Samantha, Falchion's daughter." Octavia felt equally amazed.

The orchestra struck up a lively dance tune to fill the silence left by the metal workers' departure and soon everyone was chattering loudly again, discussing this latest twist. A whole new reception line formed as sympathetic folk hurried to reassure Octavia that her party had not been ruined. Gratitude for all this concern quickly replaced Octavia's fury at the ironmonger.

Even this emotion soon ebbed away into simple exhaustion. Octavia began to wish that the night would end. Only the strict disciplines of her trade kept Octavia straight-backed and standing that last hour. Finally the last guests said their goodbyes and trickled out into the humid evening.

Halfnote greeted the end of the evening with relief as well. Her shoulders ached from carrying heavy trays all night and her head throbbed from all the shifting emotions of the day.

The orchestra played a last tune and the musicians began packing up their instruments. Mama rescued Cadie from Grandpa's shoulder, gave Halfnote a good night kiss and disappeared into the guest chambers.

The council masters finished their back room discussions and reappeared to gather up their companions before departing. Halfnote took her last empty tray back into the kitchen, happy to see the twins Annie and Alice, apprentices just a year and a half older than herself, already washing up.

Tall, bony Phyllis and nymph-like Sylvia, both older Verre House singers, helped Octavia carry the evening's largesse up to her new quarters. The rest of the household started sweeping up and dousing the lamps.

With the main chores done, Grandpa called the household together into the kitchen for a last cup of tea.

"What a wonderful party. Thank you all for your efforts. Naturally, we'll all want a bit of a rest in the morning ..."

Dreaming of the river

Halfnote doubted that she'd be able to sleep after all the excitement of the evening. Octavia's triumph did change things. Not all of the changes were good ones.

Halfnote realized this most acutely as she crawled into one of the double beds that lined the walls of the apprentice girls' room. She no longer shared a bed with her sister. Octavia had spent the afternoon moving her things to her new room upstairs.

As Grandma had made a point of reminding Halfnote, apprentices weren't allowed upstairs. Not even to visit.

Alice's breathing, already in the steady rhythms of sleep, rose up from the corner bed she shared with her twin Annie. Halfnote sighed and tried not to feel jealous. It wasn't the twins' fault that Octavia was five years older than Halfnote.

A light breeze stirred the treetops just outside. The room's clear glass windows revealed a sky ablaze with stars.

She settled in under the cotton sheet and began to count them. The night was still warm; it was nearly mid-summer after all. The solstice and its market festival were a little more than two weeks away. She'd all but forgotten about the festival in the excitement around Octavia's test.

Halfnote sighed again and quit counting. She and Octavia played another game sometimes when sleep seemed far away, by finding pictures in the stars and telling stories about them.

Halfnote could just make out her favorite shape, the one called Lyra. According to Octavia, Lyra had been a human woman who sang with the great dragon choirs. She lived in a time so long ago that no one even knew how to sing glass yet. Lyra loved music so much that when an evil mage stole her voice she used magic to transform herself into a harp played by the wind itself.

The dragons were so moved by this that when Lyra died, as all mortals must, they used their powers to give her a place in the stars next to Camyxis himself. Humans saw Camyxis as a group of stars but he was actually, Octavia insisted, the ruler of all dragons. Halfnote traced the stars that lined Camyxis' bed and, quite without realizing it, slipped into deep sleep.

For a time, she dreamed of dragons and harps singing in the wind. But the sound of the breeze playing in the trees and the humid night air soon brought her to another dream: the memory of a night when she still lived on the river.

The dream began as her waking memory always did, with an unexpected breeze springing up on an otherwise still night. The breeze woke the trees in the forest that crowded the riverbank where she and her parents were docked. The moving air carried with it a smell that she couldn't quite identify. The pungent gust ran its fingers though Halfnote's hair, providing welcome relief from the summer warmth. The raft trembled. A distant rumble crescendoed into a symphonic roar. What made a sound like that?

Could it be dragons?

"Mama?" she called.

A shadow coalesced out of the darkness. Mama snatched Halfnote up into her arms and jumped with her onto shore.

"Mama? What is it?"

"Flood," Mama gasped as she ran. Branches, invisible until too close to avoid, raked across their skin, drawing gasps as well as blood. Halfnote buried her face against Mama.

"Where's Papa?" Her heart pounded erratically. She could feel the drumming of Mama's heart as well.

"Behind us."

Mama tripped and stumbled almost to her knees. Terrified, Halfnote grabbed at her neck.

They almost overbalanced. Mama somehow regained her feet and paused long enough to improve her grip. The roar behind them, momentarily dampened by the dense forest, grew louder.

Other people called out and crashed through the thick underbrush around them. Mama, panting loudly, stumbled up a rocky outcropping. Suddenly she shoved Halfnote up into the branches of a pine tree. The rough bark cut into Halfnote's hands and legs. She grabbed hold of a branch and pulled herself further up.

"Climb," Mama gasped. "Climb up as fast and high as you can. Hurry."

"Mama!"

Halfnote woke with a start, relieved to find she was in the girls' bedroom. She turned automatically to Octavia for comfort, but of course Octavia wasn't there anymore. Marissa, now the oldest girl apprentice, slept next to her. The older girl mumbled and turned away, taking all of the sheet with her. It was warm enough that Halfnote didn't care.

The glasses had screamed two years ago, Grandpa said, to warn of the great floods on the Khelana River. Halfnote took a calming breath. The floods had snatched her from her mother's arms and flung her down the river's course, nearly taking her life and most definitely changing it.

Without the floods she might never have come to stay here. She couldn't imagine anything happening to Verre House or the stone city of Albermarle that could possibly be as dreadful as the floods. Not even fire.

Unless … could it be dragons? But everyone agreed that the dragons were Albermarle's friends and particularly friends to the glass singers. Dragon Mother Piasa helped human Father Bartholomew found Albermarle, after all. Piasa's son Falafel taught Melinda, the first glass singer, the first tones of power. How could dragons be a calamity?

The last warning didn't save anyone from anything anyway. Halfnote turned and tried to take back some sheet.

Fat Marissa just rolled over and wrapped herself up in it even more. Halfnote tucked her feet under the little that remained and gazed out the window. From the look of the stars she decided it must be near dawn. Camyxis, partially obscured by cloud, hung low over the trees.

Had the dragon ruler watched on the night of the floods?

She tossed and turned, struggling to find a more sleep-inducing position. This lasted until Marissa threatened in a no-nonsense whisper to make her sleep on the floor if she couldn't settle down. Halfnote lay stiffly on her back, afraid to move and certain she wouldn't sleep again.

Relief came, oddly enough, in the form of a storm. The wind kicked up and thunder grumbled, then faded away. The rhythmic tapping of raindrops against the window soothed her thoughts and drew her at last into dreamless slumber.

A new day

Octavia was up at first light despite Grandfather's suggestion that everyone sleep in. She found him waiting for her in the kitchen. They shared sweetbreads and tea while Alma bustled about preparing breakfast for the household.

"Now, my dear," Grandfather announced with a proud twinkle in his eye after they finished eating, "it is time for you to become familiar with the greatest treasure of Verre House."

He led her to his personal office, and for the first time in Octavia's presence, unlocked the door in the antechamber just behind it. The silver-trimmed obsidian door, reputedly a creation of one of the first singers, swung open on silent hinges to reveal a stone staircase. This led directly to the glasswork's top floor. New daylight, made gray by early morning clouds, entered through tall, narrow windows spaced at wide intervals in the building's outer wall.

Another shining obsidian door, mirror image of the first, stood at the top of the stairs. Octavia stepped aside so Grandfather could unlock it as well. The value of just one of those doors was more than the total earned by the glassworks over two or three years, Octavia knew. Even so, these were not the treasure Grandfather referred to, only the guardians of the treasure's entrance.

The second door opened to reveal a room that spanned the length and breadth of Verre House. Octavia stood in the doorway, struck silent by the sight that greeted her. Daylight poured into the room through wide, square windows in the walls and round sunports in the ceiling.

In every direction stood row upon row of ceiling-high glass shelves filled with parchment scrolls and square, leather-covered books with linen pages. Rows of glass tables, each illuminated by a sunport, occupied one end of the room. Glass readers, large squares of magnifying glass, stood here and there beside the tables, each in its own movable holder.

Scholars from throughout the area visited Verre House often to peruse the library collection. Octavia had once heard a gray-bearded grand master of the physicians' guild refer to this as the best library outside of the universities of Tulum.

"Here is the collected wisdom of our art," Grandfather said.

"Here you will find legend and truth in equal measure.
Here are challenge and learning to fulfill your heart's desire.
Our collection includes the notes and diaries of every master singer
since the creation of the art, including the original songs of Melinda
as transcribed by her grandson Ravel."

He indicated a thick scroll, tied with velvet ribbon and kept in
a gilt-edged glass case in a far corner.

"Here," he added, his eyes sparkling with mischief, "you will
discover that you have no idea what it means to be a singer of glass."

Octavia met his cheerful gaze with raised eyebrows. Of course
Grandfather was joking. Wasn't he? He smiled and handed Octavia a
scroll covered with tight, curling script.

"Begin by reading the tales of Mendosino. When you feel you
truly understand his message, come discuss it with me."

Halfnote awoke feeling surprisingly rested. Gray daylight
filled the silent room. She sat up slowly, not wanting to disturb
anyone. Then her eyes focused. The room was empty, the other beds
neatly made.

"OH NO!"

Halfnote jumped up and ran for her clothes. It was just cloudy,
not early. She'd overslept. Grandpa said everyone could sleep in a
little but not *this* late. Worse, she was the last one up. That meant
stupid cleaning chores all day and, if she was too late, no breakfast.
She stumbled into her dress and pulled yesterday's braids into a
quick ponytail. She dashed down the stairs and into the kitchen. She
got there just in time to see Robbie, the youngest boy apprentice,
finish off the last of the eggs and greens.

"You're late," Alma told her.

Halfnote's stomach gurgled sadly. The portly cook
winked and tossed her an apple.

"Eat quick, mind. We've much to do today."

"Don't worry," Robbie said through all the food in his mouth,
"I'll help you." Halfnote just glared at him. Robbie spent so much
time in the kitchen helping Alma that it almost
seemed as if he preferred cooking and cleaning to singing
glass. Octavia said that was because Robbie's mother had been
a cook. No one knew much else about Robbie's parents. The flood

that devastated the Khelana two years before also carried Robbie from his parents' home into Verre House.

"Have Mama and Papa left already?" Halfnote asked before biting into her apple.

"Yes, my love," Alma said. "They looked in on you before they left but Melody didn't want to wake you. She thought you needed your rest, after yesterday's excitement."

"I just wanted to tell them good-bye."

"Don't worry, sweetheart. You know they'll be back with us in a day or two."

Halfnote sighed.

A monster at the gate

"Of course the chores have to be done," Alma told a still sulking Halfnote after she and Robbie finished washing up the breakfast dishes. "But it isn't all a waste of time. Practice your *listening* skills while you sweep the front garden. Watch how the currents of the wind move things."

Robbie weeded the flowers and straightened the white painted rocks bordering the path from the front gate while she swept up dead leaves and other debris.

The broom's straw bristles made a light *whisk whisk* as they drew lines across the black dirt surrounding the wide stones paving the way from the visitor's gate to Verre House's main entrance. The *whisk whisk* rose in pitch when the broom crossed the stones. Halfnote heard her own footsteps crunch in the dirt and the *squeeee* of her hands rubbing against the wooden broomstick as she swept. The garden's boundary stones clicked against each other as Robbie placed stray rocks back into the smooth curving lines that marked the difference between flower space and foot space.

A light breeze whispered through the tree branches. A few more leaves floated down for Halfnote to sweep up. The brightening sun made no sound at all as it burned through the last clouds. A robin declared itself in cheery chirps and clicks from atop the apricot tree next to the gate.

Something rustled underneath the ivy vines covering the stone wall. Outside, she could hear several pairs of feet in heavy leather boots scuffing against the cobblestones. Voices called out to each other further down the street, some excited, some alarmed. It sounded as if a large and noisy crowd hurried towards the gate. The excited voices grew louder and closer. Halfnote stopped sweeping to listen but she couldn't quite make out what the voices said.

Robbie made his way out of the flower patch, wiping futilely at the dirt stains on his knees. "What's going on?"

Halfnote shrugged, vaguely annoyed by the question. She couldn't see over the wall any better than him. But amid all the uproar she could, just barely, hear something strange. She stood very still and *listened* as hard as she could.

Whatever it was sounded large and heavy, but soft at the same time. It moved slowly in the four-footed rhythm of an animal. What could it be? The noises grew closer.

"I'm going to look." Robbie pulled himself into the apricot tree and scampered up the branches until he could see over the wall. He froze, his mouth forming a silent O.

"What is it?"

"Hsssht!" Robbie, his black eyes wide, gestured desperately for silence.

"Robbie! What ..."

"Hsssht! Hsssht!" Robbie all but fell out of the tree in his haste to get down. He landed on his backside on the path next to her.

"Look at the wall," he hissed. "Look at the wall. Along the top. It's a giant serpent. A headless serpent. Look!"

"What?" Halfnote tightened her grip on the broom, ready if necessary to chase the thing away. In the dappling of light and shadow she didn't see anything strange.

Then something moved. She could just make out something long and round and grey slithering along the top of the wall. She couldn't see any eyes or ears in the dim shadows under the tree but the creature did have a dark, round opening at one wrinkled end.

"Is that its mouth?" Halfnote whispered to Robbie. He shrugged. As they watched, the grey thing grew longer and longer. How big could it possibly be?

The serpent (what else could it be?) slithered up into the branches of the apricot tree, feeling its path in a way that seemed natural for a blind creature.

But how could something have no head and still live? How did it breathe, without a nose? And where did it come from? No wonder people in the street shouted.

A clear ringing filled the courtyard: The visitor's bell. Robbie and Halfnote stared at each other in horror.

"Well?" Alma called out to them through the kitchen window. "What are you waiting for? See who's at the gate."

"Look, Alma." Halfnote pointed at the wall.

"Look at what? There's nothing there. Go answer the gate. Quickly, now."

The gray serpent had vanished. Where could it have gone? Neither Robbie nor Halfnote moved. Halfnote wondered why the person ringing the bell hadn't noticed the serpent. Perhaps it was hidden under the ivy that grew so thickly along the wall. The bell rang again. A new thought filled her with dread.

"Do you think it's the serpent ringing the bell?" she whispered. Robbie's eyes grew wider.

"Well, I never," Alma spluttered. "What has gotten into you two?" She disappeared from the window and a moment later hurried out the door wiping flour-covered hands on a white cloth.

"Alma, wait," Halfnote shouted as the portly cook shuffled toward the gate.

"Really, Alma, d...don't open it," Robbie yelled. "There's a m...monster on the wall."

"What?" Alma turned to look back at them. "What are you two going on about?"

With her back toward the gate, Alma didn't see the serpent as it reappeared above her head. The creature, still blindly feeling its way about, reached down until it touched the top of the cook's tight bun. The creature pulled back and snorted wetly, then reached down to nudge Alma's neck.

Halfnote screamed. Robbie screamed louder. Alma jumped and shouted, turned to see what touched her and screamed the loudest of all.

Assorted singers and apprentices scrambled out of the front door to see what was happening. Grandpa followed at a quick walk. Halfnote looked for Octavia in the gathering group but didn't see her. The serpent snorted again, this time in Alma's ear, sending a spray of slime across her cheek.

"Eeewww," Halfnote and Robbie said.

Grandpa just laughed. "Open the gate, open the gate," he urged Martin. The bald-headed singer stared open-mouth. "Let's not keep our guests waiting."

Martin ran a nervous hand across his scalp and then hurried to the entrance.

The serpent vanished from the top of the wall and the most amazing noise exploded from the street beyond. Most of the household jumped in surprise and stared in astonishment at the front gate, but Halfnote looked at Grandpa.

While everyone else looked astonished and a little frightened, he looked surprised and amused. Halfnote frowned. Didn't he hear it? Surely, she thought, Grandpa must hear it. That noise, whatever it was, rose and fell in exactly the same rhythm as the warning cry of the glasses.

Unexpected visitors

Martin reached up to pull the bolt to open the gate.

"Wait!" cried Phyllis, second youngest singer, no, third youngest now. Martin, his closely shaven head now shiny with sweat, looked back to see what she wanted.

"We don't know what's out there," Phyllis gasped. Her spindly fingers tugged on the front of her blouse as she spoke.

"No, we don't," Grandpa agreed genially. "So by all means, Martin, open the gate. Let us see what has come to us."

Martin jerked the bolt back and Ted, the singer just older than Phyllis, pulled the gate open. A man with a short dark beard, his hand still holding up the hammer to the bell, stood framed in the gateway. In his other hand the visitor held a short spear, the point grounded in the earth at his feet.

A spear? In town? Generally only the mountain Gorani brought weapons into town and they usually carried large knives or small axes, not spears. Albermarle's city guard didn't usually try to disarm the denizens of the mountains. Despite his beard, this man didn't look anything like a Gorani. Who could these people be?

Other people crowded up behind the man at the gate. Some of them also carried spears. They all wore brilliant fabrics of purple and gold. The bearded, balding man at the gate took a step forward and bowed deeply toward the assembled glass singers.

"All honor and glory upon this house." The stranger spoke in Albi, the language of Albermarle. He spoke well enough in a pleasant baritone voice but emphasized some of the words in the wrong places. This made his meaning difficult to catch at first. Grandpa, looking as surprised as the other glass singers, hurried forward to return the bow.

"All blessings are welcome and yours most of all," Grandpa replied in formal tones. "How may we serve you?"

"The Intan Negarawan, crown prince of Samoya, seeks the house of the glassmaker Verre." The man rolled the r's in 'Verre' in a way that made it sound as if he growled when he said it. Robbie's eyebrows rose in consternation. Halfnote stifled a giggle. Behind them a murmur of surprise broke out among the gathered glassmakers.

"Oooh, a prince," Alice whispered to Annie. "Is he married?" Halfnote rolled her eyes. Is that all they could think about? The twins were always falling in love with someone: the city guards patrolling the street, that tall astronomer, Hipparchus, and even, for a short moment, Geoffrey. Eww.

Grandfather quelled them with a glance, then made another bow to the visitors.

"And the Intan has found it. I am Fortis Verre, Grand Master of this house. Please come in. The Intan Negarawan and all his people are welcome in Verre House."

"On his behalf, I thank you. I am Chancellor Razak ..."

"Samoya?" Robbie whispered. "Where's that?"

"All right," Alma hissed from behind Robbie and Halfnote, startling them both. "Into the kitchen with you. We've important guests and they'll want refreshments. Alice, Dan, I need you as well.

Laiertes go the reception hall and put out the chairs. Get the others to help you. Hurry now."

"But who are those people?" Robbie asked as they rushed back to the kitchen.

"I'm sure we'll find out soon enough." Alma pulled out various bowls and spoons and a fresh apron. "Quick, quick. There's no time for dawdling. Robbie, check the oven fire the way I showed you. We want the coals banked and bright red for baking, no flames.

"Halfnote, run down to the store rooms for one, no for three cups each of ground cinnamon, nutmeg and … and the same of walnut meats – already cleaned, mind. We don't have time …. Well, hurry on. What are you waiting for? And don't forget to bring up what's left of the raisins."

One of the things that Halfnote liked best about Alma's kitchen was the wooden supply lift that let her ride easily from kitchen to basement and back again instead of stumbling up and down worn stone stairs with her hands full of things. The simple rope and pulley system was nothing compared to the complex system of chains, leather ropes, pulleys and winches that carried lifts of people and goods up and down the interior of Viridian Mountain. Mama and Papa rode those giant wooden platforms nearly every week. Still, she loved the smooth and easy way the kitchen lift rose or fell at the merest tug of her hand on the leather guide ropes.

The basement was pitch black and as usual she'd forgotten to bring a candle. After a moment her eyes adjusted to the darkness and the little bit of light that leaked down the lift shaft from the kitchen above. Fortunately, she already knew where most things were and the nut meats and raisins she needed were on the closest shelves. Even more fortunate was the fact that they still had some left after Octavia's party. She quickly loaded up a basket, then pulled herself back up to the kitchen. There she found Robbie standing on a chair at the heavy wooden preparation table, up to his elbows in batter. He vigorously stirred the thick flour mix while Alma carefully added a cup of fine sugar to it. The cook dropped in a handful of walnuts as well. She put the raisins aside for the moment, then set Halfnote to whisking up a frothy egg batter.

In what seemed like no time at all Alma was pulling a pan of cinnamon scented shortbread out of the oven. She sent her young crew out to the back garden pump to wash away the remains of flour and dough while she loaded the fresh-baked pastries onto three of the ornate glass trays reserved for serving the most important guests.

Name your price

Halfnote's arms ached from carrying yet another heavy tray as she led the way back into the receiving hall. Daylight flooded the hall through the giant window. Everyone gathered at that end, clustered in two groups. Despite the bright daylight the hall, shorn of its party decorations, now looked spare and empty. The grim-faced Samoyan entourage of about twenty or so clumped together in one corner. Halfnote thought they looked nervous. She wondered what there was in Verre House that could scare anyone.

Several of the Samoyans carried spears and stood at the edges of the group as if on guard. All of the Samoyans, male and female alike, wore purple and gold cotton fabrics wrapped skirt-like around their waists. The women wore embroidered blouses very like those of the Khelani while the men wore a sort of sleeveless tunic. They were dark skinned, even darker than the Khelani. Except for a grey-headed few they had thick black hair, but curly instead of straight. Most of the men were clean shaven, just like the men of Aethelstan.

Halfnote realized that she had encountered a few Samoyans before, in the marketplace of Tulum. She remembered Papa telling her that they lived on a group of large islands far across the ocean. The Samoyans traveled, Papa said, in giant winged ships carried along by the wind. The mountains on Samoya's islands were called *volcanoes* because they breathed fire and smoke just like dragons.

Grandpa sat in a straight-backed chair with junior masters Geoffrey and Lorraine standing on each side. Octavia, looking very serious and a little self-conscious, stood with the rest of the Verre House singers behind Grandpa.

"Go on, already," Alice hissed. "Quit blocking the door."

"Madam?" Halfnote offered her pastries to the closest person, a grey-haired woman nearly as short as Lorraine. The woman's heavily lined face might have seemed kindly if not for the tension that deepened the grooves around her narrow mouth and almond-shaped eyes. The woman, intent on the words of the man addressing Grandpa, started when Halfnote spoke. She nearly upset the tray of pastries. Others in her party seemed caught off guard as well. One man's hand dropped to the hilt of the large knife he wore at his waist.

The speaker, a young man with long, curly hair that glistened with some kind of oil, turned and glared at them. Halfnote froze in embarrassment. So did the woman.

"Apologies," the woman stuttered. She spoke in Albi but with a heavy accent. "I ... apologies." She snatched a pastry from Halfnote's tray and gestured for others in the Samoyan party to do so as well. Other visitors hurried to comply.

Grandpa glanced at Halfnote without expression, then returned his attention to the gaudily dressed speaker.

It's not my fault, Halfnote wanted to protest even as the nervous guests quickly emptied her tray. *Alma told us to offer refreshments. I don't know why that lady got so scared.*

Strangely enough, the incident did seem to relax the Samoyans. Those not participating in the discussion took the proffered refreshments and began to look around the hall at the glassware on display. They appeared particularly impressed by the tree-shaped candelabra and the wall-sized window. Halfnote and the other servers, in response to a frown and a wave from Alma, backed up to stand against the wall near the kitchen, out of the way but ready to serve again as needed. The speaker, who wore gold, snakelike bracelets around his upper arms and a golden coil on his head, continued in a slightly nasal voice pitched to second tenor.

"That must be the prince," Robbie whispered in Halfnote's ear. She nodded. The Intan ... something ... the man at the gate had called him.

The Intan snapped his fingers and the man from the gate, Chancellor Razak, hurried forward. The balding chancellor carried a large leather bag in both hands. The Intan grabbed the bag and flung it down on the floor in front of Grandpa. It landed with a loud thud against the oak floorboards. Phyllis and the other Verre House singers gasped as an amazing quantity of jewels and gold coins spilled out.

"As I said," the Intan made an extravagant gesture, "you can name your price. We will pay anything you ask for the creation of the *Hygeia paraphasis*."

Grandpa's frown deepened. "The cost would be considerable, Intan Negarawan, but I assure you it is not a matter of price."

"Do not waste time with these petty tactics, old man. I told you, haggling is unnecessary."

Halfnote gasped aloud at his rudeness. Grandpa's eyes flickered in her direction before he replied to the Samoyan prince in a voice tinted with danger.

"Beware the hasty promise, Intan. The cost for supplies needed to make the piece you seek is quite high. But these arguments are irrelevant. As you say, negotiation is pointless. I am unable to accept the commission. At any price," he added with a nod toward the treasure spilled out across the floor.

"The creation of the *Hygeia paraphasis*, the so called healing mirror, is banned by our guild and by the rulers of every country that I am aware of – including Samoya."

"While my father lies ill, my word is law in Samoya. I tell you now, make the mirror."

A what? Halfnote wondered. What did they want?

"What's a *Hygeia p...p ....*?" Robbie whispered. A sharp look from Annie hushed him. Halfnote shrugged. She didn't know either.

The woman with the worn face and grey hair, the one who nearly upset Halfnote's tray, stepped up. She glanced at the Intan.

"My physician." The Intan waved her forward. "Argana. She will help you create the mirror." An unhappy look, quickly suppressed, passed across Argana's face. Grandpa inclined his head politely and she bowed deeply in reply.

"My lord glassmaker." The healer spoke in a low, timbered alto. Halfnote decided that she liked the woman's voice, and therefore the woman. She didn't like the Intan's shrill tones at all. "I will do anything to help you make the *Hygeia paraphasis*. The physicians of Samoya were helpless against this most dreadful disease."

"Do you understand the risks involved in the healing mirror's creation?" Grandpa watched her expression with narrowed eyes.

"Not all, perhaps." Argana ignored the Intan's angry look and met Grandpa's sharp gaze with calm self-assurance. "But I do understand that I could die in the making of it."

"As could I. As could anyone else involved in the project. In fact, making the *Hygeia paraphasis* would risk the life of everyone here, including the lives of these innocent children serving pastries. The mirror in its most dangerous phase could swallow our very souls. Do you consider this an acceptable risk?"

Halfnote heard Robbie gasp and struggled to keep her own features as calm as possible, the way Octavia would. Glass that could swallow souls? She'd never heard of such a thing, not even in the scary stories Marissa told in the apprentice room when they were all supposed to be asleep.

Octavia, standing next to Martin and Sylvia, also struggled to keep her expression calm. Had she heard Grandfather correctly? No wonder he looked so grim.

There were natural dangers inherent in glass singing, especially from fire, but she had never heard of any piece that could kill just from the making. People sometimes accused glass singers of sorcery. She had always dismissed those charges as nonsense. But glass that could swallow souls?

What else have they kept from me?

And how was such a thing possible?

She *would* find out. She meant to learn everything about glass singing and this news just made her more determined.

Just let anyone try and stop her.

"But you've done it before," the Intan protested, his voice becoming even more shrill with frustration. "In Tulum they say that you, Verre, have made several healing mirrors. With this experience, surely failure is unlikely."

Grandfather's voice turned bleak. "As a young maker, I helped my master create three such mirrors. The first two took form easily enough. Our third attempt, however, failed horribly. The incomplete mirror devoured my cousin Devin, an apprentice of great talent and unfinished training. It took no more than a moment's distraction to create tragedy. In an instant the *Hygeia paraphasis* became a *Hygeia mortolo*, a cursed and horrible object. Its ravenous appetite threatened all of Tulum. We had no choice but to destroy the mirror and Devin with it. Did they not tell you that as well?"

Devin? I've heard that name before ... but not how he died.

"I do not care to face such a choice again," Grandfather continued. "Two other singers died in the struggle to destroy the piece. Find a mirror already made if you must have one."

"Where are they? Do you know? Of course we sought them even as we travelled here. One mirror went to Samoya, years ago. It was destroyed in a house fire." Grandfather's eyebrows twitched as if in surprise but he said nothing. "The glass singers in Tulum said the second mirror went to Malmesbury, to a rich vintner."

Grandfather nodded. "That is my understanding."

"We dispatched agents to Malmesbury. They have not found anyone who knows of any such mirror. Most say they have never even heard of a healing mirror. In all our searching we found no word of any others. Our people are dying. We dare not delay."

"Master Verre." Argana stepped forward again after a diffident glance at the Intan. "We understand your concerns. But all Samoya stands in danger now of losing cousin, brother, mother. Many are dead already. The king himself lies ill. No one can find a remedy against it. We have tried every possible cure and none have had any effect. Naturally you care for your household. Surely steps can be taken to protect them. In Samoya our families have no protection. Without help, they will die. All who contract the disease die."

A new star in the heavens?

"All right," Alma hissed from behind, startling Halfnote into nearly dropping her tray again. "Back into the kitchen." The cook set her apprentices to washing this latest set of dishes while she considered how to prepare for the next meal.

"Will they stay and eat with us?" Robbie asked. Alma shrugged and frowned.

The Samoyans themselves answered that question a few moments later by leaving. Halfnote, glancing out the kitchen window, caught a glance of the Intan. His face contorted with fury as he led his people out of Verre House. The strange noise sounded again, as loud as the first time, just as the front gate slammed shut behind the last Samoyan. Startled birds scattered in every direction, chattering their complaints.

She peered out the kitchen window to see what could possibly cause such a racket. Even the portly cook glanced outside before scolding Halfnote back to work.

The mid-day meal was quiet, attended only by singers and apprentices. At Grandpa's request, Alma sent Dan and Laiertes to his office with trays of food for himself and Geoffrey and Lorraine.

To Halfnote's annoyance, Octavia spent the meal at the other end of the table. She carried on an intense conversation about the definition of harmony with Sylvia and Frank, the two oldest singers. Frank waved his spectacles about in one hand as he spoke.

Everyone expected Sylvia to test for junior master by the end of the year. Frank would probably test shortly thereafter. Skinny Sylvia always looked too frail to sing, but no one who heard her voice doubted her ability.

No one mentioned the Samoyans as they ate. No one smiled much, either, and everyone hurried away after eating as if trying to avoid something unpleasant.

To Halfnote's surprise, Geoffrey, his black eyebrows making a thick hedge line across his forehead, appeared in the kitchen just as she and Robbie finished with the washing up.

"Sorry, Alma, but I've come to take your apprentices away. They've got some real work to do. Master Verre says we're falling behind, what with everything that's happened. And," he announced, bouncing on his toes, "business is increasing. We received three new orders from the astronomer's guild just this morning."

Halfnote and Robbie regarded the junior master warily. Geoffrey actually looked happy.

"Take my helpers? Well, go on, then. It'll be cold soup for you this evening," Alma replied, her stern expression belied by the twinkle in her eyes.

"Good thing Lorraine and I planned on dinner at home." Geoffrey broke into a rare smile.

"I'll just have a quick word with Lorraine," Alma winked at Halfnote and Robbie, "to make sure it's you that does the cooking, then." Her eyebrows crimped. "Three orders from the astronomers in one day? Is there a new star in the heavens?"

"No." Geoffrey grinned. Halfnote and Robbie exchanged looks of alarm. But before they could get too worried the junior master explained: "That fool of an iron monger, Falchion, is trying to organize a boycott against us, to force Master Verre to explain the meaning of the warning cry. Only everyone's mad at Falchion for making a scene at Octavia's celebration and now we're getting even more business."

Two barrels filled with coarse, red sand awaited the apprentices in the back garden.

"Red s…sand?" Robbie said, cocking his head at the sight. "I've n…never …"

"That's right." Geoffrey cut him off. "Heavy red sand. And what do we use it for? Hmmm?" His black eyebrows formed their usual thunderclouds as he glared down at them.

"Lenses?" Halfnote half guessed. "For telescopes. The coarse sand makes a heavier glass that can hold the … the shape that makes them see so far."

"Exactly right," Geoffrey said. "For telescopes, spyglasses, reading glasses and similar items. And the word you're looking for is 'curvature.' The tightness of the lens' curvature, assuming the swirl is even across a properly polished lens, dictates how far it will see."

What? Halfnote glanced at Robbie but he looked just as puzzled. Still, Geoffrey, his dark brows sharply contracted, watched them expectantly. She took a breath, met his gaze and nodded as if she understood.

"Don't worry," she whispered to Robbie when Geoffrey glanced away, "I'll ask Octavia what he means." The crinkles on Robbie's forehead smoothed out.

"Excellent," Geoffrey said. "Now, we need all of this sand sifted into three lots, very fine, fine and grit, by suppertime. And stored in the upper supply room."

"A…all this … ?" Robbie whispered after the junior master strode off.

"We can do it," Halfnote said confidently. "I helped Mama and Papa with this sometimes."

They spent the rest of the afternoon on the task, sneezing and coughing in the dust they raised until Frank walked by. He muttered something about "that idiot Geoff" and made them tie scarves over the bottom half of their faces.

"I know it's uncomfortable in this hot weather," he added, though neither Robbie nor Halfnote complained, "but we need all our sand for glass. You get too much of that stuff up your nose and you'll end up with a permanent cough, like an old Gorani miner.

"Dan and I are on watch on the balcony this afternoon." Sunlight sparkled off the lenses of Frank's spectacles. "Give us a yell when you're done. We'll help you move it."

Learn to control those voices

That night Halfnote climbed gratefully into bed, too tired to ask the twins Annie and Alice what they were giggling about. Marissa dashed into the girls' room at the last minute and dove fully clothed into bed next to Halfnote. She jerked the pleated quilt over her head despite the night's moist warmth. Halfnote didn't have to ask why. The heavy tread that could only be Phyllis' sounded clearly in the stairwell just outside the door.

Alice blew out the last candle and they all lay down, feigning sleep. Phyllis rapped her knuckles sharply on the door frame and grated "bedtime." Marissa responded with a loud and very fake sounding snore.

Halfnote and the twins giggled. Phyllis snorted and headed up the stairs to her own quarters; upstairs where Octavia now slept.

Marissa whipped the covers off of her head and sat up.

"Guess what?" she hissed.

"Wait. Not yet," Alice muttered. The younger apprentice focused her quiet tones toward the center of the room. All of the girls, even Marissa quivering with impatience, stopped to *listen*. The stairs above still creaked with the sound of Phyllis' awkward footsteps. Other voices, perhaps belonging to Frank and Grandpa, rose up from below. The normally quiet Sylvia clattered up the steps past their door.

Annie blew out a breath of relief. "What is it?" Alice asked in soft and tightly focused tones.

"Are you sleeping in your clothes?" Halfnote asked.

"Of course not," Marissa sniffed. She hopped out of bed again. The faint glow from a stairwell lamp provided the only light but it was enough for Marissa to find her nightshirt.

"What did you want to tell us?" Annie asked.

"Oh, so now you're interested," Marissa said.

"Hush!" Alice snapped. "Focus your tones. Haven't you learned? You'll get us in trouble."

Marissa sucked in a long breath and clambered back into the bed, roughly shoving Halfnote out of the way without so much as a 'sorry' or 'excuse me.'

"But what is it?" Annie asked.

Marissa pouted a moment longer, and then relented.

"I ran an errand for Sylvia." Marissa focused her perfectly modulated *soft* tones directly toward the twins. Halfnote could barely hear her. "And Sylvia just told me that she plans to test for junior master in a few months."

"We all knew that." Alice forgot to focus her own tones. Annie hissed a rebuke.

"Yes," Marissa snapped, all voice control gone, "but did you also know that Master Verre sent official notice to the guild masters today, asking them to set a test date?

"And," she paused dramatically before anyone could cut her off, "he's going to hold auditions for new apprentices."

"What?" Annie and Alice gasped together. "When?"

The top stair step from the singers' floor above creaked ominously. All of the girls froze, listening to see if they'd been caught. Halfnote counted the beats of her pulse. She made it to 22 before Annie, the best listener among them, sighed in relief. "When do the auditions start?"

"Girls." Sylvia appeared without warning in their doorway. "You'll have to learn to control those voices if you want to keep talking after bedtime." In the darkness Halfnote couldn't see if the singer smiled, but her tones suggested it.

"Sorry," Alice said and all of the girls lay down. Halfnote frowned and considered Marissa's news. New apprentices; what would they be like? Friendly like the twins or grumpy like Marissa? And how many? Grandpa usually chose two at a time. Would any be Khelani?

Probably not, she thought with a sigh.

"When will Master Verre hold auditions?" Annie asked.

"At the Midsummer Fair," Marissa said, sitting up again.

"But that's only two weeks away," Alice said.

"That's what Sylvia said," Marissa replied.

Floorboards creaked in the hallway and everyone lay down again, but only for a moment.

"So you won't be the youngest anymore," Marissa whispered. Halfnote considered this. She wasn't quite sure how to feel about it.

"You'll like it," Annie assured her. "It means you will get to do some real glass singing and not have so many kitchen chores."

That sounded all right, Halfnote thought, and wondered how Robbie would feel As far as she could tell, Robbie preferred working in the kitchen. He would miss Alma.

"That's enough," Phyllis commanded from the doorway. "The light is out and you know what that means. No more talking. I need my sleep even if you don't."

Are you a water spirit?

The flood swept through Halfnote's dreams again. Raging water snatched her from out of the branches of the fragrant pine tree even as Mama pushed her higher into its branches. She bobbed just at the surface of the raging waters, another bit of flotsam caught in the irresistible current.

Something heavy and wooden pushed against her side and instinctively she grabbed hold of it. It rolled and she slid across it into the crook of a branch. Was it a tree trunk?

It rolled again, dipping her underneath the whirling waters. Just as Halfnote made up her mind to let go and swim for air it rolled abruptly back the other way, dragging her above the surface. The trunk slammed broadside into something that refused to give way and hung there for several minutes before scraping free.

Things unseeable in the impenetrable darkness brushed against her arms and legs. She pressed desperately against the soft bark of her unwieldy steed and shut her eyes tight against
 the sting of cold spray and despair. She never could say, in dream or

memory, how long she rode the tree, perhaps an oak, unseeing through the gloom. She did remember quite clearly the moment when she looked down at the tree trunk and could just begin to make out the outline of her own hand, wrapped tightly around a branch. A flood of relief washed through her. She wasn't blind after all.

The outlines of her hand and arm solidified against the darker dark of the tree trunk she rode.

In the first glimmerings of dawn Halfnote began to make out the shapes of other things caught in the torrent of water. Daily on the raft with Mama and Papa she watched the countryside slide by; never had it passed by so quickly. Her craft bobbed and rolled unbearably. Its branches, still carrying a wide spray of mud-covered leaves, protected her from slamming into the other debris that filled the roiling flood.

The sun rose higher, burning away the early morning clouds. The brown and silver waters spread out; did they even begin to slow down? Half a roof, its sodden thatch crumbling away, floated past. A pair of blackbirds preened themselves on its peak, apparently unconcerned by the rotation of their perch. The bloated body of a drowned cow bobbed alongside. Halfnote looked away.

Something seemed to clutch at her leg. She shuddered and kicked out at it. The tree lurched abruptly, plunging her underwater before she could catch her breath. It righted itself again, just as unexpectedly. She clung to it, shuddering and gasping for air. The thatched roof fetched up against a pile of boulders and stayed put. The cow's body bobbed on past it, carried off by the main flow of water. Halfnote's tree took her underwater again. This time she felt its whole trunk shudder and stop as if caught by something. She managed to pull herself around the trunk – which this time *didn't* roll as she moved – and up out of the water.

The tree rested halfway up a gravel bank in the middle of the churning flood. A line of half-submerged Willows marked what Halfnote guessed to be the usual border of the river. The main current flowed between the long gravel bank and those trees.

Her tree shuddered and scraped against the pebbly surface but didn't move off. A hand reached out of the water and grabbed hers. She shrieked and jerked loose.

She fell off the tree and scrabbled away in shock. Then she realized who the hand might belong to.

"Mama?" She grabbed the hand and the arm that came with it and pulled with all her strength. Just as she realized the hand was too small and dark to be her mother's, a head popped out of the water from underneath the tree. A boy, nearly naked, took a deep breath and scrambled on his hands and knees onto the gravel bank.

"You're not Mama," Halfnote said sadly.

The boy stared. "Are you a water spirit?" he asked.

Meeting the monster

The Samoyans returned to Verre House early the next morning. The strange blaring sound announced their arrival once again. Grandpa greeted them with all courtesy, ushering the party into his office and calling to Alma for refreshments. This time, however, he sent the rest of his own household on about their tasks. Only junior master Lorraine joined Grandpa in his office.

"That's all right," Halfnote heard junior master Geoffrey telling Octavia. "They'll get this settled now." Despite his mild words Geoffrey's dark eyebrows drew down together into a miniature storm cloud.

Halfnote gave Octavia a smile and a wave but Octavia didn't seem to notice as she rushed off. Halfnote bit her lip and turned to follow Robbie as he headed back to the kitchen.

To their mutual surprise, Geoffrey stopped them. "You two come with me to the back garden." He smirked at their startled looks. "Today," he announced, "you become dragons."

Robbie's jaw dropped. Halfnote instantly forgot her disappointment over Octavia's snub. She raced Robbie out the back door and into the back garden. They ran so fast that they didn't see the monster until they nearly ran right into it.

Fortunately it bellowed first. The ear-splitting sound all but knocked Halfnote off her feet. Even Geoffrey jumped back and used a word that she heard fairly often on the river but almost never in Verre House. She stumbled backwards right into Robbie and they both fell to the ground. She knew that sound; she'd heard it when the

Samoyans first arrived. She jumped back onto her feet as fast as she could and stared up at the creature. Robbie nervously followed suit.

A grey giant stood before them. The creature all but filled the garden. Its enormous leaf-like ears flapped in the wind while a snake-like nose stretched almost to the ground. It stood on four round legs that looked as wide as tree trunks.

Robbie grabbed Halfnote's arm to pull her away from it.

"Is that the serpent thing we saw on the front wall?" Halfnote pulled her arm free to point at the nose. Robbie frowned but didn't say anything more. As if to answer her question, the nose (*was it a nose?*) rose up and let loose with that same amazing sound.

"What is it?" Robbie asked. The beast was huge, much taller than the lanky Samoyan who pressed a shoulder and knee against the creature's front leg in a futile attempt to keep it from devouring more of Alma's cabbages. The behemoth reached out over the man's shoulder with its amazing appendage to rip a cabbage out of the ground and stuff it, bits of dirt and all, into its mouth.

Halfnote stared at the calmly munching creature. It appeared to hold a pair of white spears in its mouth, one on each side, even as it chewed. No, she decided, the spears simply grew out of each side of its mouth. A monster that grew its own weapons? She'd never heard of such a thing. Filigreed gold bands decorated the tips of the spears.

Looking up, Halfnote saw purple and gold tassels bouncing against the beast's broad forehead. These hung down from the purple and gold tapestries that covered the creature's broad sides and back. It also carried a polished wooden seat on its wide back. A broad umbrella, of the same purple and gold material, protected the seat. The tapestries were decorated, she realized, with the same symbols that the Intan wore on his clothing. The creature gazed back at her with dark, wise-looking eyes. It blinked and dipped its head as if in greeting. Then it raised its great … whatever it was … and made that same outrageous noise. Robbie clapped his hands to his ears. Geoffrey, in what Halfnote considered an act of amazing courage, hurried forward to confront the monster and its keeper.

"Here now," Geoffrey shouted. The man still pushed unsuccessfully against the creature's great leg. "You have to get it to stop doing that. It will disrupt all our work. How can anyone sing glass through noise that like?"

The Samoyan looked over his shoulder and waved at them. He said something to the creature. The great beast sank to its knees.

"Apologies," the beast's keeper said in strongly accented Albi. He wiped his brow and bowed to them. He wore purple and gold breaches and a tunic decorated with the same design as the creature's tapestries.

"Negarawan Gajah has found his most favorite food in all the world right here in this garden. I fear he will eat all of your cabbages if I do not stop him." The Samoyan spoke in a pleasant baritone, pitched a little higher than Papa's but better trained. He stroked the creature's … nose … fondly as he spoke. The nose rose up and draped itself around the Samoyan's shoulder.

"Yes, of course," Geoffrey huffed, "but it mustn't keep doing that … that noise. It disrupts everything we do here."

"I understand," the Samoyan replied, bowing. "I will undertake to keep him quiet."

Geoffrey's dark eyebrows drew together like thunderclouds. "Why did you bring the elephant here? And how, by all the dragons, did you get it up the lifts?"

Robbie, his eyes wide with wonder, froze as the creature's nose reached out toward him.

"Robbie, look out!"

"Do not be concerned," the Samoyan told Halfnote. "Negarawan Gajah has a great appetite but he is quite a sweet-tempered creature."

"The creature has the same name as the Intan?" Was that a polite question, Halfnote wondered too late. Mama said …

"Of course. Negarawan Gajah is a … a *palla* in my language, an ele…ah…fant," he sounded out Geoffrey's word, "in yours. He is the Intan's elder brother and the symbol of his house. They travel always together. And the lifts … they were a … a difficulty."

Geoffrey snorted. "I can imagine."

Halfnote regarded the Samoyan skeptically. "How ..." she started, but Robbie beat her to it.

"C…can we t…touch him?"

"Indeed you can." The keeper's wide smile broadened. "You are quite safe. Negarawan Gajah is as gentle with his friends as he is fierce against his enemies. But first," he held up his hand, "you must be properly introduced. What is your name, young man?"

"R…Robbie ... I mean, Robert D…Dinaldo."

"How do you do, Robert Dinaldo. And I am Maru el atta al Negarawan – the keeper of the ele…phant." Maru bowed elegantly, dipping one knee, his arm pointing out toward the elephant. The creature harrumphed and dipped its front legs as well, bowing its head toward Robbie. Geoffrey and Halfnote laughed. Robbie flushed but bent stiffly from the waist in response.

"And you, young lady?" Maru asked Halfnote.

"Oh yes, please. I am Arpeggia Melodia Verre. But everyone calls me Halfnote," she added as Maru and Gajah made their obeisance to her. She curtseyed.

"We are pleased to meet you, Robbie and Halfnote."

"Arpeggia?" Robbie asked, giving her a sideways glance.

"After my grandfather's mother. And Melodia for my mother, although everyone calls her Melody. Halfnote is just the nickname Grandpa gave me because I was so small when he first saw me." She blushed, partly because she didn't like the name 'Arpeggia' very much; partly because now she felt as if everyone stared at her. Even Gajah looked at her with his large, wise eyes.

"Indeed, a most beautiful name," Maru said. "Negarawan Gajah is named Negarawan for his house and Gajah because he is a most valiant warrior. He guards the Intan's greatest treasure."

"Treasure?" Geoffrey's heavy eyebrows quirked up.

"Indeed, yes. Gajah guards the Intan's honor."

Geoffrey scowled in obvious disappointment.

"But," Maru continued, apparently oblivious to this reaction, "Gajah is sad to discover that there are no more dragons in Albermarle. Is this true? What happened to them?"

"Myths and legends," Geoffrey said scornfully. "There were never dragons here or anywhere else in the world."

Halfnote and Robbie lost all composure in the face of this outrageous blasphemy.

"Of course there were dragons," Halfnote exclaimed. "How did Father Bartholomew ever get down Viridian Mountain to Kerguelen Lake if not with Mother Piasa's help?"

"The mountain's hollow." Geoffrey's tone made it clear that he thought this was the most stupid question he'd ever heard. "He didn't have to climb the cliff."

"But he didn't know the mountain was hollow when he got here, did he?" Halfnote replied, aghast. "Mother Piasa showed him that with her song."

Geoffrey bared his teeth. Halfnote wasn't certain but she was pretty sure this meant Geoffrey was embarrassed. Other people blushed; Geoffrey just scowled and bared his teeth.

"Anyway," the junior master said, a little too loudly, "we still have a lesson to cover."

Today you become dragons

"*We're* learning to be dragons," Halfnote told Maru proudly. "That's what we call people who take care of fire."

"So there are still dragons in Albermarle after all. We are quite pleased to know this, Gajah and I."

Geoffrey impatiently herded the two of them over to a flat quartz rock placed in the ground next to the well. Scorch marks covered its broad face. Halfnote wondered how many years this one rock had been used to teach fledgling dragons.

Geoffrey piled a handful of old leaves and dried up twigs on top of the rock. "The thing you must remember about fire is that it is a living creature. It requires food and proper living quarters just as we do. With proper care and understanding it is a great friend. Handled badly it becomes a great enemy. For the purposes of our lesson today, this rock is the fire's cradle, the leaves its food. And these," he held up his flint and steel, "are its parents."

As Geoffrey droned on, Halfnote found herself peeking back at Maru and his ele … a … fant, Gajah. The Samoyan whistled a cheerful tune as he pulled the entire saddle assemblage, tapestries and all, off the still kneeling creature.

"Halfnote, this is important," Geoffrey snapped. He slapped steel against flint to create a shower of sparks. Fire seeds, Mama called them. Geoffrey's seeds tumbled into the pile of leaves and twigs but none of them blossomed.

Behind her the well rope rattled.

The bucket dropped into the water with a loud splash. Halfnote and Robbie looked up to see Maru drawing the bucket back up with energetic pulls on the rope. He sloshed water all the way back to Gajah. The spilled liquid quickly vanished into garden soil made too dry by the hot rays of the summer sun. Equally thirsty, Gajah stuck his long nose into the bucket and emptied it with one long slurp.

"Halfnote. Robbie. Pay attention." Geoffrey snapped. "Fire, like anger or any other passion, must be understood and controlled." The junior master's dark eyebrows twitched dangerously. Maru returned to the well, whistling a cheerful tune. Geoffrey flushed and struck steel to flint again. A tiny flame bloomed among the dry leaves.

"As you can see ..." Geoffrey began but the miniature blaze failed to take hold. It died away, leaving only a tiny black mark on the back of a brown leaf. Halfnote wondered if the leaves were damp. That hardly seemed likely on such a warm day. In any case, it didn't seem like a good time to ask.

Geoffrey smashed his heavy eyebrows all together in the middle of his reddening face. The junior master muttered to himself and smacked flint against steel. Sparks cascaded over the tinder. Robbie leaned forward, cupped his hands around his mouth and called out an encouraging note. Bits of flame promptly blossomed across the pile of debris.

"Excellent." Geoffrey gave Robbie a surprised look. "Where did you learn that?"

Robbie blinked and ducked his head.

"He makes the fire for Alma almost every morning," Halfnote said. "Robbie can even bank the coals for baking."

"Halfnote, Robbie can speak for himself. Excellent work, young man. That's the calling note, the note that encourages the fire to take hold. Now we want to try the nurturing notes, the tones that encourage a fire to grow. Robbie, do you know how to do that?"

Robbie nodded and learned forward. He cupped his hands around his mouth to call out a louder series of notes.

The flames expanded, consuming the leaves.

"Ex..." Geoffrey began just as Gajah trumpeted vigorously. Robbie squawked in surprise and fire flew in all directions. Hungry flames caught Geoffrey's sleeve and raced up his arm. He fell back, swinging his arm in the air but this only made things worse.

Why doesn't he rub his arm in the dirt? Halfnote wondered. She called out the dousing notes that Mama had taught her on the raft. The flames gave off a great puff of gray smoke and went out.

"Robbie, you idiot," Geoffrey roared, thrusting his burnt sleeve at Robbie. Wide-eyed in alarm, the boy stumbled backwards out of Geoffrey's way.

"He was just trying to help," Halfnote said. "The elephant's noise scared him."

Fortunately, at that moment the back door slammed loudly enough to divert everyone's attention. They looked up to see the Intan storming out of Verre House. His guards and Argana, the Samoyan healer, followed.

Walking at a more sedate pace, Grandpa and Lorraine came outside as well. In one swift move Maru resaddled Gajah, poked him to his feet and ducked underneath to fasten the saddle straps. He came up on the other side of the elephant to stand at attention just as the Intan reached them.

Gajah appeared to straighten up as well. He trumpeted a vigorous greeting. The Intan paused beside the creature and placed one hand on one broad leg. The Intan, Halfnote thought, looked furious. He took several deep breaths, like someone trying to calm down. Gajah stroked the Intan's shoulder with his trunk.

The Intan stopped and spun suddenly on his heel to confront Grandpa and Lorraine.

"This is not the end of it, Verre. We shall return again tomorrow, and every day after until you see the sense of our proposal." The Intan's eyes blazed.

"Please," Grandpa replied in a strong calming tone, "find a more profitable use for your time. The physicians of Albermarle have agreed to consult with us tomorrow. They are quite learned. Perhaps they can suggest a solution."

"It is you who wastes time. Every day that you delay, more people die. Let that thought burn your conscience." The prince placed one foot on Gajah's bent leg and pulled himself up into the ornate saddle. Maru gave Halfnote and Robbie a cheerful wave and tapped the elephant's leg. Gajah lumbered toward the front garden.

"Master Verre," Geoffrey asked after the Samoyans left, "you are just holding out for the best price, aren't you?"

Tiny Lorraine glared up at her husband. Geoffrey pretended not to notice, but Halfnote saw his eyes flicker toward the disapproval in his wife's face and away again.

Grandpa blew out a breath. "No, Geoffrey, I am not," he said in a much sharper tone than he used with the Intan. "As I told you, I will not make the so-called healing mirror again."

"You're really going to turn them down? At that price?"

"As I said. I will not make that piece again for any price. Nor will anyone in my household."

Geoffrey blinked and looked away from Grandpa's fierce gaze. "I … I meant, I only meant, sir, well, I mean, what if the sickness comes to Albermarle? What will we do then?"

"Then we shall do what we can," Grandpa replied in a much milder tone. His eyes still burned with anger. "The mirror is not the only option. What happened to your sleeve?"

But some fish do fly …

Octavia had been encamped in the library from first light. She felt as though she'd barely begun reading when the elephant's renewed trumpeting pulled her attention away from Mendosino's tight, looping script. She felt cross-eyed from staring through the reading glass that made the tiny letters a little less tiny. Worse, the writer's apparent point confused her. She understood the literal meaning well enough. At least she thought she did. But could an artist like the legendary Mendosino truly believe that every piece needed a flaw to perfect it? Not all pieces were perfectly symmetrical even though those were the easiest to make. But to create deliberate flaws? Mendosino must be joking. Perhaps he meant this as some kind of philosophical puzzle.

She stood up to stretch her overtight muscles and took a moment to glance out the window at the back garden. The elephant was nowhere to be seen. How had the Samoyans gotten it up the mountain? And why bring such a creature all this distance from its homeland? Grandfather stood talking with Geoffrey and Lorraine.

Something about the set of his shoulders made her think he must be angry.

Halfnote and Robbie stood to one side of the adults. As usual, Halfnote watched Grandfather and, Octavia couldn't help smiling at the sight, little Robbie watched Halfnote. Not for the first time Octavia wondered why her grandfather had made Robbie an apprentice. The boy sang about as well as the elephant. Of course Verre House would always look after him, she didn't question that, but to make a singer of him?

You might as well try to teach a fish to fly.

"But some fish do fly," she could almost hear Halfnote's earnest voice chipping in. "In the ocean. Papa says …."

"Enough dawdling," Octavia chided herself.

Grandfather knew what he was doing. If there was a way to make Robbie a successful singer of course Grandfather would find it. She had her own assignment to complete. And it was daunting enough.

Be still and listen

"So, Geoffrey showed you a bit about fire today, did he?" Grandpa asked Halfnote and Robbie. They nodded together warily. Would Geoffrey tell Grandpa that Robbie set his sleeve on fire? It wasn't Robbie's fault, Halfnote thought. The elephant's unexpected noise startled him.

"Didn't need any help from me." Geoffrey gave a hearty and completely false laugh. "Turns out they already know how to start a fire, and how to stop it."

"Excellent." Grandpa beamed down at them. Robbie ducked his head. Halfnote allowed herself a cautious smile in return. "Now, if the two of you will please go with Lorraine to the main creation room, Geoffrey and I need to talk."

The underground creation chamber normally felt a little cooler than the outdoors on a hot summer day. Today, however, Halfnote started sweating as soon as she entered the room. Temporary melting boxes on iron frames stood in a clear pattern around the largest making chamber. Brass fire bowls held simmering coals under the melting boxes. Most of the other apprentices were already there, hurrying about with various tasks.

No one looked particularly surprised to see them.

"Today you will learn how to help with the making," Lorraine told them. Robbie and Halfnote stared at the blonde junior master in astonishment.

"B ... but ..." Robbie began.

"Octavia said we had to learn all about fire first," Halfnote finished for him, emphasizing 'all.' "We haven't learned about building flames or melting or ... or anything."
She found herself grinning from ear to ear. Most apprentices didn't get to make anything until they were nine or ten.

"It's all right," Lorraine said. "You already know the most important lesson."

"We do?" Robbie was so surprised he didn't even stutter.

"Yes, you do. Do you remember the first thing I told you when you arrived at Verre House?"

Halfnote and Robbie looked at each other uncertainly.

"Think back. You had just arrived and you were scared and unhappy and you expressed those feelings very well. Master Verre brought you into the kitchen and that's where we first met. What did I say to you then?"

Robbie frowned. Halfnote drew back a little. She didn't like thinking about that day. Lorraine, barely half a head taller than Halfnote, gazed at them with her firmest expression.

"You s... said, you said, 'D...don't b...be scared'," Robbie offered after a moment. "You s...said, 'Everything's g...going to b...be all right.'"

"That's right," Lorraine's expression softened. "And what did I say after that?"

"Be still." Halfnote said. Everyone looked at her. She blushed. "I mean, that's what you said. You told us 'Be still and listen.' "

"Yes. And that's the first thing that you need to do today. Don't be nervous or afraid," she said, smiling at Robbie. Halfnote stilled a jealous twitch. "And be still. Listen.

"The rest will come to you out of that. Watch and listen to what the others do. Listen to what they tell you. Listen to how they use their voices. If you start to feel confused, be still and remember your breathing exercises."

Halfnote looked for Octavia but didn't see her sister among the ten or so glassworkers present.

Lorraine sent Robbie to work with Ted, the lead dragon for the day. Halfnote joined Martin. *A singer. I get to work with a singer!*

Galliard, the oldest boy apprentice, completed their trio around a temporary melting box. Marissa acted as their dragon. Halfnote took her place and looked around, trying to absorb everything at once. She listened intently, but could barely hear anything else over the excited roar of her pulse in her ears. Lorraine touched Halfnote lightly on the shoulder and she jumped. The junior master handed Halfnote a leather scarf.

Everyone else already wore one; even Martin with his clean shaven scalp and cheeks.

"Tie this around your hair. See how Marissa and I have it? It protects your hair from sparks. Always put one on as soon as you enter the making room to work. They hang on that hook next to the door. And one more thing…"

"Yes?" Halfnote struggled to tie the scarf around her thick braids as quickly as she could.

"Breathe." Lorraine gave her a wink. "Take slow, deep breaths from your stomach the way we showed you."

Halfnote drew air into her lungs slowly, counting out the seconds. She mentally aimed the breath at the pit of her stomach and felt her lungs balloon out.

"Halfnote," Martin said.

She felt the air pressing against the top of her ribs and gulped, trying to force just a little bit more into her lungs.

"Halfnote," Martin said a little more loudly.

She allowed the breath to seep softly out of her nostrils, just a little at a time. It blew gently across her top lip.

"Halfnote," Martin snapped. She jumped. All of the air she held so carefully in her lungs escaped. Someone behind her laughed. She realized that everyone was looking at her and cringed.

"Halfnote," Martin said, his blue eyes sharp. "Pay attention. Listen. We're about to start. This is a simple round, a three note melody without harmony.

"Let Galliard and I start it and then you come in when you've got the note. Blend in as well as you can, understand?"

Halfnote flushed and bobbed her head.

"Ready?" Lorraine called from the center of the room. On a glass pitch pipe she blew a short note, a middle C that expanded until it bounced off the walls. Halfnote forgot all about breathing as the tone vibrated inside her ears.

Energy filled the room. Galliard and Martin hummed gently. Other voices took up the note. The vibrations of rising sound lifted the hairs on Halfnote's arms and neck. Entranced by the beauty and purpose of the music, she joined in very quietly. She carefully blended her voice in with the others. The reverberation of tones tickled her nose. Her teeth trembled lightly against each other.

She focused all of her attention on Martin. He stood on the opposite side of the making box, balanced on the balls of his feet. He held his hands at his sides with the palms out. His humming tapered off as he completely emptied his lungs before taking in another long breath and resuming the tone.

She noticed that Martin and Galliard never took their breaths at the same time. This kept the vibration of their combined efforts constant. She did her best to do the same. Soon it seemed effortless, humming and breathing and breathing and humming and feeling the vibrations climb up and down her spine.

Halfnote allowed her eyes to travel from Martin's smooth shaven cheeks to the making box. The yellow grains of sand filling the box trembled precipitously. She watched as two lemon-colored bits worked their way across the edge of the vibrating box and fell into the fire below. The sand looked coarser, more yellow than the sand Octavia used for her test.

Papa could probably tell which beach that sand came from.

She became aware of Marissa sitting by the brazier, dropping in bits of coal and stirring the fire. Marissa was upset. The energy of her emotions created ripples that bounced erratically through the smooth tones of the makers.

Doesn't she realize what she's doing?

Halfnote felt a little perturbed herself. She watched as her sense of annoyance rippled out through the vibrations of her humming. Martin glanced at her and changed the energy of his own voice just a little. His ripples merged with hers and smoothed them out. Then he returned to his original notes.

The energy of her amazement filled and expanded the pulses of her sounds. Martin, watching her through narrowed eyes, smiled. He made a small damping motion with one hand.

Halfnote gulped and struggled to pull back on her growing sense of excitement. The vibrations of her humming skewed slightly. She panicked and they collapsed.

Oh no, she'd gone off-key. She'd broken the rhythm. She'd ruined the making! But even as Halfnote gathered herself up to run, hide or burst into tears, a large hand took hold of her own.

She looked up through brimming eyes. Martin, still humming, still smiling, pointed at the ball of molten glass hanging just above the melting box. It remained in place despite her mistake. Martin and Galliard adjusted their tones to smooth out her disturbance.

Martin squeezed her arm just enough to get her attention. He mimed taking a breath and frowned a little. Halfnote stared at him a moment and then realized what he wanted. She took a deep breath. She started to let it out but Martin, still holding her hand and his own sound shook his head. She held the breath, the air pressing against the inside of her lungs until it hurt. Finally the singer nodded and Halfnote let it out. At Martin's silent urging she took another breath; held it, let it out. And again.

She felt calmer. The energy of the making sound took hold. She could hear the humming of the other glass workers over the ringing in her own ears. Martin let go of her hand.

Halfnote listened carefully to catch the right note and began humming again. The singer smiled encouragement and she dared to hum a little louder. Something changed in the vibrations and she realized that they were nearly done.

Their molten ball was now a simple wine bottle. Martin harmonized now with Galliard instead of blending. His variation wrapped protectively around the newborn bottle. With their tones they gently lowered their creation into the cooling bath. The bottle gave off a satisfying sizzle as it hit the water. The making energy faded away.

Halfnote stared at the cooling bath, dizzy with relief. Marissa, muttering a few damping notes, slid a brass lid speckled with air holes across the fire bowl. Galliard retrieved the completed bottle with a small net and carried it over to the drying racks by the wall.

"Halfnote." She looked up in alarm. She'd done very badly,

she knew it. Her stomach sank and her eyes filled with tears. They would probably never let her make anything ever again. And who could blame them?

"You did very well," Martin said. "You held the vibration and stayed on key for almost the entire time." Halfnote stared at him in astonishment.

"But I did lose the key. I got mixed up ..."

"You're excited. You've never made anything in a group before and you just found out how much fun it can be." He grinned. "You should have heard me at my first making. I was off-key the entire time. I had no rhythm at all my first year. They threatened to make me a full-time dragon. Of course you made mistakes. You've never done this before. That's why they put you with me. I'll keep things smooth while you learn.

"Now. Stay calm. Pay attention. Put aside any other concerns. Focus on the work. We have a lot to do today."

And they did. They melted, molded, cooled and racked a new bottle every few moments in a quick and steady rhythm. After a while, Halfnote didn't know who looked more tired – the makers as they sang or the dragons as they raced to rack the bottles, then refill the melting boxes and fire bowls.

At first, the crackle of making energy sustained Halfnote. She only became aware of the physical drain of making between songs. After the third making or so it became routine:
catch the key, blend in, breathe and stay calm. But the longer they worked the harder it became for Halfnote to ignore Marissa's annoyance and the way it affected her own energy. Worse, Martin didn't seem to notice it at all. Halfnote made up her mind to tell. But just as she drew in breath to speak, Lorraine clapped her hands and called a halt for lunch.

That afternoon, Halfnote and Robbie ran errands.

"No, this kind of sand," Halfnote told Robbie when they both ended up down in one of the lower basements looking for supplies. "See the difference in the grains? Feel it with your fingers. This is coarser and the color is a different."

"How do you know?" Robbie asked.

"They're making distillery equipment now. This is the sand Grandpa always tells Papa to buy for distillery orders."

The entire household, including Alma, gathered around the staff dining table for the evening meal. To Halfnote's surprise even Geoffrey and Lorraine joined them.

Halfnote, Robbie and Dan, under Alma's stern direction, produced a sturdy stew filled with almost as much meat as vegetables. They served it up with chunks of a hard, pale cheese and fresh-baked rye bread.

Halfnote's eyes stung from chopping up onions. She and Robbie sat next to Alma at the end of the table closest to the kitchen so they could fetch more food as needed. The Samoyans and their request – and their elephant – filled most of the conversations taking place around the table.

She kept glancing at her grandparents. They sat at the other end of the long oak table. Octavia, she noted with a minor twinge of jealousy, could actually speak to them if she chose, now that she sat with the other singers. But Octavia spoke intently with Lorraine and Martin throughout the meal, barely glancing at anyone else. As Halfnote watched, Lorraine smiled broadly and reached out to pat Martin's smooth cheek.

Grandpa spoke to no one and showed little interest in his food. Geoffrey turned suddenly to him.

"I still can't believe you turned them down. They'll pay anything you ask." The junior master's dark brows knitted together in a frown.

The table fell silent and all eyes turned toward Grandpa.

Halfnote put her spoon down and waited with the rest for his answer. The moment stretched out painfully.

"Their people are dying," Sylvia broke in with her soft but resonant voice. "You heard what they said. Even their king is ill. How can we not help them?"

Grandpa's lips thinned. He looked around the table. Only Sylvia, her delicate brown eyes clear and unafraid, dared to meet his angry gaze.

"We have a duty, also," Grandpa said finally in a tight voice, "not to expose our own people to certain danger." He took a last drink of tea and pushed away from the table.

"But Master Verre …" Geoffrey protested.

"Leave him alone," Grandma said in her firmest tones. Her red curls, a fairly simple arrangement tonight as she had no performance scheduled, bounced as she spoke.

"He has given his answer. He will do what he can for the Samoyans but he will not create another healing mirror.

"He has already asked the masters of the physicians' guild to meet with the Intan in the morning. The matter is settled. Now let us talk of something else."

The rest of the meal passed in uncomfortable silence.

Halfnote dreamed again of the flood. Unseen currents swirled around her as she clung to the bobbing tree. Chaotic waters did their best to drag her from the bucking, rolling trunk. Rough bark scraped her arms and legs. She called out into the impenetrable night for Mama, for Papa, for anyone, but the flood's roar drowned her voice.

Halfnote woke fighting for breath to find the first light of dawn peering through the window.

Flailing her arms as if swimming, she fought her way out from under the sheet and out of bed. Marissa mumbled and rolled away to the other side, taking all of the quilt with her. Halfnote forced herself to breathe calmly. It was just a dream. That's what Octavia would say. She washed and dressed as quietly as she could and tiptoed down the stairs before any of the others stirred.

"And a good morning to you, my dear," Alma greeted her, showing no surprise at her early arrival. "You're just in time to light the oven. Can you bank the coals?"

It did seem a bit unfair to have to do kitchen chores when she was the first one up today, and not the last. Surely she wasn't going to get stuck on housework again today, was she? After all, she'd begun making yesterday. *Making!* Still, every dragon needed to know how to bank coals and, she realized with a twitch of jealousy, all of the other apprentices knew how – even Robbie.

As it turned out, kitchen duty was the least of her worries. Grandpa entered the dining room just as everyone gathered for breakfast and called them all to order.

"Will you all eat quickly please and then gather in the main making room. As soon as the breakfast dishes are washed," he added, with a glance at Alma. The cook gave him a relieved look.

"And if Robby and Halfnote will come with me to the main

creation room." Everyone looked at Robbie and Halfnote in surprise. They stared at each other, then back at Grandpa.

"Y... you m…mean Halfnote and Octavia, d...don't you, s...sir?" Robbie managed to ask.

"No, no. I mean you and Halfnote. Octavia will observe with the others. As soon as you've finished eating, please."

Robbie gulped down an enormous bite of eggs and nearly choked himself. Halfnote was too excited to eat any more. They passed their plates to Alma and ran for the creation room.

There they found Grandpa pouring a fine, whitish sand into the melting box on the main platform, the same platform where Octavia took her test. They called it sugar sand, Halfnote knew, because it looked just like the fine sugar Alma used to make icings and candies. It came from Biruni, a little island just south and west of Tulum.

"Just in time." Grandpa smiled. "Robert, I understand you have some talent with fire?"

Robbie turned scarlet and shrugged. "I ... m...my m...mother showed me ..."

"Yes, he does, Grandpa," Halfnote chimed in quickly. "He builds the fires in the oven for Alma all the time. And he called fire yesterday when Geoffrey couldn't."

"Excellent. You'll be my dragon today."

Robbie gulped and took a determined breath.

"We need a small melting fire for fine sand, and a banked fire under the cooling bath. What fuel should we use?" Robbie blinked and Halfnote poked him.

"S...sir, a…a s...slow b…burning wood like oak for the bath, and c...coal for the m...melting?"

"Exactly right.

"We've coal already up here but you'll need to go choose your wood from the back garden. We're going to make a small mirror," Grandpa told Halfnote as Robbie dashed off. "I understand that you know how to hold and maintain a piece."

She swallowed. "Yes, Master Verre."

"Excellent. We are about to give a demonstration of technique. At several points in the process I will withdraw from the making to explain what we're doing to the others. You will maintain the holding chant while I speak."

"Yes, Master Verre."

Octavia wouldn't blink an eye at something like this. Halfnote did her best to look composed. Her stomach betrayed her with a great nervous growl and she blushed.

"Perhaps some calming breaths first," Grandpa said.

Grandpa had just finished checking Robbie's fire under the making box when the rest of the glass singers filtered in. He gave Robbie a satisfied pat on the shoulder.

"Excellent, Robert. You handle fire as well as a dragon of several years' experience." Robbie shrugged and ducked his head. The edges of the boy's mouth quirked up.

Grandpa stepped up onto the platform and looked out over the group. "Is everyone here? Ah, yes, Alma, excellent."

A demonstration of power

"You all wonder why I turned down the Samoyans," Grandfather said. "It may seem heartless, given the depth of their need. Perhaps everyone will best understand if I show you." He gestured to Halfnote and Robbie. "Let us begin."

Power filled the room as Grandpa began the melting chant. At his signal Halfnote joined in.

She felt like a tiny leaf caught up in and carried away by the currents of the mighty Khelana River. The delicate grains of sand melted into liquid like butter in a hot skillet. The molten globe of liquid glass swirled almost immediately out of the melting box to float gently between Grandpa's outstretched hands. Halfnote, conscious of every breath, maintained the core of the making chant as Grandpa began his shaping tones. The egg-shaped, whirling glob flattened and grew wider. Grandpa glanced at Halfnote and she nodded.

She was as ready as she would ever be. Grandpa held his note until the sound naturally fell away. The newborn mirror hung in the air, held only by Halfnote's tones.

Octavia couldn't help but smile at the sight of her younger sister earnestly *making* with Grandfather. Halfnote's innocent soprano stood out clearly against Grandfather's commanding bass.

She's good, Octavia thought, surprised by the proud tears rimming her eyes. *She has the Verre gift. Already you can hear the forming power in her voice.*

Grandfather turned to address the assembled singers.

"The Samoyans' need is great. Surely we have a duty to help them if we can. And certainly," he glanced at Geoffrey, "the offered payment is exceptionally generous; more than Verre House normally earns in a year. Despite this I refused the commission. It is natural that you should wonder why. I hope this small demonstration will make my reasons clear.

"The problem, the danger, lies in the nature of the *Hygeia paraphasis* itself. The making of the healing mirror is the most dangerous task any glass singer can undertake."

Halfnote's heart surged. She felt dizzy and struggled to stay on key. It seemed as if everyone stared at her. Surely they were more interested in Grandpa's words than her singing. She gulped a new breath while the echoes of her maintaining song reverberated off the chamber walls.

The molten mirror wobbled but did not fall.

Octavia's heart faltered as she watched the infant mirror teeter dangerously. Halfnote caught it with renewed sound just in time. Relieved, Octavia released her own breath.

"An ordinary looking glass sees only the surface of things." Grandfather continued as if unaware of the drama behind him. "As a result, the base of a typical device needs to absorb very little. Thus, the appetite of a regular mirror is rarely noticed except by those who know that it exists.

"A healing mirror, however, must see into the heart of things. It must see the core and cause of the disease to effect true healing. Often it must see into the core of a person's very soul. To do this, the *Hygeia paraphasis* must be able to absorb almost anything. It is this greater appetite, this need to take in everything that makes the healing mirror so dangerous.

"There is a point in the making of the *Hygeia paraphasis* where it is necessary to allow the appetite of the not yet solid mirror to become all consuming. The stronger the appetite, once tamed, the more effective the mirror. The unformed *paraphasis* will, if it can, snatch up any life within reach."

Octavia shivered at the thought. No wonder Grandfather feared to make this piece.

"However, if it succeeds in taking a life, the mirror becomes irretrievably tainted. It becomes a monstrous, all-devouring *mortolo*. The taking of one soul does not satisfy it. As the *mortolo* feeds, like any creature, it grows in size and strength. Naturally, after the first meal is digested, the mirror hungers again. As it grows larger it needs more food to sustain itself. It reaches out for another life and another and for all it can take. Every life it devours gives the *mortolo* more power. Every life it takes makes it hungry for more.

"Once the *Hygeia paraphasis* tastes life, it cannot be tamed. It becomes a blight on the entire countryside. It will never heal. A *mortolo* is an unstoppable glutton. It will do anything it can to draw all life to itself. It will distort and deceive and destroy until there is nothing living left to eat. Ultimately, when there is nothing left but bare rock and dead soil, the *mortolo* itself starves to death.

"It dies of the emptiness caused by its own excess. It becomes its own last victim." Grandfather's voice shook. He took a calming breath. Octavia took one as well. She had never imagined that a glass object could hold such power.

"Observe our newborn mirror." Grandfather gestured toward the flattened oval hanging now just in front of Halfnote. "This is the beginning of the absorption phase. The mirror is formed but not yet bound. Normally we bind the mirror immediately, so that it has but a moment to feel hunger. Observe what happens when we delay the binding. Even this small creation, maintained by the tones of our youngest apprentice, seeks to draw all it can to itself.

"Of course it does. It's hungry."

Grandfather was right, Octavia thought. *I am only just beginning to understand what it means to be a glass singer.*

Halfnote gulped another breath as the hairs on her arms

stood straight up. It felt as if the knot on her leather hair covering was trying to untie itself. A stray hair pulled free and floated into the mirror. Specks of dust flung themselves into it.

Even the sunlight streaming in from the overhead windows seemed to bend a little in the mirror's direction.

Hold the note, Halfnote reminded herself. She clung firmly to the memory of Octavia outsinging the screaming glass. *I won't let Grandpa down.*

Octavia watched her younger sister's struggles with a growing sense of horror.

I can't believe he's doing this. And with Halfnote! I should be up there, or Geoffrey or Lorraine ...

"We deliberately exaggerate the mirror's appetite when making a *Hygeia paraphasis* so that it will take in all things necessary for curing illness," Grandfather continued serenely. "At the absorption point in the making of a healing mirror, we would provide it with herbs, tinctures, poultices and other substances necessary to it's purpose. But this is also the moment that makes the creation process so dangerous.

"Anyone who gets too close to the mirror will be absorbed. Consider what it would feel like with this desire, this drawing in magnified a thousand times. That is the power of the *Hygeia mortolo*, the *paraphasis* once it has eaten life."

Grandpa turned back to the mirror and joined his strong voice to the making tones again. Halfnote took a relieved breath. He gestured for her silence. A little puzzled, she complied. Had she done something wrong?

In a thundering voice Grandpa called out a new melody. The sense of need emanating from the still fluid mirror grabbed her. Halfnote, her mind a blur, stumbled towards the whirling creation. As if from very far away, she heard Octavia call her name.

Grandpa cried out the finishing tones. Silver glazing wrapped itself around the mirror and the completed piece dropped into the cooling bath with a splash. Halfnote, released from the mirror's pull, stumbled and fell to her knees.

Grandpa helped Halfnote to her feet. "This has given you a very brief experience of what unrestrained absorption can feel like," he told the group. "Let me assure you, the pull of the unbound *Hygeia paraphasis* is much worse."

How can it be worse? Halfnote wondered.

Devin's fate

"Grandfather." Octavia stood in front of the rest of the group, her expression a mixture of shock and rage. "How could you?" Halfnote's eyes focused on her sister.

Octavia pulled Halfnote to her side, away from Grandpa. Halfnote, still dizzy, happily accepted the embrace despite the fierce anger emanating from her sister.

"I need you to understand," Grandpa said. His voice sounded as mild as ever, but his dark eyes glowed as fiercely as Octavia's. "All of you, but particularly you, Octavia, you must see the danger of the *Hygeia paraphasis*. This is why we must not make it. This is whom we endanger, if we undertake such a project."

Halfnote watched her sister open her mouth to protest, then shut it again. Octavia hugged her more tightly. Halfnote hugged back. A hand touched hers and she turned to see Robbie next to her.

"Are you all right?" he whispered. He looked, if possible, as fiercely angry as Octavia.

She nodded. Behind Robbie the rest of the glass singers looked shocked and unhappy. Alma stood with her hands on her wide hips, glaring at Grandpa. Phyllis, her knuckles white where they clutched at the front of her blouse, peered out from behind a frowning Martin. Sylvia, Ted and Lorraine stood close together, their expressions shocked. The other apprentices huddled near them, looking confused. Dan whispered anxiously to Galliard and Marissa, who kept gesturing for him to be quiet. Annie and Alice, somehow dressed in matching colors despite the eclectic choices of clothing available to apprentices, clung to each other.

Junior master Geoffrey stood a little away from the rest of the staff, his arms tightly folded, his dark eyebrows drawn together into a tight V.

"My cousin Devin…" Grandpa began, and then sighed.

What could Grandfather be thinking?

Octavia forced herself to calm her breathing, but it did little to still her anger. That Grandfather would dare to make a demonstration of Halfnote *… and then blame me for wanting to learn … * How could he? Geoffrey might question Grandfather's decision on the mirror but she didn't. She hadn't.

Grandfather sighed heavily and sat down on the steps of the black marble making platform. He looked old and worn in a way Octavia had never seen before. Grandfather naturally wore the gray hair and wrinkles that come with age, but he never looked … defeated. She took another calming breath.

What could Grandfather be thinking?

"My cousin Devin," Grandfather continued, "was apprenticed with me at the glassworks of Madame Marcato in Tulum. He was a talented voice just a little younger than myself. He was clear toned, bright-eyed, excited with the wonder of life and singing the glass.

"Even then and even in the House of Marcato, the making of a healing mirror was a rare event. Only the best glass singers participated. Everyone wanted to be involved, of course. Devin was inexperienced but gifted, a real talent. He prevailed upon Madame Marcato to let him take part. No one thought there was anything dangerous or unusual about this, given his gift. We all congratulated him on his opportunity."

Grandfather paused, his eyes red-rimmed with grief.

"Madame Marcato was one of the best glass singers of our time; justly celebrated for the quality of her creations. She handled the most difficult projects easily. No doubt she and we, her staff, had grown overconfident.

"We used a choral approach for the making, lest any one person falter," Grandfather continued. "Every person had an understudy, and most more than one.

"I led those who chanted the melting tones. Devin, still relatively unformed, was in the group supporting the dragons. Naturally we used obsidian for the piece."

Octavia imagined Devin as a sandy-haired twin of her grandfather, perhaps still a little shorter. She pictured them as a brash, confident pair, eager to test themselves with a truly unusual project. She thought she knew exactly how they must have felt. In Devin's place she would have pestered Madame Marcato for a chance to take part as well.

Perhaps that was why ...

She drew back from the thought. Grandfather had no right to blame her for wanting to learn more about her art.

"There was no plague, only a conscientious physician who wanted the mirror for his business," Grandfather said. "We were ... less careful ... in those days. It seemed a straight-forward commission and lucrative.

"We took every precaution, or so we believed. We checked every detail, ruthlessly removing anything that might sound a discordant note. Our reflective shielding was flawless, its creation overseen by Madame Marcato herself. We rehearsed the chants until we could sing them in our sleep." Octavia, still holding tight to Halfnote, listened in dismay. In her experience, most errors in glassmaking were the result of sloppy work and inattention to detail.

"Finally, everything was ready. We each took our place in the strict order required by Madame Marcato. All flowed together in a perfect pattern of song and color. Naturally we used the best ingredients: mountain's blood for the fire, silver for the reflective surface, the freshest and strongest herbs. We made certain that nothing could go wrong." Grandfather's mouth twisted in bitterness.

"We planned for every possibility, or so we thought."

"At first, the making went like clockwork. The obsidian, normally obstinate, melted like butter. We chanted flawlessly.

"The purification ... well, it all went perfectly. And then, as you know, Devin fell." Grandfather took a breath.

"I didn't see his fall. We had begun the absorption phase. Everyone stood behind his or her shield, every voice on key. We felt the strength of the *Hygeia paraphasis* as it liquefied. Dangerous, yes, but excellent for our purposes. The stronger the absorption of the obsidian, the better the mirror.

"Then, someone cried out. The energies of the making turned hideously wrong. The obsidian's voracious pull increased ten-fold. It took all our powers just to glaze and cool the sphere. Madame Marcato hurried all of us out of the making chamber but it did little good. We could still feel the call of the mirror, even through the thick stone walls of Marcato House."

Octavia tried to imagine how it must have felt and found herself trembling.

Halfnote, still a bit disoriented, felt Octavia start shaking and gave her sister a reassuring hug. She realized with a start that she had visited the Marcato Glassworks. Both of the times she traveled to Tulum with her parents they stopped there to make deliveries and accept new cargo. The House of Marcato, new built now of white brick and larger than Verre House, sat uphill from a smaller river that fed into the Khelana. She knew the present Master Marcato as cold and unfriendly.

He sneered at Mama and snapped orders at Papa as if he were a servant. His grating voice sent shivers down her spine. Halfnote shivered now, just at the memory. How could anyone sing the glass with a voice like that?

"Once outside Madame Marcato told me of Devin's loss." Grandpa's voice, quiet but compelling, drew Halfnote back into the story. "Madame said we had no choice but to destroy the mirror. I begged her for a chance to save Devin.

"She looked me in the eye and insisted he was already dead. But Devin was well-loved and the others stood with me. Finally she relented. She gave us until dusk to find a solution.

"The usual method for destroying a *mortolo*, a haunted mirror, is by melting. But the great heat required would destroy Devin as well as the mirror, if he did still live. With every moment, despite our best protections against it, we felt the mirror's power building."

Grandpa rubbed his face.

"We settled on shattering."

Octavia put a hand to her mouth. Halfnote tightened her grip around her waist. Someone hissed. Grandfather grimaced and spread his hands in a gesture of futility.

"We decided to use the left over pieces of obsidian. We would use them as projectiles to shatter the *mortolo*. We made our decision just in time, Madame said. The mirror reached out in every way possible. People began to see ..."

Grandfather closed his eyes and reopened them. "To see Devin throughout the building, anywhere a reflection could form. Soon the *mortolo* would draw souls to itself through other mirrors as well."

"It felt as if we stood against a strong wind as we prepared ourselves just outside the creation room. I began to doubt our chances of success but there was no time to reconsider. When all was ready I opened the door. Even with reflective shielding the power of the haunted mirror began to pull me into the room. The others managed to pull me back and we began chanting.

There is a way to use music against music, as it were, to create protections with sound, although eventually even these proved inadequate. We had, we thought, two chances. First, we would smash the mirror with sharpened bits of obsidian.

"We also prepared a cooling bath holding the coldest water we could find. If we couldn't shatter the mirror with the obsidian we thought we might be able to heat it enough that it would shatter on impact with the cold water without making the glass so hot that it cooked Devin.

"It took all of our will to focus our efforts. The mirror fought as if it understood our intentions. It concentrated its powers on those of us in front of the door. There were ten of us. Still we barely managed to block it with a wall of sound.

"We threw the shards against the mirror and first it simply repelled them. One flew out of the door and smashed into our group, shattering our reflective shields and knocking Caris unconscious. Others carried her outside of the building to keep the mirror from pulling her in.

"We tried again, spinning the obsidian shards like arrows and flinging them with all our energy against the mirror. This time it simply absorbed them and made itself larger. The mirror called aloud to us by name, in Devin's voice." Grandfather's eyes filled with unshed tears.

"Kithara ... a singer of extensive experience and Devin's sweetheart ... the mirror took her next. She tore off the safety ropes and ran to the mirror of her own accord. Fugato, a singer just three months from his master's test, tried to stop her and fell in as well.

"With the addition of two more souls, the *mortolo* seemed unstoppable. It began to absorb the building itself. Every bird and small animal in the area fought to join it. Thousands of them clustered on the roof and around the foundation, desperately seeking a way inside. A child playing next door, a boy about two years old, climbed over the wall and tried to enter as well.

"Madame Marcato ordered us all out of the building. We put all of our efforts into creating a wall of sound around the house, to stop the mirror's pull from spreading. Madame sent messengers to every glass singer in Tulum begging for help.

"We managed to knock down the building but the *mortolo* remained intact inside.

"It took time for the other glass singers to arrive. Later I heard that over two hundred took part in the cleansing.

Under the direction of Master Largo, a revered grand master, we managed to force the power of the mirror back into itself. We created a great barrier of sound for protection, covered the mirror with mountain's blood and melted it into its most basic elements.

These were forced into a mirrored box, so the remains of the *mortolo* could only reflect onto itself. I and some others carried that box to the volcano that originally birthed the obsidian. We stood watch until we were certain the chest and all its contents were consumed by burning lava.

"Madame Marcato rebuilt her house but Devin, Kithara and Fugato were lost to us forever."

Grandfather got slowly to his feet. He sighed and shook the wrinkles out of his robes before speaking again.

"It is important for you to know that there is a second danger from any healing mirror. We bind the mirror with silver glazing to curb its appetite. But the protection lasts only as long as the glazing. If that cracks, the *Hygeia paraphasis*' appetite is unleashed and it becomes a horror to all those unfortunate to be near it.

"Later, we learned that all of the healing mirrors created by Marcato House eventually became *mortolo*; two through unhappy accident, one made so deliberately."

"Deliberately!" Lorraine burst out. The tiny blonde caught herself and blushed. "I beg pardon, Master Verre."

"You are forgiven. I didn't believe it at first either. But this is the final reason why making the *Hygeia paraphasis* is banned. Madame Marcato herself led the effort to make the law universal.

"An ambitious sorcerer living in one of Samoya's island neighbors' cracked a *Hygeia paraphasis* in the mistaken belief that he could control its power.

"He was the mirror's first victim. His island, fortunately small and deserted, is now nothing more than bleak rock. All of the healing mirrors that I helped create turned deadly in the end. I regret making all of them. I will not make another."

Octavia blew out a shaky breath. No wonder he feared to make another healing mirror. Still, she did wonder how it would feel to create an instrument of such power.

It's just work

They were making bottles again. Halfnote, singing with Sylvia this time, wondered how this had ever seemed exciting. She chanted the basic holding note while Sylvia created the shape with a four note call. The completed bottle dropped into the cooling bath. Laiertes, their dragon for the day, netted the bottle, balanced the fire and then they did it again. And again. And again. Even Robbie settled down into a steady rhythm, after wandering off-key the first few times. While Halfnote worked on singing loud enough, Robbie did best when he all but whispered his part.

Frank finally called a halt to the work. He pulled off his spectacles and rubbed his eyes, then he and Sylvia whispered together for a moment. To everyone's surprise and Halfnote's consternation – she was still stuck maintaining – Sylvia and Robbie switched places.

Halfnote watched the sweat dribble down Robbie's neck and drip off the ends of the leather head cloth tied slightly askew over his brown, shoulder-length braids. Frank blew the starting note on his F-shaped pitch pipe and they began.

Halfnote and Robbie both began the maintenance notes until Sylvia tapped Robbie on the shoulder. Robbie gulped but Halfnote kept the tones in place.

Robbie found his place and followed Sylvia's lead through the simple melody. Sylvia's resonant tones seemed to wrap themselves around Robbie's, and drew him effortlessly to each correct note. The spiraling ball of molten glass elongated into a clear hollow shell. Sylvia, with Robbie gamely following, changed one note and the neck formed. Robbie blinked away sweat and watched the lengthening bottle with wide eyes.

The new bottle dropped into the bath with a satisfying sizzle. Sylvia winked at Robbie, her brown eyes bright.

Robbie, his face filled with relief, grinned back. Laiertes put the completed bottle on the cooling rack and then dumped new sand into the melting box.

They began again, Robbie calling out the notes with much more confidence this time while Sylvia faded back.

When do I get my turn? Halfnote wondered.

The sand melted quickly and they raised the spinning molten ball over the cooling bath as before.

Then, catastrophe.

Gajah's unexpected trumpeting startled everyone. Robbie's voice cracked and the ball of liquid glass exploded.

Halfnote ducked instinctively and bumped heads with Laiertes. The singers and older apprentices began a buzzing sound, as if they had turned into a hive of angry bees. Sylvia hurried a tearful Robbie over to a sand-filled barrel. She grabbed a handful and rubbed it vigorously against his cheek to remove a glob of hot glass. Then she led him off to the kitchen for a cold compress from Alma.

Oh, why did that have to happen?

Halfnote knew the elephant didn't mean to hurt anyone, but Robbie had just begun to gain some confidence in his singing. And this was the second time that Gajah had startled him into disaster.

A private meeting

Octavia, once again struggled through a reading assignment. She frowned at the faded, spidery script. She'd spread the ancient scroll out under the library's strongest reading glass. The curving flare of the glass's decorative edges reminded her of Grandfather but the abrupt decline of focus at each end seemed at odds with his usually meticulous efforts.

She sighed, rubbed her eyes and tried to return her attention to the age-reddened lines of ink. In truth she'd rather puzzle out the identity of the magnifying glass's maker than struggle with the five possible meanings of each cuneiform letter required to understand Theides' dissertation on the methods for creating scented glass. Did the curlicue off the side of the letter written as a triangle inside a square mean she should emphasize the declarative tense or ignore it? She couldn't remember.

The elephant's trumpeting startled her so that she nearly knocked the reading glass off the table. The scroll underneath crumpled but didn't tear.

Thank you, Mother Piasa.

Why couldn't the Samoyans keep that creature quiet? Octavia rolled up the scroll and returned it to its case with more care than she might have otherwise, then hurried downstairs to greet their guests.

She reached the office just in time to see the door shut. A pair of the prince's bodyguards took up positions, one on each side. Octavia acknowledged the men. The taller guard blocked her path with his spear. He said something in Samoyan.

"But Master Verre needs me."

The guard shook his head and kept his spear in place.

"Oh, this is ridiculous. This is my home. You have no right to stop me. Get out of the way." Geoffrey hurried up.

"In his office?" he asked Octavia.

"Yes, but they won't let me in."

"What do you mean?" The guard met Geoffrey's glare with fierce eyes and pointed his spear at the junior master.

"No," the guard managed in rough Albi.

"What?" Geoffrey looked as astonished as Octavia felt. "Look here, you, this is our house. Our master requires our presence. You have no right to stop us."

"At least tell Master Verre we're here." Octavia realized from blank look on the guard's face that he didn't understand her. Octavia considered the smattering of Samoyan words she knew, but none seemed appropriate to the situation.

The guard held his stance. His companion, still at attention, shifted nervously. He eyed first Geoffrey and then Octavia, as if uncertain which of them might attack first.

"What's going on?" Grandmother demanded as she joined them. She wore her hair this morning in the straight and simple ponytail she favored on days when she had no performances. Other glass singers arrived as well.

Now the second guard lowered his spear towards the group. He looked grim, as if prepared to defend the door against all comers.

"They won't let us in to see Master Verre," Octavia said.

Grandmother raised an eyebrow and spoke in the lilting language of Samoya. The guards looked surprised, then relieved.

The first one answered in a firm but respectful voice. Grandmother sniffed and responded. The guard looked embarrassed, Octavia thought, but shook his head and repeated the same phrase. His spear didn't waver.

"All right, everyone," Grandmother told the gathering crowd of glass singers, "go back to your tasks.

"The Intan has ordered his men to keep everyone out of the office while he speaks to Master Verre. Geoffrey and I will undertake to guard them as well."

She sat down in a cushioned chair across from the guards and gestured for Geoffrey to take a chair for himself.

The other singers, with many looks back towards the office, reluctantly headed off. The guards, their expressions impassive, snapped back to attention. Octavia lingered.

"You too. Don't worry. Geoffrey and I will see that nothing untoward occurs."

Beware the intrigues of princes …

Still upset, Octavia stepped out into the back garden for some fresh air. If anything did happen, what could Grandmother or Geoffrey do? The Samoyans were as bad as the mountain Gorani, apparently. Lost in thought as she hurried down the garden's familiar path, she didn't pay much attention to her surroundings until someone shouted. She looked up just in time to catch an enormous amount of cold, stinking water across the face. She drew in breath to scream in protest and instantly regretted it as water filled her lungs instead of air. Loud trumpeting echoed off the garden's stone walls as she gagged and fought for breath.

"I am so very sorry," someone said in Samoyan-accented Albi. "Gajah is bathing and we didn't see you in time." It took Octavia, still coughing and struggling for air, another moment to get the water out of her eyes enough to see the speaker. The elephant's keeper, a tall, bearded man wearing a purple headband, stood with one hand on the side of his creature.

"Maru?" Was that the elephant keeper's name?

"Yes." He patted the elephant and said something to it in Samoyan. The elephant snorted loudly and shook it's head. The great ears flapped noisily.

"Again, I must apologize. Gajah enjoys his baths. He makes a game of them."

"Where's your bucket?" Octavia squeezed the water out of her sleeves. At least the summer afternoon was warm, but now she would have to bathe and change and take time to wash out this dress when she was meant to be studying.

"Ah. The elephant's trunk is most useful. It is hand and bucket all in one. Gajah bathes himself. I assist only by pumping the water up from the well."

"Now I know you're making fun of me." Octavia turned to leave. She hoped Alma or someone would be in the kitchen and could get her a fresh dress. Otherwise she would have to drip musty smelling water through the glassworks and upstairs to her room.

"Please ..." Maru called after her, but loud voices cut him off. Intan Negarawan, his face contorted with fury, strode out of the back door of the glassworks and down the garden path.

The two bodyguards and a number of other Samoyans, all looking deeply unhappy, hurried after the Intan. Grandfather, looking much more composed, followed. Maru jumped to attention beside the elephant.

The Intan turned back to face Grandfather, his face dark with rage. "I say it outright. You are a coward, old man. All the wealth of my kingdom is yours in exchange for the mirror. If gold truly means nothing to you, think of those who will die because you fear to act."

"I prefer to think of those who will live because I refuse to create too dangerous an instrument." Only Grandfather's narrowed eyes revealed the passion behind that mild voice.

Octavia barely stopped from crying out when the prince's hand dropped to his sword. Grandfather cocked his head to one side, as if simply curious to see what might happen next. The two men locked eyes. For a moment Octavia thought they truly might come to blows. Where were Geoffrey and Martin and the other singers? Grandfather stood alone against at least four armed men and an elephant, in his own home. She took a step forward, casting about for something to say, anything that might break the tension.

The kitchen door slammed and Alma hurried out.

"Master Verre," the cook said, wiping her hands on her apron, "forgive me, but he won't be put off. He says he must

see you this minute, and the Intan, as he's still here."

"Who?" Grandfather asked, frowning slightly.

"The head of the Metal Workers League, that Master Falchion. He's here with others, a delegation of the council."

"Surely their business is with Madame Verre."

"It is not," Falchion himself announced. The beefy metal worker had followed Alma out of the kitchen. He brushed past the cook and planted himself on the path in front of Intan Negarawan and Grandfather. Several well-dressed men and women, all wearing the green stole of council membership, joined him.

"Intan Negarawan, Glass Master Verre," the iron monger announced in his rusty baritone, "I am here to enjoin you, in the name of the Council of Albermarle, against any attempt to create or to cause to create, or to give to any other party the means to create, any so-called healing mirror. This is an instrument of death, as Master Verre knows full well. Shame on you, Verre, for allowing greed to cloud your judgment."

"But he didn't ..." Octavia objected.

"All monies paid for such an object are to be turned over to the council immediately." Falchion continued as if she hadn't spoken. He bounced on his toes as he spoke, an evil smirk lighting his face. Clearly he was enjoying this moment.

Intan Negarawan wrinkled his nose at the iron monger as if he gave off a particularly offensive smell. The prince gestured to his people and turned to leave. Falchion stepped into his path. The Intan's guards advanced, hands on their weapons. Octavia, certain again that blood would be shed, put her hands to her mouth.

"No, Falchion," Grandfather said in his mildest voice, "You have misjudged the situation. No money has exchanged hands. As I was just explaining ..."

"I'm not a fool, Verre. All Albermarle knows why the Samoyans are here and what they will pay for this piece. You will desist from making this sorcerous mirror, you will give all payment to me ... to the delegation," he amended hastily, "and the Samoyans, Lord Negarawan, will leave this city at the earliest moment possible. If you do not find your own way home today the city guards will be along to your inn at first light tomorrow to escort you to the lifts."

"Surely this is an over-reaction," Grandfather began.

"We shall never accept such an insult," the Intan growled. He coughed, then, and seemed to have trouble catching his breath.

"The council commands it," Falchion smirked. "You have no choice, Intan."

"Step aside," the Intan snarled. He wheezed as he spoke.

"I shall not. Even visiting royalty must abide by the council's orders within the city borders. You must go."

"I cannot," the Intan replied in a slightly more reasonable tone, "so long as you block my way. Shall I have my men clear the path?"

The bodyguards tensed. Falchion turned pale and stepped aside into the mud of the vegetable patch. The Intan and his party swept away toward the outer gate. Maru smiled at Octavia and spoke a word to the elephant. It trumpeted loudly and lumbered after the Intan, forcing the rest of the council delegation into the mud as well.

Grandfather glanced at Alma and Octavia. Understanding his meaning, they followed him back up the path to the kitchen door.

"Verre! I'll have that payment now."

Did that man never quit? Octavia wondered.

Grandfather turned back but waited for Octavia and Alma to pass before replying. "There is no payment. I refused the offer. You see, Falchion, I have not forgotten the death of my cousin. I told the Samoyans I will not make the mirror. Albermarle is safe from me. Thank you for bringing the council's message. I'm sure you can find your own way out."

Alma locked the kitchen door securely behind them, slamming the bolt into place with more force than necessary. Grandfather blew out a breath. His face cleared a little.

"Beware the intrigues of princes and politicians, my

dear." It sounded like a quote, but she couldn't place the source. "Too much ambition can be the death of a man; or of many, if he persuades them to follow."

"What will we do about the Samoyans and the council?"

"Madame Verre will deal with the council. I'll speak to Harmon; know Master Brin, our representative, don't you? Interesting that he was not among those who visited today. By their own rules the council should have at least informed Harmon and your grandmother before sending us this deputation. And we received no written warning. Falchion may yet find himself embarrassed by his hasty actions."

Grandfather *tcched* and accepted a steaming cup of tea from Alma. The cook handed a cup to Octavia as well before taking one herself. Octavia inhaled the lovely fragrance of rose hips and something else.

Could it be orange peel, at this time of year?

"What of the Samoyans?" she asked.

"Well, according to Falchion the Samoyans will leave in the morning. Perhaps the iron monger has his uses after all."

"And if they don't? What of the plague, Grandfather? Their people are dying. Is there really nothing we can do for them? Have you spoken to the physicians?"

Grandfather traded an unhappy glance with Alma.

"Albermarle's physicians say that they are aware of the illness and have been seeking a solution for some time. When it first struck the Samoyans naturally sent messengers in all directions, hoping someone might have a cure."

Grandfather sipped his tea, and then frowned at Octavia.

"What happened to you, my dear? You look as if you fell down the well."

They are not our Samoyans

The visitor's bell rang as everyone gathered for breakfast the next day. Halfnote, closest to the door, ran out into the humid morning to answer it. A light mist drifted down from low-hanging clouds, dampening her hair and clothing. The bell clanged again, louder, as she hurried to the gate.

"Coming, coming," she called, irritated by the ringer's impatience.

"Verre House," Falchion's rusty voice boomed. "By order of the council, I demand that you allow us entry."

Halfnote nearly turned and ran back to the kitchen. Octavia would answer it, she thought and forced herself forward. Octavia wouldn't be scared of that mean old ironmonger. She took a breath, pulled back the lock and opened the gate, even managing to curtsey as she did so.

The square-jawed metal worker stood, his muscled arms folded, in the gateway. Behind him a squad of city guards blocked the road. In front of Falchion, her shoulders hunched and her face drawn, stood a Samoyan. Halfnote recognized her as a member of the Intan's party but didn't know her name. It wasn't the physician, but one of those who followed in the Intan's wake when he visited.

"What is it, Falchion?" Halfnote turned to see Grandma, her face tight with anger, standing in the path behind her. As it was still early, Grandma's long hair, damp from washing and not yet curled, was pulled back into a simple ponytail. Halfnote scampered out of the way. Grandma said something in gentle Samoyan to the woman. Then she glared fiercely at the ironmonger.

"You, Falchion, are not welcome here," she added in severe tones. "I ask again. What do you want?"

Halfnote moved as slowly as she dared back to the kitchen. "Council business," Falchion blustered. "Your Samoyans are still here, despite the council's order to leave."

"What is that to us? They are not *our* Samoyans. We do not command them."

"They are here because of you."

"We did not invite them."

"Please," the woman said in Albi, her voice quiet but strained. "We cannot ..." she paused, and bit her lower lip. "Please. Something has happened." She glanced over her shoulder at Falchion, then gave Grandma a pleading look.

Falchion snorted.

"What is it?" Grandma asked the woman, also in Albi. Worry

tinged her gentle tones. Halfnote crept closer to the gate to listen.

"The Intan ..." the woman visibly pulled herself together, "He is ill. He collapsed yesterday after returning to the inn. Others of our party also show signs of sickness."

"Oh, stop this nonsense," Falchion snapped. "I … The council is not fooled by this ridiculous deceit. This is a trick to delay your departure and it won't work. The city guards will have you and your people out of Albermarle today."

"Come to the inn. See for yourself."

"If they are ill, that is all the more reason for you to leave us." For the first time Falchion looked uneasy.

"Our healer says to move them now would be murder."

"If they are truly ill ..." Grandma began.

"Halfnote," Grandpa said quietly in her ear, "go back to the house. Quickly now."

She jumped in surprise and ran for the kitchen. Alma and half a dozen others stood just inside the door, all *listening* intently.

"What happened?" Robbie asked her. "Did she say that the Intan is sick?"

"Quiet," Marissa hissed. "I can't hear. What is Master Verre saying to them now?"

"Madame Verre is leaving with the Samoyan woman and Falchion," Martin reported from his vantage point beside the window. "And Master Verre is on his way back."

Everyone, even Alma, rushed back to their places around the breakfast table and tried to look unconcerned as Grandpa entered.

"Martin," Grandpa said, "run get Geoffrey and Lorraine. They can breakfast here if they haven't eaten yet. Singers will meet with me in the office chambers as soon as they arrive. Alma, we need a complete cleansing. Every inch scrubbed."

Martin ran a hand across his shiny scalp and dashed off.

"How bad is it?" the cook asked, her face pale.

Grandpa shook his head. "I fear that we may have been more foolish than we yet know." His gaze lingered a moment on Robbie and Halfnote, then he hurried out of the kitchen.

"Well, eat up you lot," Alma snapped before anyone else could say anything. "You heard him. We've a good day's work ahead of us. There'll be no dawdling, now."

Alma set the apprentices to work in pairs. Halfnote found herself knocking down cobwebs and dusting with Alice while Dan and Galliard followed with hot soapy water to wash all around. For once no one argued about what tasks they were given or who they had to work with. They began in the topmost attic and worked their way down through all the various floors and rooms, down into the deepest basement.

Alma pushed them to finish quickly so that the older apprentices could set up tall braziers filled with slow-burning herbs in every room. Halfnote wrinkled her nose against the sharp-smelling medicinal smoke. It filled every corner of Verre House. There was no escaping the caustic scent.

Halfnote and Alice put down their dust cloths and brooms just in time to help Alma serve a cold lunch at the kitchen table normally reserved for breakfast.

Grandma returned just toward the end of the meal. Grandpa himself rushed out to open the gate for her.

Halfnote, sitting at the kitchen table with the other apprentices, heard Grandpa speaking angrily to someone in the garden. He sounded as angry as Halfnote had ever witnessed; even angrier than the day when Papa told Grandpa he didn't want Halfnote to live at Verre House.

"You do this on purpose. You seek to force my hand." The main entrance slammed open.

"No, I swear it." Half note recognized the dusky tones of Argana, the Samoyan healer. She was the woman who nearly knocked over her pastry tray when the Samoyans first spoke to Grandpa. "By his strictest order, only those still healthy accompanied the Intan. No one stricken before we left Samoya would have survived this long."

"And how many more lives will this trip of yours cost?"

Grandpa's voice rumbled down the hallway and into the kitchen. "How many more will fall ill because you met them on your way? How far have you spread your contagion?"

"I tell you, all were healthy when we left." Now Argana sounded angry. "We traveled two months with no sign of sickness. I do not understand why we see it now. It makes no sense. Nothing about this plague does."

The visitor's gate clanged open again, jangling the bell. Ted half rose, as if to answer it. Alma looked out and gasped.

"What is it?" Phyllis hurried over to peer out the window with her. Octavia and several others followed her. Halfnote strained with the rest to hear the argument still raging in the reception hall.

"The guard," Alma said, "they're bringing the Samoyans here." The elephant trumpeted as if to echo her words.

Grandma came into the kitchen and looked around at the assembled group without really seeming to see anyone. She looked pale, as distressed as Halfnote had ever seen her.

"We have guests," she said. "They are quite ill, some of them. They will be placed in the guest and master suites. I'll share Octavia's room and Master Verre will take the spare room on the men's side. They'll need tending, and their meals delivered, Alma. I think they might find your hot barley and garlic soup particularly efficacious."

"As of right now, no apprentice may enter the master or guest suites for any reason. No one else should enter them except by permission from a master or Alma. We'll want extra braziers there as well, I think. Frank, Phyllis, please see to it."

"Octavia, go immediately to Doctor Hahnemann and bring him here. Verre House will pay all costs. Everyone else, continue with the cleaning or as Alma directs you."

"I'll have to send to the market for more herbs and some other supplies," Alma said.

Grandma nodded distractedly. "Whatever you need. Top up the foodstuffs as well. Don't worry about cost. We need clean bedding ... Laiertes, Annie, Alice please bring all you can find to the entrance of the master chambers. Call to me from outside the door when you get it." She hurried out. Halfnote looked at Robbie. For once even he looked worried.

It's the glass singers' fault

Octavia traded her indoor slippers for leather shoes and dashed out the front gate. She dodged through a gap in the line of Samoyans entering the front garden.

How many people has the Intan brought?

In the street she found herself face to face with Gajah. The elephant raised its trunk as if in greeting. Octavia, caught off guard, raised a hand in return. She ran on down the road toward the physicians' quarter. Normally, she enjoyed a visit to the city proper.

Normally, Octavia thought wryly, she wouldn't be exchanging greetings with an elephant. And where was the elephant's keeper? She hoped he wasn't ill.

Doctor Hahnemann's house was located in the middle of the physicians' quarter above the marketplace, next to the largest houses of healing. Octavia's path took her from the quiet lane in front of Verre House to the much noisier main streets leading toward the market. Horses, carts and pedestrians filled the cobblestoned roads.

Octavia grew increasingly uneasy. Surely it was her imagination, but she felt as if people stared at her. Angry faces came out of the crowd to glare at her and then vanished again. It seemed as if they stared particularly at her pendant.

She walked faster and ducked down a quieter street. She firmly ignored the feeling that several people followed her.

Oh stop it. The streets are always crowded. I'm just nervous because of the Samoyans.

Even so, she entered the physicians' quarter with a sense of great relief. Doctor Hahnemann's house stood half way up the crowded street. Voices murmured around her, but she disregarded them. She ran up the steps to the front door and jangled the glass bell. The hot sun burned down on her uncovered head as she waited. No one answered. She jangled the bell again and peered through the window. By the swirls in the glass it was probably Lorraine's work, she noted automatically. But why did no one answer the door?

"They're gone," a woman called from the street. Octavia turned to see who spoke. A gray-haired fishmonger peered up at her, one hand shielding her eyes from the sun. "They've all left. Fled."

"What do you mean, fled?"

"What do you think I mean? They fear the illness. Left in the night. Every single healer. Gone north, some say."

The woman couldn't be serious. "All of them? Surely not."

"Are you daft? They fled for their lives. No doubt the rest of us should do likewise. Go home, girl. Whoever you have that needs tending, you'll have to see to them yourself."

"She's not daft." A muscled man in labourers ' clothes stopped by the fishmonger. He wore a tiny copper hammer on a silver chain. "She's a glass singer. Look at her charm."

Octavia automatically reached for the dragon's head.

"No she's not," the fishmonger snorted. "Look at *her*. She's a Khelani. She's a river rat, not a craftworker."

"I'm both," Octavia snapped, despite the fishmonger's look of warning. *River rat indeed!* The woman gave a disgusted *tcch!* and shoved her half empty cart into the street to leave.

"You're Verre's girl, aren't you?" sneered the man.

"And you're a carpenter. What of it?"

*"Carpenters didn't bring plague into Albermarle and threaten the city with sorcerous mirrors, now did they, girlie?"

"What? That's nonsense." Falchion's nonsense, she realized and then understood the man's enmity. The carpenters' guild was closely allied with the metal workers
because carpenters used iron nails and hammers for their
trade. Other people in the street stopped to listen, their
expressions ranging from curiosity to anger.

"Neither have the glass singers. We didn't invite the Samoyans. And Master Verre refused their commission."

"Liar!" someone shouted. A flung cobblestone narrowly missed her cheek. It hit the window in the door behind her, and bounced onto the narrow stoop. Octavia flinched from the stone. The quickly growing crowd held her trapped against the building. The door behind her was locked; its window unmarred by the rock.

Albermarle was known far and wide for the peacefulness of its citizens. Would this mob really attack her?

"Here now, what's this?" A gruff voice, obviously used to giving orders, cut clearly through the crowd's angry grumblings. Sharp whistles sounded at the periphery of the gathering mob.

Thanks be. Octavia felt weak with relief. The city guard had arrived and were calling for reinforcements.

"Make way, make way I say." A burly man with short cropped brown hair and beard shoved his way through the crowd towards her. He wore the brown uniform of the city guard and an orange sergeant's insignia on his shoulder.

People refused to move aside for him until he grabbed two and physically shoved them out of his way.

"She's a glass singer! It's *her* fault the physicians are gone!" an anonymous voice. Angry muttering filled the air.

The sergeant clambered up on the stoop beside Octavia and looked her over. His focus sharpened on her pendant.

"Are you hurt, miss?" he asked quietly.

"N…no."

Another missile, a ball of mud or something worse, splattered against the side of the building. Octavia didn't see who threw it but a pair of guards did. They fought their way through the mass of people, grabbed a youth and began dragging him away.

"That's enough of that," the sergeant shouted. "You'll keep the peace in Albermarle or face the council for breaking it. We've the miscreant in custody and will see the matter through. You'll go on about your business now, you will, or face the council yourselves."

Miscreant? Did he mean the boy who threw the mud? Surely he didn't mean … Octavia opened her mouth to protest but closed it in the face of the sergeant's sharp frown.

Most of the crowd began to dissipate. A stubborn core, centered on the carpenter who first accosted her, remained.

"With me, miss." The sergeant jerked his head at a trio of guards. The three forced their way to the front of the angry knot and pushed them back. The sergeant took Octavia by the arm and led her down the steps into the street. He hurried her down a tiny alley.

Angry shouting broke out. The sergeant increased his speed, dragging Octavia with him.

Something smacked into the stones behind them. They turned abruptly down another alley, splashing through the trickle of water that ran down its center. They came out onto the main boulevard that rounded the main marketplace. The sergeant whistled and waved. A horse-drawn carriage for hire pulled up beside them.

"Official council business," the sergeant snapped to the driver. He shoved Octavia into the carriage and slammed its door shut behind her. The driver swore.

"Official business. Free ride, you mean, for you and your honey," the driver complained.

"I'll give you a receipt," the sergeant, still standing in the street, said in a bored tone. "Take it to the council for payment." Up close Octavia could see the crow's feet around the sergeant's eyes and the gray hairs in his beard. He was older than she'd first thought.

"Verre House will pay," Octavia told the driver. She leaned out the window to speak. "Please, I just want to get home." The sergeant swore and shoved her back out of sight.

"Have you no sense at all? Stay hidden, if you want to stay safe. Draw the blinds, for both our sakes."

"Verre House?" Now the driver sounded more alarmed than angry. "I'm not going there. Not for any money."

"What? What is wrong with everyone today?" Outrage replaced her earlier fear. "We haven't done anything."

The sergeant grabbed the driver by his shoulders and pulled the man bodily out of his seat and onto the road. He jumped lightly up onto the carriage to take the driver's place.

"I'll return this to you in due course," the sergeant called to the driver. He took up the reins and clucked to the horses. They trotted into traffic while the outraged driver shouted curses after them.

To Octavia's great relief no one followed.

Quarantined

They made their way through Albermarle's crowded streets easily enough. It took just minutes to reach Verre House. Octavia, still shaking, stumbled out of the carriage. Only then did she see the city guards at the entrance. A large parchment carrying the council's gold seal blocked the gate.

"What is it? What's happened?" Octavia felt light-headed, as frightened as she had the day of the floods, before word arrived that her family was safe.

"You're under an order of quarantine." The sergeant dropped down, tossed the reins to another guard and took her arm again. "You should not have left Verre House."

"I ... didn't know. There was no order when I left."

"An oversight." The sergeant hurried her to the gate. A guard pulled away the parchment while another rang the bell.

"What do you want now?" Alma called angrily.

"To return one of your own," the sergeant replied.

Octavia heard the scrape of the bolt being jerked back.

"Is that Octavia? Is she all right?"

"Yes, Alma. I'm fine."

The gate crashed open and Alma clutched Octavia against her ample bosom.

"Thanks be, thanks be. We've been so worried."

"Go on inside, then," the sergeant said in firm but more gentle tones as he nudged them through the gate. "By order of the council, you cannot leave the confines of Verre House."

"For how long?" Octavia pulled free of Alma's grip to stare at the sergeant's grim face.

"Until the order is lifted."

"But we've done nothing wrong."

The sergeant refused to meet her eyes.

"Then it's for your own safety. You saw the mob. Do you want to face them again? Stay home until things settle down."

"Mob? What mob? Chevalier," Alma grabbed the sergeant's arm. "What mob?"

"The mob he rescued me from," Octavia explained, "outside Doctor Hahnemann's house. People blame us for the Samoyans' plague." Octavia started to push past Alma, then turned back to the sergeant. "Thank you for helping me."

"Just doing my job," he said with a shrug.

"Have all of the physicians truly fled?"

The sergeant nodded. "All that I'm aware of."

"Chevalier," Alma said. "What are we to do for supplies in the meantime? We have over fifty people behind these walls now and half of them ill. Do you mean to starve us?"

"You'll have to take it up with the council," the sergeant said in the same bored voice he used with the carriage driver. "I just do what they tell me. The market's all but empty in any case," he added in a different tone. "Those who came in this morning unaware are packing up to leave. Everyone's afraid."

Octavia left them arguing at the gate. All she wanted at this moment was a cup of tea in Alma's comfortable kitchen.

The physicians have fled

Halfnote, the twins, and Dan and Laiertes spent the afternoon washing every piece of Verre House bedding and clothing in hot sudsy water before hanging it all out to dry. Fortunately the summer sun had made short work of the morning's clouds. Everything dried quickly. The apprentices took turns practicing their dragon skills by maintaining the fire under the washing tubs.

Maru, one Samoyan who still appeared quite healthy, removed Gajah's finery. With the elephant's help he pulled down several dead trees in the thicket behind the glassworks. Together they dragged the trees into the back garden. He then cheerfully helped Frank and Galliard chop the dry timber into firewood. Gajah stood obediently in the corner assigned to him and tucked into a pile of old lettuce.

By the end of the afternoon Halfnote felt as if she had spent her whole life scrubbing. She was soaked from head to toe with soapy wash water. Her fingers ached from the heat of the water and too many accidental scrapes against the rough rubbing board. She responded with relief when Alma called her into the kitchen to chop herbs for the smoking braziers.

A Samoyan woman came to the kitchen for more Soup for the ill. From the long shape of her face and her silver belt, Halfnote recognized her as the woman at the gate.

"Healer Argana asks for word of your physicians," the woman told Alma. "Do you know when they'll arrive?"

Halfnote turned in surprise. Didn't the Samoyans know? Alma caught Halfnote's eye. "That's enough," the cook said. "Go fetch more garlic from the storeroom." She scampered away obediently.

"The physicians have fled," she heard Alma say.

To Halfnote's surprise the Samoyan woman only sighed.

"They are wise. In Samoya, the physicians were among the first to die. The only survivors were those who ran away. But what shall we do?"

The right price

To save time as always, Halfnote climbed into the kitchen's supply lift. She lowered herself smoothly and soundlessly into the cool, dark basement. She pushed open the wooden door and hopped out. She waited a moment for her eyes to adjust to the dim light that leaked down through the lift shaft. As usual, she'd forgotten a candle. After a moment, black lumps and lines resolved themselves into barrels of wheat and barley flour, woven bags filled with apples and parsnips or hanging strings of dried apricots.

A pair of footsteps, one set a sharp click of hobnails and the other a scraping of soft leather soles sounded on the stone steps that led into the storeroom. Voices murmured. Halfnote recognized Geoffrey's fluid bass; a Samoyan lilt shaped the second speaker's tones. It was Razak, the Intan's chancellor. Halfnote started to call out but Chancellor Razak spoke first.

"We are alone here?"

"Yes, yes," Geoffrey said impatiently. "It's a storeroom. There's no one else here."

Halfnote's stomach tightened. Geoffrey wouldn't appreciate stumbling over an apprentice in the middle of what was clearly meant to be a private conversation.

She faded back into a nook between two barrels and squatted down out of sight. She hoped Geoffrey wouldn't take too long. She didn't want to keep Alma waiting either.

A light flared.

"Put that out. They'll see it upstairs," Geoffrey hissed.

The room went dark again.

"What's your offer?" the junior master demanded.

"You are certain you can make the mirror?" Chancellor Razak asked. Halfnote stifled a gasp. Surely he didn't mean...

"For the right price. Verre taught me everything he knows. And the records of every making are in the library upstairs. Yes, we can do it. It will require a certain investment in advance, however."

Chancellor Razak snorted. "You shall have everything we offered the cowardly Verre as soon as the mirror is made."

"The ingredients are costly. I cannot simply take them from house stores. Their absence would be noticed. Verre would know why they were taken. Coward or not, he's no fool."

"Here," the Samoyan snapped. Halfnote heard the clink of coins. "Will this help you begin?"

"Oh, yes." Halfnote heard the triumph in Geoffrey's voice. "When the mirror is done …"

"All Samoya will celebrate your accomplishments."

"And my own glassworks …"

"Save us from this plague and nothing will be denied you. The Intan swears it."

Halfnote waited long moments after the sound of their steps vanished up the stairs before leaving her hiding place.

She could barely believe her own ears. Geoffrey meant to make the *Hygeia paraphasis* despite Grandpa's warnings. She should tell him. Just in time she remembered to snatch up a string of garlic before jumping back into the lift. She pulled so hard on the guide rope that the platform flew past the kitchen and half way up to the next level before she could stop it.

The Samoyan woman still sat with slumped shoulders at the kitchen table. Heavy tears rolled silently down her face.

"Go on." Alma pushed Halfnote toward the preparation counter. "Get to it. All of this garlic needs mincing and there's chamomile to brew for tea." For once Alma didn't ask what had taken so long.

"I need to see Grandpa, I mean, Master Verre. It's about the *Hygeia paraphasis*. I'll come back right away."

"It won't make any difference," the Samoyan woman said. Her tears gathered unsteadily on her chin then dripped into a small puddle on the table. "Nothing will. The plague will take us all in the end."

"But you survived. You're not sick. What did you do?"

"Hush," Alma said. "Don't be impertinent. Do as I say."

"But I need to see Master Verre. It's important."

"You'll see him at supper. And that will have to do."

Mama has the sickness

But Halfnote didn't see Grandpa at supper. Or Grandma, or Octavia. None of the masters or senior singers attended. The Samoyans, even those still healthy, ate in the sick rooms. Everyone who did come to the table looked tired and worried.

Despite the day's lingering heat, Alma served up hot barley soup redolent with onions and garlic. The soup smelled and tasted strongly of herbs known more for their healing properties than for their tastiness. Only Robbie tucked into his meal with any real energy.

Halfnote dunked a bit of bread into the soup. She had to tell Grandpa, or at least Octavia, about Geoffrey. She would find them after the meal, if she could avoid getting stuck on kitchen duty again before bedtime.

She watched as the orange soup spread through the soft brown bread until it foundered against the dam created by the thick, dark crust. How did Geoffrey think he could make the *Hygeia paraphasis* without anyone noticing? Even apprentices felt the energy created by ordinary work chants. It didn't matter where they happened to be in the building. Glass workers were chosen for their sensitivity to the creative energies, after all. The singing of a piece like the healing mirror would take incredible power. Even Alma would likely feel it and she was just a cook.

Steam wafted out of Halfnote's bowl and off the bread. She might welcome hot soup on a cold winter's night, but not on this warm summer evening. The soaked bread reminded her of something, but she couldn't think what.

"Eat your food," Marissa snapped from across the table. Halfnote glared back. Fat Marissa couldn't tell her what to do. She might be older but she was still just another apprentice.

"Are you feeling all right, dear?" Alma gave her a worried look. Now everyone at the table stared at her.

Halfnote blushed and took a quick bite of the soup-drenched bread, careful not to let anything spill. In fact, she didn't have much appetite. She wanted to see her grandparents or Octavia. The barley soup tasted too much like sick room fare. Did Alma expect them all to get ill as well?

Halfnote looked around the table. Marissa, her face still red from the afternoon's laundering, unhappily shoved a spoonful of soup into her mouth. Galliard sat at the end of the table closest to the kitchen, his food all but untouched. He stared out the door towards the sick rooms. Dan chewed thoughtlessly on his lower lip while stirring his soup with his spoon. The twins ate mechanically, without once giggling or whispering or kicking Halfnote under the table. Robbie, his bowl nearly empty, smiled when she glanced at him. He, at least, seemed unaffected by the day's dark mood.

Everyone jumped at the sound of shouting outside. The gate banged open; it smacked against the wall as if kicked.

"I thought we were under quarantine," Dan said.

"We are," Alma said. She jumped up from her seat and rushed outside. Indecipherable words voiced in a desperate baritone echoed against the walls. Halfnote took a breath.

That baritone sounded very familiar … could it be?

"Bring her in this way," Alma told someone. The front entrance clattered open and the desperate baritone reverberated down the hallway from the main reception area.

Halfnote gasped and dropped her bread.

"Papa!"

She knocked over her chair as she jumped up and dashed down the hallway, unaware of the other apprentices following close behind. Rough hands grabbed her just as she reached the reception hall.

"No, Halfnote." Geoffrey's thick fingers bit painfully into her shoulders. "You mustn't."

What? Had Geoffrey seen her in the storeroom after all? She twisted and kicked out, but his bruising grip held.

"Let me go!" she screamed. "Papa!"

"Ouch, stop it," Geoffrey yelled as her foot connected with his shin. His hold loosened and Halfnote pulled free. She sprinted for Papa, then skidded to a stop at the sight of him.

Papa stood in the middle of the well-lit reception hall, his face gray. He held Mama in his muscular arms. A dark-haired young man in the woolen trousers and tunic common to Aethelstan held Mama's legs. Mama's head rolled back, with only the whites of her eyes visible. Her long brown hair fell untidily around her shoulders. Her labored breathing rang out harshly in the rasping cough that even Halfnote knew as the mark of the Samoyans' sickness. Sweat darkened the front of Mama's brown travel dress. Geoffrey caught Halfnote's arm, but she didn't fight him.

Mama had the illness.

Halfnote's heart all but stopped.

Mama had the illness that no one knew how to cure.

"It's all up and down the river," Papa said. "It struck without warning two days ago. People fell ill everywhere at once. No one knows what to do. Thousands are sick. They're burning the bodies of the dead and the homes of the afflicted in Malmesbury and Aethelstan. In spite of all that the disease keeps spreading."

Halfnote put her hands to her mouth. Mama had the illness. And Alma said there were no physicians left in Albermarle. What would they do now?

"Mama," she whispered.

Grandma and Grandpa rushed out of the office. Their cries of dismay brought out the other singers. Grandma cradled Mama's head in her arms while Grandpa pushed aside the dark-haired townsman to take her legs.

"We dodged the city guard all the way," Papa continued. "All Albermarle is under quarantine. The guards say they'll kill anyone who breaks it, even to seek food or medicine."

"Octavia, run tell Alma …" Grandma began, then realized the cook stood beside her, helping to hold Mama.

"No, go find Argana. She's in the sick room. Tell her... No. Of course we'll take Melody there. Sylvia, prepare another bed. Octavia, see to Halfnote before she bites Geoffrey."

Halfnote opened her mouth to protest this slander even as Octavia caught her up in a rough hug. Geoffrey released her with a relieved look.

"I want to see Mama," she said.

"You can't." Octavia hugged her tightly as the adults carried Mama away. "Mother is sick. You must keep away from her until she gets well, or you might get sick too."

"Will she get well?" Halfnote sobbed.

"Shhh, what kind of question is that? Of course she will,"

Octavia said in her most calming voice. She wiped Halfnote's tears away with her hand.

Octavia makes a promise

Octavia felt her heart turn cold even as she spoke. Could Mother recover? Would anyone in the sick rooms survive? Argana and the other Samoyans didn't think so. Albermarle's physicians obviously didn't believe it either.

Stop it. Despair helps no one.

They would find a way. The library held medical manuals from every part of the world. Every sickness had a cure and they would find it. Grandfather would leave no stone unturned. He might not make the healing mirror but he would find a cure. She didn't doubt that.

"Don't you worry, Mother will get well," Octavia told Halfnote and deliberately plated her words with command tones made of steel. "We'll make sure of it, won't we?"

"Yes, we will." Halfnote's voice trembled just a little.

Octavia thought her heart might just crack when she saw the trust in her sister's eyes. Mother was sick of a disease no one knew how to heal; the entire city was under quarantine; the physicians had fled rather than face the illness …

…and I just promised Halfnote that I'll find a cure.

Well, no one ever accused her of too little ambition.

"Good." Octavia managed a smile. "Now wash your face and make yourself useful. Alma needs all of our help."

Octavia fiercely blinked back her own tears as her sister dashed to the kitchen.

I will find a cure, Octavia vowed. *I will not let Mother die. Whatever it takes, I will do it.*

She turned to see Geoffrey rubbing his shin.

"Your sister takes after you."

In spite of everything Octavia almost laughed.

"I haven't kicked you in years."

Geoffrey just shook his head. "Will he change his mind now? About the mirror?"

Octavia turned cold again. "I don't know. I'll ask."

"And if he won't?"

Octavia turned away to keep Geoffrey from seeing the anger – or was it fear? – in her eyes.

"I told you, I'll ask."

And if Grandfather says no? Octavia put that thought aside as well. She would find the cure. One way or another. Mother would survive and once the cure was found, so would everyone else. She hurried into the master chambers.

What thieves know

"We learned this from thieves," Argana was telling the singers clustered around Mother's bed when Octavia arrived, "those who made their living robbing the wealthy dead. Alas, we'd lost most of our physicians by the time we learned it."

The Samoyan healer dipped her hands into a wide-mouthed bowl filled with a golden liquid. Vinegar, Octavia realized from the smell. Argana held up her arms, now bare, and let the liquid run down nearly to her elbows before wiping it up with a towel. The smell of vinegar nearly overpowered even the sharp fragrance of the smoking herbs.

"Wash always, before touching the ill, and after."

Argana placed the back of her hand against Mother's forehead. Octavia bit her lip as Mother moaned.

"She has fever. She needs tea brewed from the flowers of yellow goat weed, if you have it."

"Goat weed only flowers in early spring here," Alma said, "and we've none in our stores. We've plenty of chamomile or laurel, though."

"Laurel, then." Argana's eyes remained focused on Mother. "It also eases breathing."

Mother's breath whistled painfully as if responding to

Argana's words. Octavia found her own breathing difficult. The healer's calm manner eased her fears a little, but even Argana with all her knowledge could only delay the outcome.

Will Grandfather consider making the mirror now? Octavia looked up to find her father, pale and red-eyed, watching her from the other side of her mother's bed. The lines around his eyes and mouth were drawn tight with worry.

"Octavia," Grandmother's crisp voice called her to attention. "Take Trader Breydon to the kitchen and get him something to eat. I imagine he'll want a bath as well. And clean clothes, after."

"Bathe first, Trader," Argana commanded. "In hot water with two cups of vinegar added to the water. For your own safety, girl, do not touch him until he is clean."

"I am not sick," Father muttered.

"You are not sick *yet*," Argana replied calmly. "The bath is a precaution. Pray that it works." She met his angry gaze with a look, Octavia thought, that communicated both the detached attention of a healer and somehow also the gut-deep grief of someone who has lost too much. Father expelled a breath and looked slightly less angry.

"Come on, Father." Octavia mustered her most business-like tones. "You know Mother is in good hands."

An argument renewed

Once bathed, shaven and dressed in clean townsman's clothes from those he kept at the glassworks, Father returned to the kitchen. Exhaustion and something else Octavia refused to call fear muted his usual restlessness. Muscular in a taut, lean way, Father was a man used to moving about.

Halfnote happily served him a meat pie and poured out steaming mugs of chamomile tea for each of them before settling possessively onto Father's lap. Robbie and Dan stood at the sink washing the supper dishes while Alma, Sylvia and Martin carried food and tea to the sick rooms.

The dark-haired young townsman who arrived with Father,

now also freshly bathed and wearing clean clothes, sat at the other end of the preparation table with Annie and Alice. The trio sat with their heads together and spoke in low tones.

How bad is it? Octavia desperately wanted to ask Father, but hesitated to do so in front of Halfnote and the others.

"How did you get past the guards?" she asked instead.

Father grimaced. "It pays to have friends. And I know a few paths the guards don't."

"Papa," Halfnote asked, "where are Mischa and Cadie?"

"I sent them north, with Aunt Lily." Father blew on his tea. "You should go as well. They have no sickness there."

"Are they well?" Octavia asked.

Father nodded. "That healer; she's Samoyan, isn't she? On the river, the wagging tongues blame the Samoyans for the disease. Even calmer heads insist it started there. They say a great party of Samoyan royalty traveled up the Khelana last week. Complete with an elephant, if you can believe it, leaving the sickness in their wake."

"It's true, about the royal party, anyway. They're here, in Verre House. The elephant is in the back garden."

Father choked on his tea.

"An elephant in Alma's garden? I can't believe she allows it," he gasped, once he stopped coughing. "How did they ever manage to get it on the lifts?"

"Gajah's smart," Halfnote piped up. "He knows how to behave. Maru had a long talk with him and now he leaves the vegetables alone. And he doesn't make nearly as much noise as he used to." Father's eyebrows went up in that comic look he had when surprised. "I like him," Halfnote added. "He has a confident voice. His legs feel funny, though."

"Do they?" Father laughed. "Now I've heard everything: An elephant in Albermarle on a first name basis with my daughters. It's enough to make you think the dragons really will return." He glanced around the kitchen and then leaned toward Octavia.

"What do the Samoyans want?" he whispered.

Octavia looked around as well. Robbie and Dan, up to their elbows in sudsy water, were engrossed in some low-voiced argument. The twins and their dark-haired visitor continued their own intent conversation.

Octavia shrugged. "It's no secret," she replied in a normal

tone. "They want us to create a healing mirror, to help them find a cure for the sickness. They readily admit that it struck first in Samoya. They insist, though, that only the healthy traveled with the Intan. I'm certain they didn't expect the plague to follow."

The twins and their visitor looked up.

"So they would say." Then returning hope washed some of the darkness from Papa's eyes. "Of course; a healing mirror. What supplies do you need? The sickness has brought chaos in its wake but I know who to contact. What do you need?" He straightened in excitement and nearly unseated Halfnote. She squealed a protest and clung to him.

Octavia shook her head. "Grandfather refused the job."

"He *what?* I think you'd better get down," Father told Halfnote in a deceptively mild tone. She reluctantly did so.

"Did I misunderstand you?" Father leaned forward and placed both hands on the table as if about to stand. His voice rose in disbelief. "Verre *refused* to make a healing mirror? In the face of this plague?"

"It is a sorcerous piece." Octavia unconsciously backed away from the table and the storm in Father's face, "banned by every country, even Samoya. The council just renewed the ban, to make certain we do not create it."

She realized, vaguely, that Robbie and Dan had stopped their washing to stare at them. The twins and their dark-haired visitor watched as well, the young man's expression tight with dismay.

Halfnote stood uncertainly between herself and Father, as if not sure which way to run. Octavia heard a noise in the doorway and knew somehow that Martin had started to enter and then retreated.

"He refused …" Father repeated as if still unable to believe his own ears. His large hands clenched into fists. "Surely now … Melody … his own daughter … he must surely make it now. He's made these mirrors before, hasn't he? He can hardly refuse now that the life of his own daughter is at stake. I'll go talk to him."

"Father, no…"

"Trader Breydon, wait," the dark-haired young man with the twins called out. "Verre's right, you know."

But Father had already left the kitchen.

"Octavia …" Halfnote tugged at her sleeve.

"Not now."

Octavia pulled free of her sister's hand and ran after Father. *Not again.* The last time Father and Grandfather openly disagreed their argument raged for days. She didn't want another fight between them. Not with Mother ill.

Halfnote watched in dismay as Octavia rushed after Papa. *But I need to tell you about Geoffrey*, she didn't dare say out loud. She started to follow Octavia but Alma's firm hand stopped her. Where had she come from?

"Will they fight?" Dan asked. His eyes were bright, as if he found the idea exciting.

"When did they ever stop?" bald Martin snorted. He entered the kitchen from the hallway. "Here we go again."

"Stop it, all of you," Alma commanded. "It's between Master Verre and Trader Breydon and no one else's business."

Dan flushed. "Is there anything to eat?" he asked.

"It's our business if Verre decides to make the mirror," Martin retorted. "We're the ones who will do the making and we're the ones who will face the council's wrath for it, after."

"But they can't, they mustn't," the stranger said. "You wait here," he told the twins, "while I talk to Master Verre."

"Sorry," Martin said, fixing less than friendly eyes on the visitor, "but who are you?" Halfnote had wondered that too.

"I'm Peter." He gestured toward the twins. "I'm Alice and Annie's brother. Our father sent me to bring them home when we heard that the Samoyans were coming here to buy a healing mirror. Aethelstan has seen what a *Hygeia mortolo* can do. We fear the mirror more than the plague."

"But Master Verre refused …"

"Yes, yes, I know that now." Peter waved his hands in a placating gesture. "The twins told me. But wild rumors are flying everywhere. No one in Aethelstan believed Verre would refuse the Samoyans' offer. They came to us first, you know, hoping to buy a mirror already made. We know how much they will pay for it."

Halfnote pulled free of Alma's hand, dizzy with the thoughts swirling through her head. Mama was sick and no one knew how to help her. Grandpa didn't want to make the healing mirror, but Papa did. So did Geoffrey. He had taken money to do it in secret. Grandpa would be furious when he found out. And he would find out, Halfnote knew. Once the making began, everyone in the glassworks would know. The energy would be unmistakable.

Without the mirror, how would they help Mama?

Everyone who got sick died. The Samoyans had been very clear about that. Halfnote knew about death. She'd seen the lifeless bodies bobbing down the Khelana River after the flood; cold, bloated cows and dogs and even people who stared unblinking at the clouded sky...

Mama ... Did helping Mama mean helping Geoffrey?

Octavia promised that we would find a cure. And her sister never lied. Once she made up her mind to do something, Halfnote knew, nothing could stop her. Ever. Octavia would find the cure for Mama even if no one else could.

The twins' brother, Peter, stood talking with Martin and Alma, his face and tones intent. He agreed with Grandpa; that the mirror would do more harm than good. And Grandpa was almost never wrong, especially when it came to glass.

If Grandpa wouldn't make it to help the Samoyans she doubted that he would make the mirror for Mama. Grandpa always helped other people when he could. He'd given Robbie a place when no one could find his parents, even though Robbie sang about as well as an angry cat. Grandpa didn't care what the other singers said about Robbie's voice. She looked up to see Robbie watching her. He smiled. She tried to smile back.

Did Robbie ever dream of the river?

It's not your fight

Octavia hurried up the corridor. Her footsteps echoed faintly off the stone floor, muted only a little by the woolen tapestries draping the walls. In the reception hall Father bellowed in the voice he normally reserved for shouting orders across the wide Khelana: "Verre! Where are you? We need to talk."

"Father, please calm down," Octavia called. A hand

caught her arm as she passed the entrance to the master suites.

"Let them be." Grandmother stood in the doorway to the newly converted sick chambers, a shawl around her slumping shoulders. She still wore her long, thick hair in the morning's practical ponytail.

"But you know how angry they get," Octavia protested.

"It's their fight. You have no right to interfere."

Octavia gave Grandmother a doubtful look. *No right?*

"It's between them," Grandmother gestured dismissively. "They've fought this way since before you were born. You'll only get hurt if you try to get between them. Come, tend to your mother."

Will Grandfather make the mirror now, Octavia wanted to ask. She couldn't find the courage to speak the question aloud. Even so, Grandmother looked back as if she had.

"Child, you know that your grandfather and I will do everything in our power for your mother."

Octavia nodded, still unable to speak. Grandmother stopped and gazed into her face intently.

"You understand why he won't make the mirror, don't you?" she asked in gentle tones. "The evil it would cause far outweighs any benefits. You understand that, don't you?"

"Yes, Grandmother." Octavia forced the words out through her constricted throat.

Grandmother sighed and put a hand on Octavia's shoulder. "Melody is our daughter, Octavia. Just because ..." her voice trailed off and she sighed again. "I promise you, we are doing everything we can. We will not abandon her."

Octavia nodded again but her eyebrows crimped. Just because ... what? What did Grandmother not say? Of course they wouldn't abandon their daughter ... just because ... Fear twisted her stomach.

Caring for Mother

Octavia watched Mother stir fitfully in Grandmother's bed. She moaned and pushed off the blue linen sheet. Her red flushed face stood out against the cream colored pillows.

Sylvia, who sat in a straight-backed chair next to the bed, returned the sheet to its place. Octavia traded places with her.

Sylvia reached out to give Octavia a sympathetic pat on the shoulder, then caught herself. She turned and instead rinsed her hands thoroughly with fragrant vinegar from a glazed bowl on the bedside table and dried them on a cloth.

"We bathe her periodically with the vinegar to keep the fever down," she whispered to Octavia. "Argana says a mild fever is actually good. It seems to slow the progression of the other symptoms. So long as the fever doesn't go too high."

Octavia nodded, her eyes focused on her mother's red cheeks. The caustic smoke of herbs burning in a hastily positioned brazier in the corner stung her eyes and throat.

Sylvia and Grandmother traded whispers. They spoke to her before leaving, but she barely noticed. She dipped a cloth in the vinegar and wrung it out before gently wiping Mother's burning forehead and cheeks. Mother flinched when the cool cloth touched her, and then sighed deeply as if comforted.

I promised Halfnote that I'll find a cure.

Octavia watched her patient struggle for breath. What would Mother say to that? Don't make promises you can't keep? And what had Grandmother kept herself from saying? Just because … just because of what?

Grandmother answered her question about the mirror as surely as if she asked it aloud. Perhaps Grandfather was right to refuse. Octavia remembered the mob. She shivered. That was Falchion's fault; spreading lies to further his cause. Except that, in this case, Grandfather and Falchion apparently agreed with each other.

That didn't stop Falchion from turning people against us.

Octavia refreshed the cloth with vinegar and laid it across her mother's forehead. How many times had Mother done this for her, Octavia wondered and then paused.

Had Mother ever done this for her? Grandmother and Alma tended her through the few colds, scrapes and the one serious fever Octavia could remember. On the river … she barely remembered life on the river. She knew Mother and Father more as visitors than parents. That thought felt … strange.

She could not imagine leaving the glassworks to make a life on the Khelana River as Mother had. Octavia knew without question that her mother relished the life her choices brought. At times it did strain her relations with Grandfather and … well, mostly with Grandfather. Yet Mother sent both of her daughters back to Verre House and the life she abandoned without apparent regret. Despite Father's objections...

Mother's chest rose and fell. The wheezing eased; perhaps thanks to Alma's potent concoctions. If only Alma could provide a medicine that eased emotions as well. Fear for Mother warred with … of course she wasn't angry with Grandfather. Mother was his daughter. Grandfather wouldn't leave Mother to die.

What a thought.

Mother coughed suddenly. Great wrenching spasms shook her whole frame. Octavia managed to turn Mother on her side to keep her from choking as Alma had taught her in the past. Sylvia hurried back into the room. She used a pair of tongs to carry a steaming pot.

"Argana recommends this for the cough."

"It's too hot," Octavia objected as Sylvia poured out the liquid. The white steam wafting out of the cup carried a caustic odor that stung her eyes. "It will burn her mouth."

"Argana says the heat is necessary." Sylvia blinked away sweat and wiped at her eyes with one hand.

Together they managed to get Mother to drink a cupful. Sylvia left to aid the others. The wracking cough eased but soon Mother's face reddened. Heat radiated off her skin.

Octavia bathed her face and neck again with the vinegar but this time it seemed to have no effect.

A mild fever might be a good thing but surely this high fever was too much. Mother moaned and tried to push away her hands. Octavia barely kept her from upsetting the vinegar. Heat burned through Mother's thin linen night shift. She stopped sweating. Surely that was a bad sign.

"Grandmother!" Octavia called in a carrying voice. "Madame Verre! Argana!" No one answered. Of course they wouldn't. Octavia struggled to stay calm. They tended the others. Mother was her responsibility. But what could she do?

As much to calm herself as anything, Octavia began to hum the cooling song. This was something she learned from Mother almost before she could speak. Mother used it to calm everything from over-enthusiastic cooking fires to rowdy young children.

Octavia remembered her surprise, in her first days at Verre House, in learning that the glass singers used the same notes to calm their work flames. Octavia's heartbeat and breath slowed as it always did when she repeated the simple tune. Mother sighed, her features relaxing. The horrible redness of her face eased.

Encouraged, Octavia trilled a variation of the calming song used to cool newly formed glass. Mother used it to cool soup. The redness in Mother's face and the fever that caused it eased. The horrible whistling of her breathing grew quieter. She rolled onto her back and opened her eyes.

"Octavia?"

Octavia caught her hand. "It's all right, Mother. You're in Verre House. We'll see that you get better."

"Where's Paul? Where's your father?"

Octavia's mouth twisted. "Talking to Grandfather."

"Arguing, you mean?" Mother rasped, the ghost of a smile brushing her lips. Octavia's heart leaped. Mother couldn't be too sick if she could still smile.

"You know how they are," Octavia said, smiling back.

Mother shook her head. "It's my fault," she whispered in that same raspy voice and slid back into sleep.

"What?" Did Mother really blame herself? How could that be? Perhaps it was just the sickness talking. At least she looked as if she actually rested. Octavia sat back in her plush chair and closed her eyes as well, just for a moment.

What have you done?

"What have you done?" Argana demanded. Octavia started out of a deep sleep. The Samoyan held Mother's hand in her own, frantically testing her pulses. Octavia jumped to her feet. How could she sleep at a time like this?

"Is Mother all right? She's been quite calm and her fever dropped. It seemed a good sign," Octavia all but babbled. "She even spoke to me a little." In fact, she thought, Mother appeared healthier at the moment than the exhausted healer.

"Yes, an excellent sign. What herbs did you give her?"

"Only the tea Sylvia brought for the cough. She was terribly hot so I wiped her face and chest with vinegar. The fever still felt too high so I tried the cooling tones and that seemed to help."

Horror filled Octavia. Was she wrong? Had she harmed her mother by reducing the fever?

"You did what?"

"I sang the cooling tones," Octavia said in a faint voice.

"The cooling tones? What tones? What do you mean?"

"Like this." Octavia took a full breath and sang the tune. Mother sighed. The deep lines of exhaustion in Argana's face eased and Octavia's fears faded a little.

Argana stared at Octavia. "Do that again." Octavia complied. Argana sighed. The tension in her shoulders eased.

"This is wonderful," Argana exclaimed. "I never thought … Come with me. We must do this for the others."

"I cannot leave Mother."

"She is fine. We'll send another to watch her."

A new hope

A babble of animated voices woke Halfnote and the other apprentices the next morning.

"What is it?" Alice asked. "What's happened?"

"Dunno," Annie mumbled through fabric as she pulled her dress on. "I'll go see."

"I'm coming with you," her twin said. She and Halfnote hurried into their clothes and ran down the stairs after Annie.

"What's wrong?" Halfnote asked the singers they found clustered at the bottom of the stairs. Martin, Phyllis and Sylvia stood talking excitedly. "Is it Mama? Is she all right?"

"Yes, yes." Sylvia's voice was rough with fatigue but bright with joy. "Your mother is better. All of the patients have improved. Octavia discovered a way to help them last night. We think we might be able to find other ways to help the sick by singing."

"That's wonderful," Alice said.

"Is Mama cured?"

"No, no, not yet," Sylvia said. "But she is better."

"Maybe Master Verre is right," bald Martin said. "Maybe we don't need the mirror."

"Of course it would be Octavia," Phyllis muttered in a less than happy voice. She folded her arms against herself.

"Sure and why not, it's her mother that's sick." Sylvia gave scowling Phyllis a reproving glance. Halfnote was too happy that Mama was better to care about what cranky Phyllis might say.

"Can I see Mama?"

"No, Sweetie, not yet," Sylvia said. "She's still sick."

"Oh." Halfnote's spirits drooped again.

"Where's Marissa?" Phyllis asked, her voice still sharp. "Halfnote, go check on Marissa. Why didn't she come down with the rest of you?"

Halfnote turned and hurried up the stairs.

"Honestly, Phyllis." Calming tones resonated through Sylvia's voice. "Was that really necessary?"

"I can't stand the way she whines," Phyllis sulked.

"You won't do yourself any favors in this house by picking on a Verre," Martin remarked.

Halfnote quickened her pace up the stairs so she wouldn't have to hear any more. Why was Phyllis always so angry anyway? Surely helping the sick was a good thing.

"Marissa," she called when she reached the door. "Are you awake? Phyllis wants you."

She found Marissa still in bed, the comforter pulled over her head. Halfnote pulled it off and shook her when Marissa didn't respond. The older apprentice moaned and turned over to reveal a bright red face. She gulped a breath and let it out with a piercing whistle. Halfnote bolted for the door, yelling for help.

Finding out what doesn't work

The birds had only just begun their morning chorus when Octavia hurried into the kitchen to gulp down a steaming bowl of porridge. She found her grandfather there, consulting with Argana.

"Up already? You need your rest to stay healthy."

And when did you rest, she wanted to ask him.

The healer glanced up to give Octavia a nod. Argana appeared more rested than when she sent Octavia off to bed the night before, but Grandfather looked exhausted.

"I could hardly sleep," Octavia admitted. "I'm too excited by what we discovered last night. Do you really think we can use the tones to cure the illness?"

"The results that you discovered, my dear," Grandfather acknowledged, his expression a mix of pride and hope. "We shall certainly try. No one I know of has ever considered using the tones in this manner. I am most impressed."

Octavia took a calming breath but her cheeks went pink.

"Master Verre." Frank dashed into the kitchen, holding his spectacles in place as he skidded to a stop. "It's not just Laiertes. Marissa is sick too."

The lines around Grandfather's mouth tightened. "Bring her to the sick rooms. Clearly, we need to get to work."

Octavia gathered with the other singers in small groups around various patients. They tried different tones and tunes as directed by Grandfather and Argana.

Even Phyllis, whose fiery temperament meant she spent too many hours as a dragon, did nothing but sing. They sang the fire breeding songs as a tonic to the blood; cooling tones to reduce fever; curing tones to maintain a mild fever during the early stages as this seemed to delay the worst symptoms; and purification tones in hopes of removing the cause of the illness altogether. Over time, Octavia's elation ebbed. For all their efforts, none of the patients recovered.

"Well, no one's died," Martin noted at the end of the week. He rubbed the reddish stubble covering his normally bald head.

Octavia sat with Argana and the other singers – those still healthy, anyway – at the kitchen table late that afternoon. Even a steaming mug of Alma's restorative tea couldn't raise her spirits. She felt completely drained.

"No one's improved, either," Phyllis muttered, with a pointed glance at Octavia. "How much longer can we go on? People keep falling ill and still we have no cure."

Octavia moodily considered the steam clouds rising from her cup. She agreed with Phyllis. Three apprentices, Marissa, Dan and Laiertes, had fallen ill. So had Sylvia, the house's strongest singer after Lorraine. Of the Samoyans only Argana and the elephant keeper remained well. Outside of Verre House the streets stood eerily quiet. Not even the curt shout of city guards on patrol broke the silence. Did they still march or were they all too sick as well?

What are we missing?

They had found no cure; not even a preventative. What would they do once there were no more voices left to sing? Who would care for the sick when all were ill? She looked up to find Lorraine watching her. Lorraine gave her a supportive smile and a comforting pat on the hand. Phyllis blew out a breath and looked away.

"We haven't found a cure but we have kept the sick from getting worse," Lorraine said. "At least we know more about what doesn't work. It takes time to work out a new process."

Octavia forced herself to nod despite the uneasy clench in her gut. Still, she admitted, some good had come of her discoveries. Father quit badgering Grandfather to make the healing mirror. He made himself useful now by chopping up the endless amounts of firewood needed in the sick rooms and Alma's ever busy ovens.

Is patience really a virtue?

Halfnote, sent by Alma to fetch water, was delighted that afternoon to find her father talking with Maru and Gajah in the back garden. The sun hung just above the glasswork's stone walls, throwing long shadows across the garden. Papa gave her a fierce hug. Maru cheerfully offered to pump the water so that she and Papa could have a moment together.

"Have you seen Mama?" Halfnote asked.

"Yes. I left her room a few minutes ago to get some fresh air. She sleeps peacefully, as she has since Octavia first used the calming tones. Who knew that a simple tune could have such power?"

"Is she better?"

"She's not worse. And she is resting well."

"But is she better?"

Papa looked away. One hand clenched into a fist. "No. She isn't worse. But she isn't better."

The scrape of wooden buckets on the rock path startled them. "Sometimes healing takes time," Maru said.

Papa's eyes focused on something in the distance. "Sometimes, I wonder whether patience is really a virtue."

Halfnote bit her lip. So far she hadn't told anyone about Geoffrey's plan to make the forbidden mirror. But that was because Octavia's discovery about the healing tones had made the mirror seem less necessary. If the tones didn't work ...

If Geoffrey did mean to make the mirror he'd done an excellent job of hiding his preparations. None of the necessary items were missing from the house stores. Could he get supplies from somewhere else in spite of the quarantine?

Papa could. But could Geoffrey?

Octavia's discovery also meant that she was always too busy to talk to Halfnote. She only left the sick rooms to snatch a few hours' sleep. Every time Halfnote tried to slip up the stairs to her sister's room someone came along to chase her back down again. And they were all so busy that she didn't get many opportunities to try. No one in Verre House was getting much sleep these days.

She considered her father's worried frown. What would Papa do if she told him? She couldn't bear the thought of another horrible argument between Papa and Grandpa. But Mama wasn't any better. No worse, but no better. What if she never got better?

"Papa."

"Halfnote," Alma called. "Where's that water?"

"Better go." Papa gave her a quick hug.

"But Papa ..."

"Go on, now. Alma needs the water."

"Papa, there's something I really need to tell you."

Papa's eyebrows crimped. "All right. Let's take Alma her buckets and then I'll tell her that we need to talk."

It's time

Octavia found her father waiting for her by the stairs as she headed for bed. She bit back another yawn, bid Phyllis good night and followed Father into the now darkened reception hall to talk.

"Can anyone hear us in here?" he asked.

Octavia *listened* a moment, then led Father to another corner of the large hall. Some parts of the ornate gallery were built to carry sound, others to dampen it.

"We can speak privately here, Father. What is it?"

Father glanced around, then spoke softly into her ear. "It is time, Octavia, to make the mirror." Octavia gasped.

"You know Grandfather won't."

"No, but you can."

"What? No ... no, Father, no."

"You have delayed the course of your mother's illness," Father said, his eyes and voice intent, "but still it persists. Without a cure Melody will die, Octavia. All those stricken do, in the end. If you stood with me on the roof of this building tomorrow morning you would see that the sky is black with the smoke of funeral pyres in every direction. Only the mountain winds keep us from choking on the stench of death here in Verre House. I'd make the damn thing myself if I knew how. Make the mirror, Octavia. It's our only hope."

"I can't make it alone, Father."

"You don't have to. Halfnote told me she saw Chancellor Razak pay Geoffrey to make it. Maru confirmed it. He says Geoffrey's preparations are nearly complete."

"He has no right. He's not the master of this house. He's betrayed Grandfather."

"People are dying, Octavia. To withhold a potential cure is nearly the same as murder, isn't it? Geoff needs your voice. You know the others will follow your lead. Join him in the making and it won't matter what Verre does. All of the others will sing if you do. Most will sing even if you don't."

"I … I need to think about it, Father."

He caught her arm but she pulled free and all but ran from him up the stairs to her room. Fortunately Grandmother was still tending the ill downstairs, so Octavia had privacy to think. After what seemed like hours of pacing she finally threw herself into bed.

How could she possibly choose? Betray Grandfather to save Mother or stand with Grandfather in hopes of finding another cure. And if they failed … her mind shied away from that thought.

No. Look at it.

If they failed, Mother died. She felt like the dragon mother, Piasa, alone and at the brink of starvation; torn between the need to protect her children and the need to leave them in search of food. Who could make choice like that?

What if she, Octavia, betrayed Grandfather to help Geoffrey make the healing mirror and it became the monster Grandfather feared? How would she feel then? What if she made the mirror and Mother died anyway?

How will I feel if Mother dies when I know there was something else I could have tried and didn't? If I try to make the mirror and Mother dies anyway, at least I tried.

And if Halfnote fell ill … or Father … or Grandfather? And what of the others in the household who were already sick: Sylvia, Marissa, Laiertes? What if one of them died?

Have we truly tried all other options? What are we missing, with the tones?

She had felt such hope when the calming tones eased Mother's fever. Why didn't the other tones help? Cooling, heating, forming, these all changed the shape of the glass to the maker's intent. Why couldn't they change a person's health to the healer's intent?

Is that what the tones for the *Hygeia paraphasis* did? Could they heal the sick by using the tones for the mirror without the piece itself? But how could she find out? Grandfather flatly refused to discuss anything about the mirror with anyone.

Octavia threw off the sheet and pulled on a dressing gown. All records pertaining to the *Hygeia paraphasis* vanished from the library the day after the Samoyans arrived. In Grandfather's place no doubt she would hide them as well. But she could probably guess where he put them.

Octavia slipped out of her quarters, past the room where Phyllis snored fitfully and down the stairs to Grandfather's office chambers. She started guiltily when a stair board creaked loudly underfoot. If she were still in apprentice quarters, she thought with a wry smile, she'd remember which steps to avoid. And if she were still in apprentice quarters she would never have gotten this far without her sister sneaking out after her.

Halfnote. I've hardly seen her these last few days.

The memory of the trust in her sister's eyes stabbed her with guilt, but also filled her with fresh determination.

I have to try. I promised Halfnote we would find the cure. I cannot leave this stone unturned.

She found the glassworks dark except for the glow from the door to the sick chambers. Even the kitchen's usual lights were out. She paused at the door to the office chambers to *listen.* She caught the faint tones of calming from the sick rooms. Lorraine's voice. The tension in her shoulders eased.

If music calms the sick, why can't it heal them?

Could tones used to create the healing mirror heal without it? What gave the mirror such a potent appetite if not the music? If music creates form, why not the form of health?

She'd been right once before, following her instincts with Mother. Why not again?

Grandfather's private office was next to the stairs that led up to the main library. In the center of the office stood a large glass desk created by Grandfather's great-grandmother to settle a bet that glass singers could shape sharp corners as well as curves.

By feel and memory, Octavia found and lit the little oil lamp in the corner. Its light reflected off the frozen heads of dragons and birds that sprang out of the flat sides of the desk at unexpected intervals. They looked very like the decorative rainspouts that adorned the Albermarle Council Hall and other important buildings.

Grandfather said that great-great- ... great ... grandmother Verre could never make anything so simple as a square box, no matter how practical. Octavia thought the desk ought to be one of the center pieces displayed in the reception hall. Grandfather always laughed and said he worried that the grimacing decorations might actually scare off customers.

There was, of course, another reason why Grandfather kept such an amazing work out of main sight.

Octavia composed herself and *listened* a moment further to make sure she was truly alone. She placed her hands atop the heads of two snarling dogs, and trilled middle C, then D-flat three octaves down. Something chimed and clicked.

Octavia pulled on the two heads and hummed the same tune as the chime, just making the G sharp instead of flat. The side of the desk pulled smoothly out to reveal a deep drawer. Stacks of ink-covered parchment filled it nearly to the top.

Octavia blew out her breath. Now she felt certain that Grandfather didn't realize that she knew about this drawer.

She'd seen him open it years ago and at that moment naturally became obsessed with learning its secret. Now, perhaps, this knowledge would help her solve another puzzle.

She lit a second, smaller lamp and used its light to scan the lines of once black looping calligraphy now fading to red. The pile of browning parchment and crumbling linen pages stood nearly a foot high. Could she find her answer before morning? She found a square magnifying glass on a nearby shelf and, swallowing a large yawn, began to read.

Another idea

Octavia started awake to find the office filled with the gray light of dawn. On the other side of the desk in the visitor's chair sat – not Grandfather, but Lorraine.

"Of course you would know Verre's hiding places."

Octavia wiped her cheek with one hand. Oh dear, had she drooled on the parchment?

"What do you want?" she mumbled.

"The same thing you do," Lorraine said, her blue eyes afire despite her obvious exhaustion. "The secret to making the healing mirror. I wish you'd told me what you intended. We've wasted too much time already."

"I'm not going to make the mirror." Octavia struggled for clarity through the heavy fog of sleep that still blanketed her thoughts. Lorraine snorted.

"Don't insult my intelligence. What's that, then, that you've made a pillow out of?"

"Listen. Perhaps there's another way. To heal the sick, I mean. If the cooling tones can ease a fever, why can't the healing tones heal? Without the mirror, I mean."

Lorraine's nostrils flared suspiciously at first, and then she frowned. "I never thought of that. If that's possible, why hasn't it been done before?"

"Why didn't anyone try cooling tones on a fever before?"

Lorraine cocked her head to one side. "Point taken. Let me think this through. The mirror focuses the healing properties. The mirror doesn't heal; it only shows the way to healing. It holds the energies within itself; releasing the energy without proper focus distorts it. If releasing unfocused energies causes harm, then wouldn't using the tones alone do the same thing?"

"According to Grandfather, Madame Marcato's singers practiced the making tones for their mirror for several weeks before the creation. He didn't say anything about practice being dangerous."

"An undistorted mirror reflects a clear picture. A focused mirror does heal. It's the focus that matters, isn't it?"

"How is the energy focused? Without the mirror?"

"We focus it. We're the mirrors. We focus the tones with our intentions. That's what we do with a normal piece, isn't it? 'Hold the shape in your mind and it can't help but come out in the music,' that's what Grandfather always says. If we hold the patient's health in our minds while we sing, why can't we create health?"

Lorraine frowned. "We create health by focusing the tones with our minds?" She shook her head. "I know how to create the image of a mirror. That's simple. But what is health? What image do we create? What does it look like?"

"Perhaps it is not an image, but a feeling."

Lorraine rubbed her forehead. "I don't know, Octavia. We have too many questions and too little time. We're wading through deep marsh here and I have no idea how to find the firm path. One false move in any direction and we drown. Worse, we drown those we mean to save."

"You may be right. But what else can we do? Grandfather believes the mirror is evil. You have to admit, he's not often wrong."

Lorraine eyes slid away from hers.

"Master Verre is cautious, but the time for caution is past. My Geoffrey has the sickness now. I will not simply stand aside and let my husband die. I don't know how you've stood it this long, watching your mother ..."

Octavia winced.

The junior master bit off her words. "Sorry. I'm sorry. Listen," she said, before Octavia could respond. "This is what we'll do. We have to practice the tones before making the mirror, regardless. We know from Master Verre that that's been done safely enough. We'll prepare for the making, but try the tones first. Then if they don't work we're still ready to make the mirror."

"Grandfather will feel the energy, when we sing."

"Oh, I have the cure for that."

"Really?" Octavia was shocked that Lorraine knew better than herself how to handle her grandfather. "What is it?"

"Your father. You know he wants the mirror made. We'll set him on Master Verre, get the two of them arguing. That's sure to keep old Verre thoroughly distracted."

Octavia grimaced but couldn't argue.

"Your father is in the kitchen having breakfast with the others. There's no time to waste. We'll get started directly."

"Indeed," a deep bass voice agreed.

"Grandfather," Octavia gasped. He stood, his arms folded, in the office doorway. How had he managed to come upon them unawares? She looked down guiltily at the parchment spread out across the desk. The door to the secret compartment stood wide open. And, oh dear, how much had he heard?

Lorraine's hand went to her mouth, then she dropped it and met Grandfather's direct gaze quite calmly.

"This is my fault," Octavia said.

"Don't be ridiculous," Lorraine snapped.

"Master Verre, my husband is ill and I will do anything necessary to save him. I will lead the making of the *Hygeia paraphasis* even if you won't."

Grandfather opened his mouth to speak and then closed it again, as if uncertain of his words. He looked, Octavia thought, as old as she had ever seen him.

"Lorraine," he finally managed in a rough voice, "we are all concerned about our loved ones." The junior master flushed, but did not drop her gaze.

"Now." Grandfather's voice steadied. "Let us see if we can put this amazing idea of Octavia's to work."

Discord

The music meant to create the healing mirror began with major discord. Halfnote cringed. The dissonance bounced off the walls to rattle the bits of discarded equipment under the main creation room's black marble stairs. Her muscles quivered with the sense of unbearable tension and she couldn't get control of her breathing.

She sat, arms wrapped around her knees, in the same tiny hiding place from which she observed Octavia's test. She sat beside the same dusty pair of bellows. No one ever thought to clean this little nook. That's what made it such a good hiding place. The sand barrow with the broken wheel was gone; either repaired or reduced to firewood. She might be easier to see, as a result, if anyone looked. She really didn't expect them to, in this cacophony.

She fled to this spot after being blocked yet again from the sick room, this time by Papa. As before, she knew she ought to be in the kitchen helping Alma.

She should be chopping up mountains of herbs or helping to prepare soup for all the people now abed in the sick chambers or filling the smoking braziers outside those rooms with some of those same herbs or mopping, sweeping or washing an unending mound of bedclothes in near-to-boiling vinegar-scented water.

Instead, she sat here, gritting her teeth against this discord and hoping that the small group of singers creating it would somehow find a solution to the plague.

But how could this be *making* music? It didn't *flow*. This … sound … did not create the usual energetic currents caused by any normal making. She felt no life at all in the noise.

Alma would look for her soon enough and accuse her of ducking chores. But it had been days since she'd seen Octavia. Days of knowing Mama was ill and that Octavia had done something to help but not quite enough and no one … no one who really knew anything … would speak to her about it.

Of course everyone, Octavia included, was terribly busy and she knew not to bother the singers too much but if no one told her anything soon she would sneak in and see Mama for herself.

Yes I will. Just let anyone try to keep her out.

She'd told Papa about Geoffrey but that didn't seem to have made any difference. Was it because Geoffrey was sick now? Did everyone else agree with Grandpa? Papa didn't, she knew, but he'd also stopped arguing with Grandpa about it.

Halfnote watched intently as Grandpa, Octavia, Martin, Lorraine, Phyllis and Ted stood in a circle next the black marble making platform. Grandpa directed the group through each interval. He stabbed at the air with one finger as if hitting the key of some invisible musical instrument. From the sound of it, he and his choir were hitting all the wrong notes. Where were the other singers? Could they really all be sick?

"Are you sure this is music?" Martin asked with uncharacteristic impatience.

A deep frown replaced his usual cheerful expression and his voice rasped from too much singing. The reddish bristles covering his normally bare chin had grown nearly long enough now to look like a proper beard. A stiff bristle of the same color covered his normally bald pate.

"It will be," Grandpa said, "once we put all the pieces together. This is only the beginning. This is the frame into which the rest of the piece is poured."

"How does this promote healing?" Lorraine asked.

"As I told you previously …."

"Right, it's the framework." Lorraine put up a placating hand. "I understand. At least I hope to," she added in an aside to Phyllis, who sniggered knowingly.

Grandpa's glare silenced both of them.

"Pay attention. The sounds will make more sense to you once you know the whole work. The next notes go like this ..."

Halfnote wasn't aware of falling asleep. The tones filling the making room bounced off the white walls, They fell all in a heap into her dreams. The sounds didn't create song, this time, her dreaming self realized, or even glass. Instead, they created a heartbeat. Or, she thought, they created a heart and it beat as all living hearts do.

In her dream it seemed as if Grandpa and his choir sang up a body of sound that was somehow going to take on a life of its own. It just needed the right spark. Some notes became veins filled with musical fluid. Some became the lungs, taking breath and expelling it. No wonder the music sounded so funny. It wasn't actually music. What Grandpa called the framework, sleeping Halfnote realized, was in fact the creature's body.

What sort of tones, she wondered, would it think with? Would the mirror, when they made it, become its eyes? But something was missing. The creature needed something. What could that be?

She woke an uncounted amount of time later in a dark and empty room to the sound of someone calling her name.

The voice echoed softly. Footsteps sounded above her, then descended. Halfnote held her breath. How long had she slept? Had her dream creature come to life? Yellow light followed the steps, which stopped just in front of her hiding place. Someone held a candle up and looked around the room. Someone short, Halfnote realized just as he squatted down and peered into her hiding place.

"Halfnote? Are you there? Everyone's worried."

Halfnote scrambled out. At least it was only Robbie. He grinned. She ducked her head and tried not to smile back. After a moment they both laughed, their giggles reverberating off the walls as well as any music.

"Are you all right? Are you sick?" Robbie asked.

"No." Halfnote's heart sank. Of course that's what everyone would think. What would Alma say? Or Grandpa? Would he notice? "Is Alma very angry?"

"I think she's too worried to be angry. She is upset. But you'll probably have to do all the washing up yourself."

That didn't sound too bad.

Defining health

The next day, with notes and their meanings now thoroughly committed to memory, Octavia and the other singers began learning how to focus the tones. Octavia's stomach hurt and she barely managed to eat any breakfast. Would this work? Could it work?

At Grandfather's insistence, they practiced first on plants. Anything blighted or wilting or overwhelmed by insects – any plant Alma normally uprooted from her garden, in other words – found its way into the making room.

And there they encountered a new problem.

"But," Phyllis said, "What image, precisely, should we focus on? I mean, what form does health take? And won't it be different for a plant and a person?" She scowled as usual, but Octavia knew for once that Phyllis wasn't just in a bad mood. All the singers genuinely struggled to understand this point.

And I don't know how to answer her.

Neither did Grandfather.

What was health, after all? Was it enough to vanquish the beetles with the shiny black shells devouring the leaf? That still left the leaf half eaten. And, according to Alma, the real problem was root rot. A healthy plant didn't draw beetles. And if the questions were this difficult with a rose bush, Octavia wondered, how would they heal people?

Halfnote managed to put the tray down without spilling anything before running over to Grandma's side. She still breathed, though with a raggedy wheezing. Bright red splotches covered Grandma's face. She lay in a heap in the corridor just outside the sick rooms. Halfnote drew Grandma's hair out of the way and gently stroked her cheek.

"Grandma? Wake up." Grandma wheezed and moaned. Her cheek felt terribly hot against Halfnote's warm hands.

"Octavia! Grandpa! Papa! Someone! Help!" No one answered. Torn between staying and running for help, Halfnote patted Grandma's cheek one more time and dashed to the kitchen. No one was there. Still shouting for help, she dashed back through the dining room and into the reception hall. The door to the office opened. Alma hurried out.

"What is it?"

"Grandma fainted. Outside the sick chambers."

To Octavia's great frustration the plants did not react at all at first. Even so, Grandfather kept them at it.

The poor rose plant, still overrun by the tiny black beetles, simply wilted further. The beetles did eventually vanish into the soil, apparently unaffected. The singers put the rose plant aside and focused their tones on a pot of leeks.

For the longest time, the leeks seemed unimpressed. Then they burst into flame. Martin doused the fire.

The singers tried again with another fading rose bush. The under-nourished bush suddenly put forth an army of buds. These swelled into bright pink blossoms that filled the room with a wonderfully refreshing scent.

We've done it. Octavia's exhausted spirits blossoming.

The chanters' voices swelled in excitement. In response, all of the petals and leaves turned abruptly brown and dropped in a clump onto the table. The remaining stems shriveled up and crumbled away to dust. Even the pot holding the plant cracked and fell to pieces. Nothing remained of the tiny bush but a pile of dry soil, brown dust and a few shards of clay from the pot.

"Perhaps," Grandfather said after a moment of heavy silence, "now would be a good time for lunch. Octavia, please alert Alma. The rest of us will clean up in here."

Out of time

Octavia hurried to the kitchen, grateful for a moment's privacy to compose herself. If this is what the tones did to plants, what would they do to people?

She found Alma, her eyes dark with grief, seated at the kitchen table. Halfnote lay curled up in a tight ball in the cook's ample lap, sobbing. Robbie stood next to them, one hand on Alma's shoulder, his face all but empty of expression. He bounced nervously on one foot, then the other.

"What is it?" Halfnote dove headlong into her arms. Dread stabbed her heart. "Is it Mother?"

Alma, her mouth tight, shook her head. "Madame Verre is ill now as well."

Octavia nodded, too overwhelmed by relief and horror in the same moment to speak. Mother still lived ... but Grandmother...

"But she is only ill, isn't she?" She held Halfnote close.

"Alive still, thanks to you and Argana. Although ..."

Octavia's eyes stung with tears of disappointment. "Alive but not well. We're running out of time, aren't we?"

Alma's expression turned grim. "Our stores of medicinals are nearly used up and even your father can not replace them."

"Father?"

"While you work on finding a cure he has left us twice to seek new supplies. No one will sell what little they have left, not for any price. Not even to Paul."

"So much for the quarantine ..."

Alma's mouth quirked. "The quarantine still holds. Your father knows more ways in and out of here than anyone."

Somehow, Octavia thought, that didn't surprise her.

"Where is he now?"

"In back, chopping firewood. Since Peter took ill ..."

"Peter? Who's he?"

"The twins' brother. He was the young man who helped Paul bring your mother here."

"Oh, of course." Octavia blinked. "And where are the twins? I haven't seen them since ..."

"Sick as well." Alma shifted uncomfortably in her seat. "As are Dan and Galliard."

Octavia took in a breath.

"But that's ..." she glanced down at Robbie and Halfnote. "That just leaves ..."

Alma nodded. "It's time to make the mirror. Past time."

Heartsick, Octavia could only agree. Did they have enough voices left to do it? How much had she cost them in wasted time and effort with her stupid, stupid ideas?

Grandfather took his lunch in the sick chambers at his wife's bedside. The rest of the staff gathered in the kitchen for a meal of little more than day old bread and hard cheese.

"Octavia, I'm sorry," Lorraine began but Octavia wouldn't let the junior master continue.

"No, *I'm* sorry. You were right. We should have started on the mirror three days ago. All I've done is waste time."

"At last, she admits it," Phyllis said, with a bitter smirk.

Octavia swallowed a sharp response.

"Don't be so hard on yourself, Octavia." Frank gave Phyllis a severe frown. Light glinted off the lenses of his spectacles. "We needed time to learn the chants properly, no matter what we use them for. We could hardly have learned them any faster."

"Are we all agreed?" Lorraine looked around the table. "With or without Master Verre, it's time to make the mirror."

"I vote yes." Frank gave his spectacles a determined shove back into place.

Martin and Phyllis nodded. Martin scratched nervously at his new-grown beard. Ted pushed away his plate and shrugged. Even little Robbie weighed in. With the somber expression befitting a judge passing sentence, he said quite clearly, "Yes, I think so." Everyone stared at him in astonishment. The boy flushed and ducked his head, but recovered when Alma smiled and patted his hand.

"You're right," Alma said. "Several Samoyans are near the end. We cannot keep death at bay much longer."

All eyes turned toward Octavia and Halfnote. They sat together at one end. Octavia nodded. "Yes. We've tried every other option." At least her conscience was clear on that point.

Halfnote gasped. "But what about Grandpa?"

"I'll speak to him," Octavia and Lorraine said at nearly the same moment. They looked at each other and laughed.

"We'll both speak to him," Lorraine said.

"I'll go with you." Alma stood up. "I've known him longer than anyone. Longer even than Madame Verre. He'll listen to me."

"Do we have the supplies for it?" Martin asked. "I mean, the store room shelves are getting pretty bare. No point in disturbing the old man if ..."

"We have everything," Lorraine said grimly. "Geoffrey

made sure of that."

"Even obsidian?"

"Oh yes. The Samoyans themselves brought that. A nice big piece, nearly pure."

Martin ran a nervous hand across his head. His hand jerked away from the reddish bristles as if still surprised to find them there.

"I guess we really are ready." He looked worried.

In the end, everyone went to speak with Grandfather. They found him at his wife's bedside, his food untouched.

Octavia fought back tears at the sight of her grandmother lying helpless, her usually animated expression gone slack and dull. Grandfather, his face gray, looked nearly as ill as Grandmother.

"Grandfather." Octavia's heart ached. How could she betray him at a time like this?

He looked up at her with red-rimmed eyes. His gaze sharpened on the little group that stood before him.

"Halfnote, Robbie. You should not be in here."

Octavia looked down in surprise to see her sister standing so close as to be half hidden in her skirts. Robbie stood next to Halfnote, clutching her hand. Halfnote seemed not to notice. An expression of rare defiance crossed her face.

"What difference does it make? The sickness is everywhere."

"Halfnote found Madame after she fainted," Alma explained, "I made her wash in vinegar, afterwards. But we're nearly out of the old wine. We're nearly out of good wine, for that matter. Fortis, we've delayed long enough. Too long." Grandfather frowned at her.

"We're making the mirror," Lorraine said, "with or without your permission. We cannot wait any longer. Our patients are going to die. Outside Verre House, people are dying already."

Grandfather looked from one determined face to another. Frank took off his spectacles and vigorously polished them on the hem of his tunic. Martin nervously scratched at his new beard and looked away. Phyllis, at the back of the group, became suddenly engrossed in the backs of her hands.

Ted's eyes widened. He glanced back at the door as if he wanted to run. Octavia looked down at Halfnote and found unexpected strength in her sister's determined gaze.

"We have no mountain's blood, to purify the obsidian. It's the only fuel hot enough. We cannot make the mirror without it," Grandfather objected.

"We have it," Lorraine said, triumph in her voice. "The Kerguelens would not sell Trader Breydon food or medicine at any price but they had mountain's blood to spare."

At first, Halfnote thought that Grandpa must not have heard Lorraine. Then he moved towards her, slowly, as if in great pain. He looked old. Not old as in 'older than Papa' but ancient and brittle like a piece of centuries-old glass.

"So," he said. "All right, then."

He pushed himself up and stood before them, one hand holding the back of the chair as if for support.

"If you are going to make the mirror with or without me, Lorraine, I think the better choice is with me. I have the experience. I know what mistakes were made. I know why Devin fell. I know what we must do to protect ourselves."

Lorraine nodded. She looked relieved.

"We ... I ... I have lived in fear too long" Grandfather said. "The past is past. Mind, this is still the most dangerous task any of us has ever undertaken. We must take every precaution. The sick must be moved as far from the making as possible. I would send them out of the house entirely, if we could. We will make a place for them in the lowest basement, until the process is complete. That is our first task.

"Then these suites, the entire house, must be cleansed, purified in preparation for the making. We must make the entire house a sounding chamber. Every note, every sound must harmonize with every other. There must not be one note of dissonance in the making of the *Hygeia paraphasis*."

Getting ready

They began their preparations at once. Alma, Robbie and Halfnote used the lifts to send the last baskets of cheese, vegetables and herbs from the lowest basement to the next level. It took both Robbie and Halfnote to carry just one basket. Halfnote was relieved to find they had so few to move but Alma pursed her lips in worry.

"We need an end to this, and soon. We're feeding fifty people from supplies meant for twenty and we'll be out of everything we don't grow ourselves in another day or so."

The underground space naturally lacked windows and ventilation. Just one iron ring by the door allowed a torch. By its wavering light they swept and then scrubbed the entire converted cavern with hot, soapy water. Robbie and Halfnote carried down several candle holders taller than themselves from the library. From attic storage Alma produced a gross of beeswax candles as long as her arms, and twice as wide.

"I meant these for the midwinter's celebration." Alma stared unhappily around the empty space, hands on her hips.

"It's not near enough light. And they'll want more heat. It's too hot outside and too cool in here. And too damp. We'll bring the braziers down, of course. There'll be little enough air for breathing, once we get all those bodies down here.

"I suppose they'll keep each other warm." She shook her head doubtfully. "It's a bad situation, all around. I hope they don't stay down here too long. Well, come on. There's still too much to do before supper. We need more firewood and whatever medicines we can get from the back wood."

An unjust attack

Halfnote sighed with relief as she stepped out into the kitchen garden and fresh air. Robbie looked equally relieved as he followed her. To Halfnote's great delight, Papa agreed to join them on their expedition so Alma could stay behind to begin preparations for supper. Maru and his elephant decided to join them as well.

"Gajah needs to stretch his legs," Maru said. "And he enjoys carrying things."

"B … but w…what about the quarantine?" Robbie asked nervously as they headed for the back gate.

"The wood belongs to Verre House. The guards have seen us out there before and haven't objected," Papa said.

For this trip Gajah left most of his finery behind. Instead, he carried a pair of very large saddlebags. They filled these with all the wild herbs, roots, mushrooms and anything else edible or medicinal they could find. They also gathered as much firewood as they could from the coppiced beech and alder trees that grew between the glasswork's back wall and the sheer edge of Viridian Mountain.

Halfnote's feet sank nearly ankle deep into the carpet of decaying leaves and pine needles. She drew in deep breaths of pine-scented air. Gajah chose each step with care as his heavy legs sank even more deeply than Papa's into the detritus of the forest floor.

Some birds squawked and fled from a line of bushes near the glassworks. Something *hmmmed* just below the level of hearing and Halfnote took a breath. So did Robbie. Even from here they could feel the energies change as the singers began *making*. She recognized the energy pattern even if she couldn't quite hear the song. By the patterns, she thought the singers must be making mirrors. But why make ordinary mirrors at a time like this?

Papa and Maru didn't seem to notice. Gajah, well, Gajah raised his trunk as if scenting the air but then looked down again as if deciding where to put his foot next.

Gajah took another careful step and then looked back over his shoulder. Maru stopped and looked back as well.

"What is it?" Papa asked.

Three crows perched on the back wall took to the air screeching. Something *zzzzipped* past Halfnote and struck a tree near Gajah with a heavy *thunk!* The elephant trumpeted. With surprising speed he lumbered around to face the source of the sound.

"Get down!" Maru shouted. He shoved Halfnote behind an old log. Papa pushed Robbie down beside her.

Another *zzzip* and *thunk!* knocked bits of bark off the log. Maru chirruped to Gajah.

The elephant charged a cluster of trees. Maru, his machete drawn, dashed after him. The ground trembled under the elephant's heavy footfalls. Men shouted nearby.

"What is it? What's happening?" Halfnote cried, raising her

head up so she could see over the top of the log.

"Keep still. Be quiet." Papa hissed. He forced her head back down with a firm hand.

"It's the city guard," Robbie whispered. "They're the only ones who use black crow feathers in their arrows."

"But why ..."

"Hssht, you two," Papa snapped. "Keep down!" Gajah trumpeted loudly.

"Call off your beast!" someone shouted. "Call off your beast." That voice sounded so familiar that Halfnote barely kept herself from looking up again.

"Hoy, Trader Breydon," Maru called, "Gajah has convinced these foolish attackers to put down their weapons and speak to us instead. Come and see who it is."

Papa climbed slowly to his feet. After a moment he waved to Robbie and Halfnote. They scrambled up as well. Once they got past Gajah's imposing bulk and twitching tail, they could see that the elephant held a squad of the city guard against a tight line of beech trees. Their bows and short spears lay scattered on the ground around them. They looked pale and exhausted, Halfnote thought. They stood dark-eyed with fatigue, the men unshaven. Mud and other stains covered their usually crisp brown jerseys.

Only one guard, a woman with shockingly bright red hair, remained uncowed. She'd managed to climb up an oak tree and now lay across a thick branch just out of Gajah's reach. She aimed a loaded crossbow directly at Maru's chest.

"I will take it as a great favor, ma'am," Papa said, "if you put that bow down."

"You're breaking the quarantine."

"We are not," Halfnote said, outraged. Robbie stared at her as if she'd just acquired another head. "This is Verre House property. We come here every day for firewood. You're the trespassers."

"As my daughter says," Papa's mouth quirked up a little, "we have a right to be here. You don't. You just tried to kill two children. What are we to think of you after that?"

"You're no glass singer," someone muttered from within the group. Halfnote stared at the bulky, strong-jawed man.

"It's that metal worker that tried to ruin Octavia's party. What are you doing here, Master Falchion?"

Papa looked at the speaker, his eyes narrowing. Falchion turned several amazing shades of purple and pink.

"I don't answer to you, you little ..."

Papa was on him so fast that even Maru looked startled. The guards scattered out of his way. Papa grabbed the metal worker by his broad shoulders and slammed him up against the tree. Falchion had width on Papa and the muscles of his trade but he was no match for Papa's wiry, angry strength.

"You attack my family, metal worker," Papa spat. "I am Paul, a trader of Clan Breydon. Do you challenge me?"

Falchion snorted and blustered. For a moment Halfnote thought it might really come to blows. The iron master glared back at Papa and then slumped in defeat. His eyes darted from side to side, looking for an escape. The guards stood back. They looked disgusted. The red-headed woman put away her bow and dropped to the ground.

"I do not challenge you, Trader Breydon," Falchion said in a husky voice, "only that sorcerous bastard Verre. Trader Breydon," Falchion said again, in a different tone. He looked at Papa with a startled expression. "Breydon. You married Melody. You're Verre's son-in-law."

"That's right. What's it to you?"

"Look at you." Falchion stared at Papa, then Halfnote and Robbie. "All of you. You're healthy. I knew it. That sorcerous glass bastard. I knew he'd do it."

"What are you talking about?" Papa let go of the man.

"He's mad," Robbie whispered. Halfnote agreed.

"And you." Falchion turned his angry gaze to Maru. "You *Samoyan*." He spat out the word, as if saying something nasty. "You brought this plague. How dare you stand before us in good health?"

"We came to Albermarle seeking help for our people." Maru stood perfectly still, one hand against Gajah's side. "The sickness followed. My well-being is in the hands of the gods."

"God's hands? You mean Verre's hands, don't you? He's done it, hasn't he?" Falchion's breathing grew more rapid and his eyes widened. "That sorcerous bastard. He's gone and done it."

"Go home," Papa said. "There's nothing for you here."

"Home?" Falchion rasped. "Home? My wife ... my children ... you'll not keep me from it." He shoved Papa

roughly aside and bolted for the glassworks. Papa stumbled
backwards, swore and dashed after him. The guards looked as if they
wanted to follow but Gajah and Maru stood in their way. The oldest,
the one with a sergeant's insignia on his shoulder, stepped forward.

"We're going to Verre House, Samoyan."

"What do you seek? We have no cure for the illness."

"Then why aren't you sick? Or them?" The sergeant pointed at
Halfnote and Robbie. "Like Falchion said, Verre's
own aren't suffering. Your grandfather made the mirror and found
the cure, didn't he, little girl?" he asked Halfnote. "I don't blame
him. I would too. But the rest of us need healing too and we've come
for it. The least Verre can do is share.

"Come on," the sergeant told his people, "they won't stop us."
The guards hurried off. Maru shook his head and urged Gajah
forward. Halfnote and Robbie followed as quickly as they could.

How many dead?

Octavia took over as dragon while Phyllis and Martin
completed their mirrors in one of the smaller making rooms. The
shouting began just as she damped down the making fire. They'd
heard and ignored the elephant's trumpeting earlier, but this
disturbance sounded much closer. Octavia quickly slid the snuffing
lid into place while Martin placed the last mirror on the cooling rack.

"That sounds like that metal worker," Phyllis said after
cocking her head and *listening* for a moment. "The one that made
such a fuss at your celebration, Octavia."

"Yes it does." Octavia wasn't likely to forget that rusty voice
any time soon. "We'd better get out there."

The doors to the other creation rooms remained closed
and the murmur of chanting still sounded from within.

Clearly, the others could not be disturbed. The shouting grew
louder. Alma's valiant alto rose up against the rasping roar. Then the
back door banged against the wall and Father's baritone joined in.
The three singers ran for the kitchen.

"If there's no mirror," a red-faced Falchion demanded of an equally furious-looking Alma and Father, "why aren't any of you sick? Look at you. Look at them." He pointed at Octavia, Martin and Phyllis as they entered the kitchen. "Healthy, all of you."

"Don't be ridiculous," Alma snapped. "Of course there are ill among us. We have the Samoyans to care for, thanks to you. Madame Verre is ill and Trader Breydon's wife as well. These you see standing here are just about the only healthy individuals left in Verre House."

"Raquel? Verre's wife? And Melody? His daughter? I don't believe it. Show me …"

Father stepped up, his fists clenched. "You'll not disturb them, iron monger …"

"Ha! I knew it."

Octavia moved quickly between the two men.

"No, Father. Show him. Master Falchion needs to see. We'll never get rid of him, otherwise." She met the metal worker's glare with an icy stare. Falchion took a step back.

"Rid of me? Why should you need to be rid of me? What sorcery goes on here?"

Octavia rolled her eyes. *Honestly* … "Come with me."

"But quietly," Alma snapped.

"Down there?" Falchion demanded as Octavia headed for the basement stairs. Father treaded silently behind him. Alma hesitated and then followed. She waved Martin and Phyllis back.

"Make tea. And keep an eye on the bread in the oven."

"This is a trap." Falchion pulled up short. "You mean to do away with me, don't you? I'm not so foolish as you think. I'll not go blindly to my own demise."

"Oh, please. Argana," Octavia called, "Can you come up for a moment?" She turned back to Falchion. The iron monger stood behind her, a foot on each of the first two steps down, his back to the wall. He looked nervously from Octavia to Father and back again. Could such a strong looking man really be this cowardly?

"Argana is the Samoyans' physician." Octavia couldn't remember if Falchion and Argana had met.

"I know who she is," Falchion growled.

"Argana," Octavia called again in a carrying voice.

"Oh, I'll get her." Alma pushed impatiently past the others, her slippers clattering loudly on the stone steps. In a moment she returned with the healer.

"I don't understand." Argana said as she and Alma entered the stairwell. "Who is ill? Why don't you bring them down?"

"Not ill. He's just taken leave of his senses. Assuming he ever had any. Falchion," Alma called up the stairs. "Here is the physician. Now do you believe us?"

"You keep your ill in the basement?" Falchion asked.

"We naturally separated the sick from the healthy as the city hoped to do with the quarantine," Argana replied. "And the basement is cooler, which helps with the fever."

Here was someone who did not look as if they were in the peak of health, Octavia thought. Heavy lines creased the healer's face. Her shoulders sagged with obvious fatigue. Her formerly well-fitting robes now hung loosely off her frame. Brown stains covered her once-immaculate leather apron.

"Come on, Falchion." Father pushed past him and Octavia. "I'll go ahead to ease your fears. If you want to see our sick, this is where you will find them."

Falchion, looking slightly ashamed of himself, pushed off the wall to follow.

It took a moment for Octavia's eyes to adjust to the gloom of the basement. Large candles set along the walls did their best to brighten the crowded room but made little headway against the heavy smoke of the herb-burning braziers. The tang of that smoke caught in the back of her throat and the miasma of too many sick bodies kept close together made breathing difficult.

Falchion walked between the beds, an expression of deep suspicion on his face. He held his arms tightly folded against his chest. He stopped here and there to peer into the faces of the ill, as if he expected to catch them at something. He stood for a long moment at the foot of the Intan's bed.

Two Samoyan guards, wheezing terribly, nevertheless stood and with trembling hands pointed their spears at the iron monger.

Falchion blew out his breath and stepped aside, glancing from Laiertes, half conscious and moaning to Dan, who lay so gray and still as to seem already dead.

"How many …" Falchion's voice caught. He coughed. "How

many have died?"

"None, so far," Argana said, "but …"

"None?" Falchion's voice rose in outrage. "None dead? And yet you still insist you have no cure?"

"None have died *yet*," Argana replied, the exhaustion clear in her voice, "and none recover. Every hour they slip further away."

"And Verre does nothing?" Falchion demanded, striding through the beds. "He holds the key to life in his hands and does not use it? I don't believe it."

"You yourself threatened him with banishment and the loss of all his goods if he made the mirror," Alma snapped. "You even threatened to take Verre House from him, as if the other glass singers would allow it."

The iron monger sniffed and turned toward the entrance.

Mother lay unconscious in the bed in front of him.

Falchion stared.

"Melody?" Octavia could only wonder at the depth of emotion that filled his voice. The metal worker dropped to one knee beside the bed, took Mother's arm in surprisingly gentle hands and felt for her pulse the way a physician might.

After a moment he got shakily back to his feet. He stared at Mother a moment longer and then at Father, who balled his fists and glared furiously back.

"And you allow this?"

"I am not a glass singer. My voice does not carry here." Now it was Father who looked ashamed. Falchion, his eyes wide in disbelief, headed unsteadily towards the exit. He bumped against another bed and the occupant moaned. Falchion's jaw dropped.

"Raquel? Verre's wife? I don't believe it. I didn't believe it. How can I possibly believe it? When does Verre listen to the council? His own wife and daughter? What can he be thinking? Doesn't he care if they die?"

Halfnote and Robbie caught up with Maru, Gajah and the guards in the back garden. Gajah stood in his corner near the back wall while Maru, one eye on the guards, pulled off the elephant's saddle bags. The city guards formed a large clump around the door to the kitchen. Phyllis stood defiantly in the threshold, looking like a soldier ready to defend her castle. Halfnote wasn't sure whether she should help Maru or stand with Phyllis against the guards.

"Your master is already inside," Phyllis said. "You'll just have to wait for him."

"Falchion is not our master," the sergeant replied. "We're here for the healing mirror. We need a cure."

"So do we all. Alas, you will not find one here either."

"W…watch out," Robbie whispered, a little too loudly, "They're g…going to fight."

The sergeant took a wheezing breath and turned to Halfnote. "Tell me truly now. Do you have sick among you here?"

Why is he asking me? Halfnote squirmed. "Of course we do. My mother and grandmother, Marissa and Dan ..."

"Even Madame Verre ..." the sergeant gave her a searching look. "And truly, you've found no cure?"

Halfnote shook her head.

"How many have died?" another guard, a corporal by the slashes on her sleeve, demanded. Her nasal voice cut a tenor counterpoint to the sergeant's baritone. "Every other house has fresh graves outside but here there are none. Why?"

"Because no one has died." *Surely that was obvious.* Halfnote wished the guards would go away. She particularly didn't like the corporal with the grating voice.

"And yet you say you've found no cure?"

"Alma s…says it's the s…soup," Robbie offered.

"Soup? What soup?"

"Hot b…barley s…soup," Robbie replied, "with g…garlic and onion and thyme …."

"Wait," the wheezing sergeant interrupted. He leaned toward Robbie. "Of course. How could I have forgotten? Alma Lemley of Dantuig is your cook. Can we speak to her?"

"Alma's our c…cook, b…but I don't know where she's from. I thought she was from here, from Albermarle."

Halfnote nodded agreement. Strange to think that Alma might have lived somewhere else at some point. She couldn't imagine her anywhere but in Verre House.

The sergeant's face cleared. "Right. Now I begin to believe you. Alma's cooking is almost as good as a cure. If we cannot speak to Master Verre," the sergeant told Phyllis, "let us talk to Alma. I trust her voice. She knows me. Tell her it's Chevalier who asks."

"When she returns. She went with Falchion, to show him where we keep the sick."

Octavia hurried after the metal worker as he stumbled out of the basement. She heard Father's steps behind her. Falchion kept shaking his head and mumbling to himself as he climbed the stone steps back up to the kitchen.

"We're lost, all of us. His own wife … Melody … even Melody. I didn't believe it. Truly we are lost."

Martin waited for them at the top of the stairs.

"We have more company." He gestured toward the kitchen door "The city guard is here as well."

"They came with the ironmonger," Father said.

"Where is Verre?" Falchion demanded. "I must see him."

"He is making glass," Martin scratched nervously again at his beard, "And cannot be disturbed until the work is complete. Even you must know that, Master Falchion."

"Making? Making? What could he possibly be making at a time like this? His own wife and daughter lay dying …"

"Distillery equipment," Martin said quickly.

Oh, good answer, Octavia thought.

"Distillery equipment?"

"To make new medicines for the ill."

"Indeed, Master Falchion," Octavia said, "you saw how many we care for here." She traded glances with Martin.

"That's why we were in the back wood," Father added, "when your guards attacked us. We were gathering anything we could find to use as medicine."

"Attacked you?" Octavia gasped

"Still, I must speak to him." Falchion ignored Octavia. "The council's order is rescinded. He must make the mirror."

Octavia's eyebrows rose. For all his ambition, Falchion was but one voice on the council and could command nothing by himself. She left that thought unvoiced.

"It was never fear of the council that stopped that making." Octavia traded an ironic glance with Martin, "but fear of the *Hygeia paraphasis* itself. It is too easily turned from an instrument of good to one of harm. As Master Verre tried to explain to you many times."

"I ... I was wrong," Falchion said in a voice so low that Octavia barely heard it. "I thought ... I thought we could deal with the illness another way, but all our efforts have failed. When will your grandfather be free? I must speak with him."

"A making takes as long as it takes," Martin said with a shrug. He even managed to look bored in a way that reminded Octavia of the guard sergeant who saved her from the mob. "Distillery glasses require both bottle and spout. They can be tricky."

And indeed, the tension of creation still filled the air.

The metal workers' art differed greatly from glass singing, but Octavia wondered if Falchion could feel the music. He didn't argue, but only nodded slowly, his expression thoughtful.

"I must return home. My wife and children are ill. Have Verre come to me ...."

"And break the quarantine?" Father growled. "Your guards tried to kill my daughter gathering herbs from Verre's own wood."

"What?" Octavia gasped. This could not wait. "Is Halfnote all right?" Martin glared at the metal worker.

"A mistake." Falchion tried to wave this away. "A misunderstanding. She is unharmed. Tell Verre. He must make the mirror. Use the signal flags to send a message to the Council Hall."

"And have all Albermarle know our plans?" Father retorted. "We'd be overwhelmed by people even more desperate than you."

"I will return, later, then." Falchion forced his way past Phyllis before she could move. Once outside he started shouting at the guards. Halfnote and Robbie hurried in.

"Are you all right?" Octavia grabbed her sister and inspected her for wounds. Halfnote blinked in pleased surprise.

"Perhaps we should have agreed to use the signal flags," Martin said. "We don't want Falchion coming back."

"What about the g...guards?" Robbie asked. "They wanted to speak to Alma."

"They're leaving with Falchion," Phyllis said.

Assignments

"I have no doubt," Grandfather said after they told him about the iron monger's visit, "that he will now blame us for failing to do the thing he previously opposed."

His mouth twisted wryly. He sat at the kitchen table, his eyes red with fatigue, surrounded by every healthy person left in the glassworks. Even Argana joined them. She usually ate in the sick room. Octavia winced at the hoarseness of Grandfather's voice.

"This is as good a time as any for a break. Is supper ready?"

Alma twisted her hands and nodded. "Or just about. Soup's done but the bread needs a few minutes more."

"Now," Grandfather said as they ate, "before we begin to make the *Hygeia paraphasis* we must complete our defense against it. We need the reflective shields for everyone who participates in the making and for the door to the sick room."

"And what of us?" Alma asked, with a wave towards Halfnote and Robbie. "What shall we do?"

"Alma, you'll be with the ill and so behind the shield to the sick room. I have a particular assignment for Robbie and Halfnote. With Trader Breydon's help, I hope."

Father's eyes narrowed suspiciously, but he nodded.

"Whatever you need."

"And I?" asked the elephant keeper. "How can I help?" He smiled at Octavia in response to her glance. In the press of her duties these last few days she had almost forgotten about Maru and his elephant. He and Argana were the only two Samoyans still untouched by the illness.

Argana almost never left the sick room. *And yet she remains well. Why? How?* Maru's health made more sense. The elephant keeper spent most of his time outside with Gajah.

"I would take it as a great favor," Grandfather said, "if you will make it your task to defend the sick room door."
Maru straightened to attention, like a soldier taking orders.

"You honor me."

"It is most important that no one, not even Physician Argana or the Intan, leave the sick room during the making.

No matter what they say or do, you must not allow it. It would be their death, and possibly the deaths of others, if they answer the mirror's call."

"They're sick," Phyllis snapped, "and unconscious. Near to death, most of them. How could they possibly leave?"

"This is the danger of the *Hygeia paraphasis*." Grandfather's eyes blazed despite his mild tone. "And we must all must be aware of it. In the absorption phase, it will call everything alive to itself. The ill and semi conscious will be the least able to resist. We must stop them, at any cost, from falling into the mirror. The reflective shield will deflect the mirror's power, but it might not be enough."

"I still don't understand," Martin said. "We use mirrors to defend against another mirror? How does that work?"

"Thank you," Phyllis muttered. "That's my point exactly. None of this makes any sense."

Then you haven't been listening, Octavia thought, annoyed.

Grandfather ignored Phyllis. "This is a fact born of the mirror's own nature. Even a small reflection turns the power of the *Hygeia paraphasis* back on itself."

"Won't that increase the *Hygeia*'s power?"

"No, because the power stays in motion. It passes back and forth between the mirrors and never settles. Now ..."

He stopped suddenly to gasp for breath. The air in his lungs rattled loudly.

No, Octavia thought in horror. *Not now. Not Grandfather.*

He cleared his throat. "Having chosen this course it would be suicide to delay. We are too weak as it is. We must not lose another voice." He coughed roughly.

"Grandfather ..." Octavia all but whispered.

"I'm fine," he rasped. "Well enough to complete this piece, anyway. We continue. The house has been cleansed," he glanced at Alma who signed agreement, "the sick have been moved to the safest possible place. The reflective shielding is complete." He took a breath. It only whistled a little. "Next we must purify the obsidian. Only the purest glass can be used in this making. Any flaw could distort its gaze and fatally skew its reflections."

"We dare not delay but we must not over tire ourselves. We will work in shifts until time to make the *Hygeia paraphasis*. Tonight, Lorraine leads in refining the obsidian."

Lorraine nodded in grim determination. Phyllis gasped, then waved away the others' glances with an embarrassed look. Octavia understood Phyllis' surprise and hoped it didn't show on her face as well. Lorraine, assuming she succeeded in this task, had just been promoted to full master.

She's ready.

"Tonight," Grandfather continued, "Phyllis, Ted and I rest. Octavia will be head dragon in the purification. In the morning, Phyllis, Ted and I will make the final preparations while Lorraine and her crew rest. Then, when all is ready, we will all gather in the main creation room for the making."

Grandfather, his face pale and pinched, took another wheezing breath. Octavia winced.

"Obsidian is a wild creature that will fight to hold its own shape just as any of us would. Bringing it into malleable form is much like the breaking of a horse or perhaps even," he managed a wan smile at Maru, "the taming of an elephant.

"A firm hand is necessary, but be careful. Brute force will only turn the beast against us. We must coax it carefully into the bridle, always gentle but always in control. Anything that is not pure glass must be removed in such a way that the glass remains sympathetic to us during the rest of the making. Mistress Lorraine's nature is gentle and yet quite firm. This is why she leads tonight. She will also lead the making tomorrow, if I cannot."

Halfnote took a breath. Octavia glanced at her sister.

"But Gra… I mean, Master Verre, what about me and Robbie? What will we do?"

"Ah yes," Grandfather shifted a little to look at Halfnote, "you will help Alma until she sends you to bed, for you also need your rest. Robbie will assist Octavia in her dragon duties during the purification, then rest with Lorraine's crew. Tomorrow I have a special task for both of you. We will discuss it then."

Robbie stared wide-eyed at Grandfather. Halfnote frowned and opened her mouth as if to complain, but Octavia caught her eye and gave a warning shake of the head. Of course Halfnote would be jealous of Robbie's role but now was not the time for pettiness. Octavia hoped Phyllis could put aside her jealousy at Lorraine's unexpected promotion.

For that matter, what would Geoffrey think, when he

recovered? He'd been a junior master for a year longer than Lorraine. Assuming he recovered, of course.

I guess I must really expect Lorraine to succeed. Octavia felt her spirits rise a little. *And the rest of us as well. If only Mother and the rest can hold on just a little while longer…*

Robbie's voice

Grandfather called Octavia back as everyone else left.

"A moment, please, my dear. I want to make sure you understand your task."

"Of course, Master Verre." Octavia stood very straight.

Grandfather smiled. "I regret, sometimes, the disciplines we impose on you and your sister. They seem necessary, but I am still your grandfather."

"I know, Grandfather." Octavia returned his smile. She sat back down beside him.

"About the purification; the dragons have a most important role in the melting. The fire must burn at exactly the right temperature. Mountain's blood burns much hotter and stronger than any other fuel. It is a wild fuel and so naturally creates wildfire. Somehow this must be channeled, focused directly onto the obsidian itself.

"This will challenge you, Octavia. I considered making Frank or Martin head dragon as they have much greater experience with fire. However, there is a particular reason why I chose you. I'm making Robbie a support dragon."

"Yes, Grandfather, I did wonder about that."

"You, Octavia, are disciplined and controlled. That boy is anything but. You will complement each other quite well. Robbie is as untamed as anyone here. He is all awkward impulse and unformed passion. The two of you are natural opposites. And yet, you are the only singer he is truly comfortable with."

"Me? You mean Halfnote, I think."

"Not at all. Your sister, for all her promise, is still only an apprentice. But of course you are partially correct. Halfnote is the key. She is the reason Robbie is comfortable with you."

"I don't understand." Octavia gave him a doubtful look.

"Robbie loves your sister. She loves you. So, by extension, Robbie loves you too."

Octavia frowned as she considered Grandfather's words.

"That seems … I mean, I never realized. Are you sure?"

Grandfather looked amused. "You are very focused on your work, my dear." Octavia's brow crimped again at this, but Grandfather continued his instructions. She would have to consider the meaning of that particular statement later.

"Now, as to Robbie. You must be careful. Remember how young he is. He is that very rare thing, a natural fire-caller. He will instinctively send his energies into the blaze. Monitor him closely. He must not give too much, lest the fire consume him. But you must channel, not block him. Get in the way and you could be burned as well. When it's time to stop, cool him gently. Don't just douse him."

Octavia frowned over these instructions. And to think she'd felt momentarily jealous that Lorraine would lead ...

"I always wondered why you made Robbie an apprentice. He's not a … a natural glass singer."

"We could hardly abandon him. If we had found his family I would have sent him home."

"Well, of course we'll take care of him, but to train him up as a glass singer? Do you really think we can? He can barely hold the tune in even the simplest chants."

"After the floods," Grandfather shook his head, his eyes distant with memory, "when we feared the worst, when truly we thought Halfnote was lost … Of course, you were there. You know how frantically we looked."

Octavia shivered. Those had been terrible days.

But they heard from Mother and Father by the end of the second day after the floods and recovered Halfnote the day after that. So many Khelani were lost it still seemed a miracle that all of her immediate family survived. Poor cousin Mischa lost everyone: his parents, three brothers and an infant sister.

"We sent all of Clan Breydon who could be spared in every direction to look for her," Grandfather continued, "promised any reward ... I doubt that I could describe to you how I felt the moment that I saw her in that crowded, stinking marketplace. It was packed with people; refugees and others like myself seeking lost family. There was no food or water.

The local guard had vanished. The worst sort of ruffians naturally took over. And there in this horrible place, among a large group of unclaimed children, sat Halfnote."

Octavia barely dared to breathe. Until now she had known very little about the details of that search. She knew only that, upon hearing of Halfnote's loss, Grandfather himself joined it. He returned more quickly than anyone dared to hope with Halfnote and, unexpectedly, little Robbie.

Grandfather had never shared the details of that terrible time. More surprisingly, Octavia realized, neither had Halfnote or Robbie. Grandfather blinked, his eyes watering.

He shook himself impatiently and continued his story.

"I ran to her. But as she turned towards me, up jumped this ferocious little boy, ready to defend her at all costs."

"Robbie? Little Robbie was going to fight you?" Octavia tried to picture shy, diffident Robbie challenging her very tall and imposing grandfather. Even after two years of Alma's cooking Robbie still stood half a head shorter than Halfnote.

"Oh yes. Barely six years old, nearly naked, exhausted and starving; still he was prepared to give his all for her.

"He roared his challenge with the most amazing voice. Once Robbie receives the proper training, my dear, I believe you will find yourself quite impressed by that youngster. Now, enough. You have work to do and I must rest."

Octavia looked up sharply at him.

"Yes, you must. You … don't look well."

"I am well enough for this, my dear."

Halfnote chopped at the pile of garlic so vigorously that Alma came over and took the heavy knife from her.

"We're not so short of meat that we need to add your fingers to the soup, child. Whatever is the matter?"

Halfnote glared at the cook through red eyes and took her breaths in short, heavy gasps.

"Dragons preserve us. Are you ill?"

"No. It's just not fair. Why does Robbie get to be dragon with

Octavia? I'm better than him at … at everything!"

"Ho, now." Alma sat by the table and pulled Halfnote into her ample lap. "Everything? Really? Didn't Robbie show you just a little bit about fire a few days ago, right here in this kitchen? He's really good with fire, that boy is."

"I taught him everything else. He can't stay on pitch. He can't find the key. Nobody would work with him. But I did."

"And good for you. That's what we do for each other here at Verre House. Don't you worry. You'll have your chance. Master Verre says he has a special task for you
tomorrow. You heard him. Half rest tonight while the other
half work. Tomorrow we switch places. We're taking turns,
that's all. What's wrong with that?"

"But with Octavia. I never get to see her anymore."

"Ah, there now, now I understand," Alma said in her most soothing voice.

Purification

Octavia found the others waiting for her in the main creation room. Martin and Robbie stood beside their already prepared fire bed. Martin rubbed his bristled head and gave her a nervous grimace that was probably meant to be a smile. Robbie stood next to him, bouncing from one foot to the other.

Octavia glanced at Lorraine. The junior master – master-to-be, now – looked even more determined than usual.

Lorraine indicated that they were ready to begin. Octavia took her place next to Martin and Robbie. They stood underneath the making platform and just to one side of the fire bed. In a rare moment of nerves she almost asked Martin to take over as head dragon. As an apprentice Octavia naturally served her allotted time in dragon duties, but the early recognition of her creative talents meant she had less experience with fire than most. She took a calming breath.

Relax. Channeling is channeling.

Argana stood next to Lorraine. The healer's presence was required for every step of the making. To Octavia's surprise, elephant keeper Maru arrived carrying an intricately carved flute. He smiled at everyone before taking up a station behind the dragons.

Octavia smiled down at Robbie. He blinked and looked away. His meticulously built up fire bed reached exactly the right height. A line of perfectly placed tinder would carry the first spark to the rest of the fuel. A pair of sand barrels – and not water, which would only spread a fire fueled by mountain's blood – stood nearby.

Martin glanced in irritation at Robbie as the boy continued his nervous bouncing. Octavia gave the apprentice what she hoped was a reassuring wink.

Lorraine clapped once, sharply, for attention. Time to begin. The tiny blonde nodded, to Octavia's surprise, not to Frank but to the elephant keeper. Maru began a simple and repetitive melody on his flute. Octavia gestured and Martin struck the flint.

The spark struck the pile of tinder soaked in pine pitch and sizzled out. Octavia glanced sharply at the singer and saw how his hands shook. They had two more tries before tradition said … on a whim Octavia took the firestarter from Martin and handed them to a wide-eyed Robbie.

Do it, she mouthed as Maru's flute picked up the pace. She felt Martin seethe in shame. *I'll calm him later.* Robbie took a breath and struck iron to flint as hard as he could. The flint shattered; three sparks jumped to the tinder and flamed, then vanished.

Why won't they take? Octavia wondered but before she could do more Robbie stepped forward and sang out a discordant note. The tinder burst into flame.

Robbie opened his mouth and then glanced nervously at Octavia as if for instructions. She urged him on with a wave of her hand, curious to see what he would do. *This is hardly the time to experiment, but...*

Hot energy crackled up as Robbie called to the flame in a mournful minor key. The notes fit his unique voice very well for all that they clashed with the flute's elegant melody. The flames bubbled up and spread in all directions across the face of the mountain blood, exactly as intended.

The smell of burning fuel caught in Octavia's nose and the back of her throat. Robbie pursed his lips as if thinking hard, then raised his hands and all but howled. The fire exploded, consuming its meal in a giant blaze of flame and heat. Octavia, caught off guard, remembered her channeling notes just in time. She chanted into place a barrier of sound around the fire bed.

The heat within bounced off the walls of that barrier and gathered itself into a great whirling tower. The heat rose up against the iron floor of the melting box. The metal reddened as it grew hot.

Martin raced to refill the flaming pit with fuel. *Already?*

Did they have enough? Octavia couldn't see what was happening with the obsidian. Lorraine tell them when to stop.

In the background, as if from very far away, Octavia could hear the makers' singing. Their melody sounded strange, just a pair of notes growing in intensity. They needed to find the key and volume that caused the obsidian to vibrate at exactly the right rate. Too strong and the obsidian would shatter. Too low and it would not melt, even at the temperatures created by the mountain's blood.

As the wild glass turned liquid – *if* it turned liquid – it would rise in a whirling mass from the melting box just like ordinary glass. If they did the job properly, matching heat and tone and energy, only the molten glass would rise, leaving all impurities behind. They would exchange the first melting box for a clean one and repeat the process twice, just to be certain.

Lorraine called out the finishing notes; Martin, using tongs and heavy gloves, quickly changed boxes. Octavia, with Robbie following gamely, began the maintaining song. This banked the flames, until the next melting. It might save them a little fuel. They had already consumed more than half of the night's supply.

In theory, the second and third meltings ought to be easier and require less energy. Octavia could only hope for this. They would not be able to renew their supplies of mountain's blood any time soon. There were other fuels, of course, but none as effective.

During the third heating, Octavia stepped back a little to watch Robbie. He encouraged the flames and the heat into their proper place with little apparent effort.

For almost the first time in Octavia's experience, Robbie seemed completely unself-conscious and comfortable in his role. While Martin stood exhausted beside her, Robbie seemed little affected by the heat and tension of their work. Octavia tried to imagine him as Grandfather described, small and starving but still rising up in Halfnote's defense.

Under his deft handling the heat didn't show the desire to escape that she always fought in her own dragon work. The melting plate turned and remained a glorious red. The ball of liquid obsidian should be rising once more.

Please, Mother Piasa, let us complete the cleansing with this third try. They didn't have fuel for a fourth attempt and didn't dare take any of the fuel set aside for the actual making.

Outside, Gajah trumpeted. She did her best to ignore this and what it might mean. What if Falchion returned? Maru, apparently unconcerned, kept playing. The fire basked smoothly under Robbie's care. Bright Lorraine's notes turned from making to monitoring.

Octavia stepped out from under the platform to see how the obsidian looked. The molten ball, clear enough to see through despite its whirling movement, hung just over the cooling bath. Octavia cleared her thoughts and joined her tones with the singers. The whirling globe felt as heavy as anything she had ever worked with. It's once discordant energies now circled smoothly, running as strong and clear as the deepest channels of the Khelana.

Now this is glass worth working with.

She felt a little sorry she had missed participating in the first melting. Carefully she allowed her tones to die away. She stepped back to check on the fire. Perhaps they could succeed at this desperate project after all. Lorraine called out the completion notes and the ball dropped into the cooling bath with a satisfying splash. Octavia and her dragons breathed out the suppressing notes for the fire with a joint sense of relief.

Lies

The transparent orb of obsidian still glowed from the heat of its purification. Lorraine slowly circled the cooling rack, peering through a strong reading glass at the piece.

Martin and Octavia each took a turn inspecting the obsidian as well. Frank peered through the reading glass first with spectacles on, then took them off for a second look.

"Well?" Lorraine demanded.

"The glass is absolutely clear," he said. "You've done it."

"Yes, it's flawless," Martin said. "Congratulations."

"Absolutely perfect," Octavia agreed.

Lorraine let out a breath of relief. She didn't look very happy, Octavia thought and wondered why. Under Lorraine's direction they had purified the chunk of wild obsidian into a flawless piece of pure domesticated glass.

This accomplishment made Lorraine a full master. She could take on any work she wanted now; even start her own glassworks if she wished. But if Lorraine felt any joy over her promotion she did an excellent job of hiding it. She looked angry and worried. Octavia pushed aside a chill of unease.

Surely she's just tired. We all are.

Everyone gathered around the new master to offer their congratulations. Argana patted Lorraine on the shoulder.

"I am happy for you but now I must see to my patients."

"Yes," Lorraine said. "You do that." She gave the healer an odd, angry look and Octavia's sense of unease increased. The Samoyan woman hurried out. Maru gave Lorraine his usual cheerful bow and followed Argana.

"What ..." Martin started to ask but fell silent under Lorraine's sharp glance. The diminutive blonde set everyone to cleaning up the room as quickly as possible.

They worked in silence as no one dared ask Lorraine any more questions. Once done, the group found Alma waiting for them just outside the creation room door.

"The guards are back. They've brought those of their own number who are ill as well. They want us to help care for them."

"What? They can't be serious." Frank polished his spectacles on his tunic. "Why, by all the dragons, should we? They attacked Halfnote and Robbie just this afternoon."

"*Can* we help?" Martin asked. "The basement's full. And we're nearly out of medicines."

"How many?" Lorraine rubbed her temples. "And why can't they take care of their own?"

"Three ill, two healthy," Alma said. "They say they can't go home until everyone recovers. It's death for all if they try."

"It's a trick," Frank said. "They mean to spy on us."

Lorraine sighed. "I assume Master Verre is asleep."

"I'll not wake him, not even for this. He's …" Alma stopped and took a breath. "He needs to rest."

Lorraine nodded. "We dare not tell them about the mirror," she said, almost talking to herself. "But we're only a day away from finishing it. Once it's done and the cure is known …" She bit her lip. "Under normal circumstances we would help them. They'll wonder why if we don't."

"These are hardly normal circumstances," Frank snapped. "We can't afford …"

"We can't afford to have them asking why we won't help them," Octavia said. "Thanks to Falchion everyone in town already blames us for the sickness."

"Then why do they come to us?" Martin asked wearily.

"No deaths," Octavia said. "That's why Falchion thought we had a cure. None of our people have died."

"Yet," Frank said darkly. "It's just a matter of time."

"Even if we send them away," Lorraine said, "there's nothing to stop them or Falchion or someone else from coming back."

She took a determined breath. "This is what we'll do. We'll take them in and keep the two healthy ones so busy they don't have a chance to think. They can take over the heavier duties of caring for the ill; under your direction, Alma, if that's all right?"

The cook grinned. "Don't worry. I have plenty of work for them to do. Truth to tell I'll be glad of their help."

"Good. Have them keep a watch as well, for other intruders. We can't afford any interruptions tomorrow. Where are they now?"

"Outside the back wall. Trader Breydon is with them."

"But what will we do once the making starts?" Octavia asked. "How will we explain locking everyone up in the basement?"

Everyone fell silent for a moment. Then Alma laughed.

"Don't have to explain it. I'll just bring them down and give them a dose of my sleeping tea. I'll tell them it's a preventative."

Lorraine sent the others off to rest while she, Alma and Octavia went to speak with the new arrivals. They found Father and Maru keeping watch. A guard who looked no older than Mischa, Octavia thought with a twinge of sympathy, sat in the branches of a tree overlooking the back wall. The newly risen half-moon and a pair of flickering torches lit the scene.

"I am Lorraine, a master of Verre House." Octavia noted with approval Lorraine's use of her new title. Lorraine's command tones reverberated off the stone wall. "They tell me you seek our help."

"Please, Madame. My sergeant and the others are ill. By council order we cannot return to the city until they recover."

"You said there were two healthy guards," Lorraine muttered. Alma shrugged.

"That's what he told me."

"Too many of our own are ill," Lorraine told the guard. "Including my own husband and Madame Verre. "Our supplies are low. We have no way to renew them."

"Please, Madame. I don't know how to tend them. I'm not a medic. I've only been in the guards a few months. I barely know how to bandage a cut. They'll die soon, without help." His voice broke. Octavia barely managed to keep her expression impassive.

Lorraine pursed her lips and considered the young man as if she had not already decided. Finally, she nodded.

"What's your name?"

"I am called Hugo, Madame."

"We'll help you, Hugo, if you help us." Octavia thought for a moment that he might fall out of the tree with relief.

"Yes, Madame. I'll do anything you say."

"This is Alma, your commander." Lorraine gestured toward the cook. "Whatever she says, you must do without question."

"Yes, Madame."

"Will you help carry them in?" Lorraine asked Father. He nodded, his brow furrowed.

"Are you sure about this?"

"Yes." Lorraine's mouth quirked. "Better to keep them where we can see them."

Father snorted and cocked his head in agreement.

By the look of the stars it was past midnight and the summer dawn less than four hours away when they finally got their new charges settled. Octavia, Lorraine and Alma sat at the kitchen table, each nursing a cup of chamomile tea. Their fresh washed hands stank of vinegar.

Octavia's head ached. She felt as if she could fall asleep quite happily right there at the table. They'd spent the last hour making up fresh medicines and dosing the new arrivals.

As it turned out, five guards needed care, not three. No one bothered to chastise Hugo for the lie. Lorraine set Hugo and Maru to watch over the sick and ordered Argana to bed. Octavia doubted the healer would stay there.

Octavia spoke quietly. "Alma, you will make sure Argana gets some rest tonight, won't you? We need our physician fresh tomorrow for the making."

"If only she really were a physician," Lorraine muttered, turning her cup in her hands.

"What?" Octavia demanded. "What do you mean," she dropped her voice at Lorraine's abrupt gesture. "What do you mean, she's not a physician?"

"She's a fraud." Lorraine managed to sound almost matter-of-fact. "She's no more healer than I am. I felt her energy all through the purification. Her heart is in the right place and I cannot fault her care of the ill, but I swear by all the dragons that our cook knows more about medicine than Argana does."

"By all the dragons, indeed," Alma replied, "I've never heard such nonsense. Of course Argana's a healer. Who do you think has been taking care of all of the sick in Verre House since the plague began? Not me. I just cook."

"She must know something. We've had no deaths. From everything Falchion and the guards said we've been amazingly fortunate. How can you call Argana a fraud?"

"She has some knowledge," Lorraine agreed, "but ..."

A sob made them all turn. Argana stood in the doorway to the basement, tears rolling down her cheeks. "I am sorry." She held her hands tightly to her chest. "I am so sorry."

Alma jumped up and hurried over to her side. "Shhh, now. Come and have a sit. Let's talk. I'll get you some tea."

"Eavesdropping, were you?" Lorraine demanded.

"Stop it," Alma snapped. Lorraine ignored her.

"I came up for some sleeping tea." Argana wiped futilely at her eyes, "and heard you speaking. The Intan insisted on this deceit. I argued but he is the Intan. I must do as he commands. There are no physicians still alive in Samoya. The Intan feared you would not help us, if you knew I was only a midwife. There was no one else they could send."

"We could have gotten another physician," Octavia said, "If we had known ..."

"Do you think so? When the illness came here, which of your healers rushed to our aid?"

Octavia remembered the line of shuttered doors in the medical district and couldn't think of anything else to say. She stared down at the table.

Alma bustled back to the table with a steaming cup of tea and a plate of cookies. "Eat now." She forced a cookie into the Samoyan's hand. "You need your strength. Physician or not, you've still worked harder than any of us to care for the ill."

"And made it nearly impossible for us to save them," Lorraine responded, unrepentant.

"Wait." Octavia held her head in her hands as she struggled to think through the swirl of her own fear and disappointment. "If you're not a physician ... I mean, you clearly have some knowledge of the healing arts. The way you've cared for my mother and the others ... If you're not a healer, why did the Intan bring you?"

"I told you." Argana's voice cracked. "I am a midwife. The prince brought me because there are no physicians left alive in Samoya. I live only because I normally care for pregnant women and newborn children and did not tend those stricken with the illness."

"But you tend them now," Octavia said. "You've done nothing but tend plague victims since the first of your group took ill. And yet you remain healthy. Why?"

"Who can say?" Argana made a helpless gesture. "It is the nature of the illness. Most it strikes down quickly, some after a little time, a few, a very fortunate few, never fall ill."

"But why not? Why is it delayed in some? Halfnote and Robbie are children and yet still healthy. Does their youth protect them? If so, why didn't youth protect Dan or the twins? They aren't much older."

"I don't know. No one does."

Alma patted Argana's hand and frowned at Octavia, clearly wanting her to stop asking questions but she persisted.

"Father carried Mother in his arms all the way up from

Kerguelen Lake and he is still healthy. Peter, the twins' brother, only helped carry her from the street outside and he was sick the next day. Why? Why Geoffrey and not Lorraine? Why Sylvia and not Phyllis? If calming tones reduce fever, why won't purification chants remove the illness altogether?"

"We get the point," Lorraine said impatiently.

"But not the answer. What are we missing?"

"Besides a physician?" Argana flinched and Lorraine grimaced, looking almost apologetic. "Enough," the new master said. "How does this help us make the mirror?"

"I don't know. Must we have a healer?"

"Everything I've read says we do." Lorraine rubbed her eyes and stood up. "We're too tired to find the answer tonight. Let's go to bed. We'll ask Master Verre in the morning."

Right. Best to just stay busy then …

Octavia meant to wake at dawn but the sun was well up when Halfnote shook her.

"Why didn't you get me up sooner?"

"Grandpa made me wait. He said you should get as much sleep as possible."

Octavia waved this away as she rolled out of bed.

"That's ridiculous. There's so much to do." She splashed water in her face. "It must be nearly mid-day. Get my dress, will you?"

"No, it's still early." Halfnote found a clean work dress in the wardrobe and handed it to her sister.

"It's just past breakfast time. But Octavia …"

"What is it now?" Octavia tugged impatiently as her dress caught on her braids.

"Octavia, I think Grandpa has the sickness."

"What?" Octavia jerked her head through the neck of the green cotton work dress.

"He's gotten all red in the face. He tries to hide it but he whistles when he breathes out. And he acts really tired."

"I know." Octavia's stomach knotted from more than hunger. "I could see it last night. I just didn't want to believe it."

"What are we going to do?"

Octavia shook her head. "It doesn't change anything. We can't let it change anything. It's too late to stop now. We're going to make the mirror, find the cure and heal Grandfather along with Mother and everyone else."

She couldn't quite look Halfnote in the eye as she said it. Her voice trembled despite her best intentions. "So it's time we got back to work." Octavia forced as much certainty as she could into that last sentence and hurried from the room without looking back.

Halfnote stood very still in the middle of the room for a very long moment. The reverberations of the tremor in Octavia's voice shivered down her own spine.

If even Octavia doubted their chances … Halfnote forced back tears. Octavia was still right. There was nothing left to do but to keep going and hope for the best. The youngest apprentice took a breath. Then she walked back down the stairs quite slowly, wondering if anything would ever be all right in Verre House again.

Octavia found everyone else gathered in the kitchen. Father gave her a smile as she hurried in. The only healthy person missing besides Halfnote was the young city guard Hugo.

No doubt he'd been put to work in the basement.

Assuming he was still healthy.

Grandfather sat at the kitchen table, surrounded by his staff. He looked and sounded just as Halfnote described. He took each breath with effort and released it with the illness' tell-tale wheeze.

"Grandfather," Octavia said, and then stopped, at a complete loss for words. Cold despair washed over her.

I don't know how to solve this. The Samoyans were right. We're doomed. Oh Grandfather.

"Sit down and eat your breakfast." Alma set a plate of scrambled eggs and greens on the table before her.

"I'm not hungry."

"Eat, and quickly," Grandfather said in a poor imitation of his old briskness. "You need your strength for the making."

Octavia opened her mouth to speak but sat down instead. She

looked at stern-faced Lorraine, who stood next to Grandfather, her arms crossed. "Have you told him?"

"Yes," Grandfather said quite firmly. "And the lack of a physician is a setback, I agree, but there is a way around the problem. We have what we need in the library."

"The library?"

"Yes. Eat up. We've much to do." Octavia took a bite.

The library? Grandfather has a plan. Good. But could he see it through? Grandfather shifted in his seat, the whistling of his breath all too clear. Octavia put her fork down.

"Grandfather ..."

"I am well enough," he said testily. "Now, what we need are all of our texts on healing, herb lore, physical development and the like. Fortunately we have the complete works of Celsus as well as the *Essays on Healing* by Apgar. Beyond that ..." Grandfather rubbed his head, "Argana will still stand as our healer. She *is* a midwife, after all. She does know the healing arts for the ills of women and infants, at any rate. Unless she lies about that, as well."

"I promise you, I do not. These hands have brought over three hundred living children into this world."

"Then we shall have a healing mirror that is at least wise in the ways of new life." Argana met Grandfather's gaze calmly. Octavia thought she looked much less haggard this morning. Perhaps she really had rested. Or was admitting the truth a tonic in itself?

"Now," Grandpa said, his voice firm despite his whistling breath, "On this last point we must all be quite clear. We are taking every possible precaution. However, if the worst does happen, if the mirror does take one of us, we must destroy it immediately. No matter who falls. There can be no hesitation. Do you understand?"

He looked around, forcing each person to meet his gaze. Even Robbie and Halfnote. Even Alma and Father. Everyone said yes or signed their agreement.

"It is harsh, I know. But we dare not falter. If anyone is taken, any delay on our part will only strengthen the mirror. Even if I fall, or the Intan, or anyone else. In that event the mirror must be melted down into nothingness and immediately. There is no other choice."

A strained silence followed these words. No one seemed to want to look at anyone else.

"Now, we all have our tasks. Octavia will retrieve the texts from the library and meet the rest of the singers in the creation room. Alma and Maru will close off the basement and see to the ill during the making. Martin will lock the door to the sick room from the outside and put its reflective shield in place." Grandfather paused and rubbed his forehead.

"Right," Lorraine jumped in. "Phyllis and Ted will finish blocking the ground floor doors and windows, in case Falchion or anyone else tries to visit. Frank will make check of our supplies and the layout of the creation room to make sure everything is in place. Maru, if Gajah needs anything, now is the time to take care of it."

The elephant keeper bowed and departed.

Octavia's head jerked up. "Grandfather, what about the elephant? Will Gajah respond to the mirror's call?"

"All living things do. But don't worry. Maru knows how to deal with the elephant."

Don't worry? Octavia considered just what could go wrong if an enthralled bull elephant tried to force its way into Verre House. That image was only slightly less frightening than the thought of all the things that could go wrong if Grandfather faltered during the making.

Right. Best to just stay busy then. She swallowed the last of her eggs and ran for the library, passing Halfnote on the way. Her sister didn't even look up as Octavia hurried by.

"Now, everyone, to your tasks," Octavia heard Grandfather say. "Robbie and Halfnote, please come here. Trader Breydon, if you would join us." Chairs scraped and feet clattered across the floor.

Oh yes. Halfnote and Robbie's special task. What it could be?

Verre House secrets

Halfnote did her best to ignore the fluttering in her stomach. Fresh tears trembled in the corners of her eyes at the sight of Grandpa's red face. She did her best to force them back again, the way Octavia would. What could Grandpa possibly want of them?

Grandpa put one arm around her shoulders. His other hand clasped one of Robbie's. Halfnote couldn't help but notice the way his arm shook.

"As soon as we finish speaking here, the two of you will go with Trader Breydon to the highlands. Alma has already packed your supplies for the trip."

"But …" Halfnote began. Grandpa shook his head and held up one finger for silence.

"Don't worry. You will return to us as soon as all danger has passed. You are Verre House's greatest treasure. Of course we must take all steps to protect you. I would send the other apprentices with you if they were healthy enough to travel."

"But we want to help with the making. There aren't enough voices," Halfnote said. Disappointment made her stomach hurt.

"Y…yes," Robbie agreed. "We c…can help."

"You are helping. You will be removing a great worry from the minds of all the singers. We cannot do our jobs very well if we are upset or distracted."

"But what about the quarantine?" Halfnote was pretty sure that the city guards' arrows hadn't missed them on purpose yesterday.

"Your father knows a secret path that will take you out of the city. I'm sorry I didn't send you away sooner. I feared … too many things. It is time to put aside fear."

"B…but … w…*where* are we g…going?" Robbie asked.

"To Haverley, up north," Papa said. "We'll stay with my sister Lilly. Halfnote's sister Cadie and cousin Mischa are already there. So is most of the rest of Clan Breydon."

"B…but won't they be afraid that we're b…bringing the sickness? The way the Samoyans b…brought it here?"

"No," Papa said. Halfnote caught the look he gave Grandpa and couldn't help but wonder if he told the truth.

"The cooler air of the northern highlands seems to keep the sickness at bay," Grandpa explained. "You will only be there a short time." He took a whistling breath. "Until the mirror is complete and the cure found. And the mirror destroyed again."

"But what about Octavia?" Halfnote asked.

"I will give her your love. We will see each other again soon, once all danger is past."

"But, Grandpa …"

"That's enough. You must go now."

Grandpa embraced them both and left. Alma gave them each a heavy pack and a big hug. Papa picked up his much larger bag. A bundle of six unused torches poked out from under the top flap. To their surprise he lit a seventh torch and led them, not outside as Halfnote expected, but toward the basement stairs.

"Where are we going?" Robbie, bringing up the rear, whispered to Halfnote. She shrugged, equally mystified.

"You'll see in a moment," Papa said. "Now, pay attention. What you are about to learn is a Verre House secret. You must not share it with anyone, even other house members, without the permission of a Verre House master."

"Or Alma?" Robbie asked.

Papa grinned back at them, his teeth flashing white in the torchlight. "Alma is a Verre House master."

He led them into the highest basement, now filled with all of Verre House's remaining food and medicinal supplies. Papa collected two more torches from used ones piled under the room's single sconce and walked over to the supply lift.

"This is the tricky part. I hope I still fit." Papa shook his head when Halfnote reached for the guide rope to bring the platform. He dropped his pack and unused torches on the floor and handed the lit torch to Robbie.

"Hold the torch until I call you, and then pass it to me."

Robbie held it up to provide as much light as possible. Papa climbed into the lift shaft legs first. He hung by his elbows and felt around for something with his feet.

"Ha! Got it." He abruptly disappeared from their view.

"Papa!"

"It's all right," his voice echoed up the stone shaft. "Send down the lift. Put the packs on it and lower it until I say stop."

They did as he asked. The lift barely dropped before he called stop. He sent it back up for Robbie and the torch.

Then it was Halfnote's turn. The lift dropped smoothly and silently into the darkness, but only for a moment. When the lift stopped she could still just see over the rim of the entrance to the highest basement. Just beneath that entrance was another opening in the mountain rock. Papa and Robbie, torch held high, waited there.

"Wow." Halfnote crawled out of the lift into the cavern.

"Is it a tunnel?" Papa lit a second torch from Robbie's.

"It is indeed." He stooped only a little to avoid the mossy ceiling. "Some say the dragons themselves made these chambers. Other scholars insist that the tunnels and caverns are made by the constant wearing of water that drains down here when it rains. We'll walk single file now, and mind your step. Our path is wet and slippery."

"How c…could water get down here?" Robbie asked. "The mountain is solid rock."

"Somehow water finds a way. There are streams and pools throughout the mountain. One such stream is the reason Verre House can have a well at the top of Viridian Mountain."

They followed the first tunnel to a series of long curving staircases that led to another long tunnel that led to a straighter series of steps that ended in another tunnel. Halfnote's legs began to hurt. She knew they hadn't really walked for long because they still used their first two torches. Even so, her legs ached from constantly stepping down and she wished they could rest.

The rock walls on either side of their ever-descending path began to slowly move apart. Eventually the walls vanished into a darkness too great to be vanquished by the glow of mere torches. Here, at least, the path leveled out a bit. After a while the trio reached another rocky wall that cut straight across their path.

Damp statues and friezes covered the wall around an archway leading to yet another tunnel. The images depicted the story of Albermarle's founding. Papa held his torch up high to give them a better view. A flying Mother Piasa seemed to burst out of the very rock just above the archway. Inside the tunnel they found a series of panels that showed Father Bartholomew and his companions as they set out in search of food for their people. It seemed appropriate as they were headed, Papa said, to Father Bartholomew's home village.

"Why do this where no one c..can see it?" Robbie asked.

"Some people think that the cave where Piasa and Bartholomew first met is up here. They say the one in Albermarle is just for show."

Halfnote thought about this.

"The one in town is easier to get to."

"Yes it is," Papa laughed. His pleasant baritone echoed
off the stone walls and reverberated down the tunnel. He
closed his mouth. "That was unwise. We're getting close to
our destination. We must be more careful from now on. We don't
want anyone to hear us."

Just beyond the story panels they left the tunnel and entered a medium-sized cavern – smaller than the last one, anyway – that acted as a sort of crossroads. Halfnote counted five, or possibly seven paths crossed in one spot. Papa paused in the center, his torch held high, his mouth pressed tight in thought. After a moment he shook his head.

"No, we haven't time. If you ever come this way again the cave is further up this path here." He pointed. "And that path, no the second one there, leads to Piasa's Pasture. I'm sorry we don't have time to visit them today."

Halfnote looked where he pointed but doubted she would be able to tell the paths apart if she ever did come this way again. She still hadn't figured out how Papa could tell which way to go.

He led them onto a path that turned abruptly left. It narrowed and grew steeper. In many places rough steps cut into the living rock. Papa ducked his head more and more.

"Papa, you've come this way before, haven't you?"

"Yes. Many times. Don't worry, we won't get lost."

Well of course she didn't worry about that! Not with Papa leading the way.

"But if it's a Verre House secret, how do you know it?"

"Ah," Papa said, too loud despite his own insistence on quiet. The sharp tone bounced away off the naked stone. "You are as clever as your sister." He turned to smile at her, his white teeth glinting out of a face made dark by shadow. "That is also a Verre House secret."

Back into your hole, rats!

Further down, the tunnel stank of mildew and air rarely refreshed. Halfnote tried to be grateful that it didn't smell of worse things. The torches, near the end of their usefulness, gave off less and less light. Still, Papa did not stop to change them. A creature with a brown shell and too many legs scurried away from a spot just as she started to put her foot there. She jerked back.

"Hey!" Robbie protested, bumping into her. His voice echoed eerily up the tunnel.

"Hush!" Papa snapped. They moved more slowly. The moss-covered ceiling dropped and then dropped again so that even Robbie and Halfnote ducked to keep from bumping their heads. Soon they all crawled on their hands and knees, their packs catching against the rough ceiling. The fetid water and muck soaked them through.

"Fortunately for us it hasn't rained in a few days. The river will be low." Papa stopped and cocked his head as if *listening*. He was listening, Halfnote realized. She took a calming breath, closed her eyes and *listened* as well.

At first she heard little more than her own breathing and heart beat; the occasional drip of water off the ceiling. She felt the slimy muck of the floor oozing between her fingers and around her knees.

A drop of water splattered against the back of her head, another one thumped against her pack. Something cold dribbled down her bare neck, making her shiver.

The smell of mold and mud and murky water filled her nostrils. She could feel the entire bulk of the mountain rising up above them. The skin of Viridian Mountain held most of Albermarle and its citizens. Most of the city was made of stone as well, as proof against fire, but thick forest cloaked the rest of the mountain. The forest had its own citizens, Halfnote knew. Robbie stirred behind her, creating a series of small splashes. Papa seemed turned to stone. She couldn't even hear his breathing.

She opened her eyes and found herself staring at the silhouette of the soles of his cobbled boots. On the raft Papa always went barefoot. In truth, he didn't like wearing boots any more than Mischa. His spent torch lay in the water by his hand. A circle of light glowed just beyond. Was it the way out? She sighed with relief. Papa held up a hand for a silence, then dropped it. He turned and squeezed up against the side of the tunnel, pressing his pack into the damp growth there. He waved Halfnote forward.

"We're under the wharves by the market," he murmured into her ear. "We need to go to the very end of the wharves, the north end. Uncle Cal's raft is tied up there. It's not far but it is very muddy. We need to be quiet and careful in case the guard is around."

Halfnote scrambled forward on her hands and knees. The Khelana River usually ran low at this time of year. They ought to come out onto mud flats under the wooden piers. The light ahead grew brighter and the aroma changed with the texture of the ground beneath her hands; from wet muck to damp rock to wet earth and worse things. One hand sank suddenly into thick, sucking mud.

"We're here," she called softly to the others. She pulled her arm free and moved out of the tunnel. She managed to get to her feet even though the soft mud gave way under her weight. All but blinded by bright sunlight, Halfnote caught hold of a thick wooden pillar for support.

She sank up to her ankles in the mud and struggled to pull them free. Robby, his eyes scrunched up against the light, followed her out. Something slammed into the rough wooden column with a resounding *thunk!* An arrow blossomed just above her hand.

Oh no. Not again.

"Go back," she shouted. "It's the guard!"

Her feet kept sinking. The more she struggled the more she sank. A second arrow landed in front of Robbie. Mud splattered his trousers. He tumbled over and crawfished back to the tunnel.

"Halfnote!" Papa roared. Several large figures stood silhouetted on the river bank. One cranked energetically on the ratcheting device of a crossbow. Fortunately, the guards also found the soft mud a hindrance. The one with the crossbow had sunk nearly to his knees.

"Back into your hole, rats!" a man bellowed. "You'll not break the quarantine here."

"Come back! Come back!" Robbie yelled. Halfnote stumbled as she tried to move. The thick mud held her fast.

"The next arrow bites," the gruff-voiced man promised.

"She's just a child," Papa shouted. He flung himself forward and, sprawled flat across the grasping wet earth, grabbed her arms. One foot popped free with a loud slurping sound. Papa, tugging frantically, dragged her a little ways back towards the tunnel. Robbie grabbed the shoulder of her dress and yanked as well. Suddenly she felt rock under her elbows instead of dirt. It gave her enough leverage to pull free of the mud. She scrambled into the tunnel.

Papa shoved her further on. He followed, pushing her roughly forward. Suddenly he stopped and made a noise that sounded like something between a gasp and a snort.

Halfnote turned but he pressed on.

"Go," he gasped. "Run."

"But Papa …"

"We don't need light, the tunnel's straight." He forced her on.

"Put a hand on the wall to find your way. Keep moving. Hurry. They're right behind."

Robbie vanished into the gloom, his footfalls splashing noisily. Halfnote hurried after. She hated the slimy feel of the moss-covered wall and worried what creatures her fingers might find. Thick mud pulled on her skirt. She struggled to avoid getting tangled up as she ran. The heavy pack pulled painfully against her shoulders. She tried to pull it off but every time she slowed down Papa shoved her forward again, muttering "Go, go."

Did the guards follow? She couldn't hear them over the sound of her own group's gaspings and splashes.

Robbie abruptly called out. She heard him fall, hard. Warned too late and blind in the darkness, she stumbled against his legs to fall heavily on top of him. Her chin thumped against his pack.

"Ow," Robbie moaned. "Ouch. Oh, oh, oh."

Halfnote somehow got to her feet without stepping on him more than once or twice. Papa, breathing heavily, bumped into her but managed to catch himself and they both stayed upright.

"Robbie's hurt," Halfnote told Papa. She could hear the other apprentice sobbing as he struggled to get to his feet.

"How bad?" Papa asked through harsh breaths. "What happened? Can you walk? Robbie?"

"Y…yes," Robbie said, still gritting his teeth against the pain by the sound of it. "Stairs. I didn't see them."

Well of course he couldn't see. Not in this darkness. "Papa…"

"Hsssht!" Papa snapped.

Halfnote held her breath and listened as best she could. The pounding of her own pulse in her ears nearly deafened her. A little ways behind them something large splashed through shallow water.

"Go," Papa growled. "Run as fast as you can. Don't you dare stop until you reach the place where the paths meet."

Halfnote heard Robbie scramble ahead. She felt around carefully in the darkness, found the steps, hitched up her heavy, muck-covered skirts and hurried after him. Papa followed, breathing heavily. Halfnote frowned as she scampered up the stairs, using her hands as well as her feet.

Why did Papa pant like that? She didn't think it was the illness; at least he didn't wheeze.

"Go on. Don't stop until you get to the top."

And how far away was the top? Halfnote pushed ahead despite the ache in her legs and lungs. The stairs seemed to stretch on forever. How long had they climbed? Were they even half way yet? She was about to tell Papa she needed to rest, no matter what, when up ahead Robbie grunted and by the sound of it fell again.

"Robbie?"

"W…we're here," he called back, though quietly. "I think. I c…can't reach any w…walls."

Re-energized by hope of a rest she sped up. The floor leveled out. She reached out ahead with her arms extended. Her fingers brushed Robbie's ear and he started. Behind her, Papa grunted.

"Papa?"

"Be quiet." His breaths rasped in the still air but did not echo. Clearly they had reached a wider space. She heard Papa pull his pack off. Gratefully she followed suit. "Listen," Papa hissed. "Do you hear anyone behind us?"

"No," Halfnote said after a moment.

"No," Robbie said. "C…can we make a light?"

"Just for a moment."

Steel struck flint. Welcome light flared. To Halfnote's surprise it wasn't Papa with a torch. Robbie, his face pale and pinched with pain, held up a small bit of candle. They had reached the crossroads. Robbie's trousers were torn at the knees and badly stained.

"Oh. Do you need a bandage?"

"I'm all right," Robbie said through clenched teeth, "b…but your father's hurt."

Halfnote turned to look where he pointed. One side of Papa's tunic hung in ribbons, and thick blood welled out from a long, straight, narrow cut across his ribs.

No return

Octavia stood in the center of the main creation room, making a final check of their preparations. Of course it was unnecessary. Frank and the others were quite thorough. The fire pit and additional fuel stood ready; the reflective shields in place. The purified obsidian waited on the cooling rack. All of the elements needed to create the *Hygeia paraphasis* were at hand. The glass singers needed only to gather and begin.

After some debate, Grandfather asked Maru and his flute to join the making after all.

"We have a good reflective shield on the basement door and Alma has given all of her charges a sleeping potion. That should be enough. We need your music here more."

Martin, his chin and scalp unexpectedly clean-shaven again, arrived last.

"The door to the sick room is blocked and the protective mirror in place," he reported. "Verre House is secure. Everyone is either locked in the basement or in this room."

"Excellent. Take your place, please," Grandfather said.

Lorraine, a bright column of determination, already stood in the center of the making platform. An unusually quiet Phyllis waited at her side. She would support Lorraine in singing the melody.

Martin, who would take the harmony with Frank, stepped up beside Phyllis. Phyllis gave Martin a rare smile and patted his now smooth cheek.

Lorraine, Frank, Phyllis and Martin formed a semi-circle around one side of the melting box; their protective mirrors set side-by-side created an unbroken shield against the mirror's call. In front of their shielding Octavia placed each of the healing texts requested by Grandfather. The mirror would take the texts and, they hoped, absorb the healing knowledge written in them.

"We are ready to begin," Lorraine announced. Octavia gestured to Ted. He picked up the purified obsidian with the tongs and carried it to its place of honor. Humming a lullaby as if to calm a small child he placed the ball of glass carefully atop the melting box. Then he lit each of the chest-high braziers that circled the making box. Small plates held all of the other ingredients meant to be absorbed by the hungry mirror: small piles of powdered gold, silver, copper, iron, tin, jade and clay; fragments of ruby, emerald, amethyst, sapphire, amber, dragon eyes and other precious stones; bits of Argana's blood and hair and spit; and, of course, bits of every healing herb or plant known and available to Verre House.

Ted took his place as dragon under the making platform. He lit the fresh bed of mountain's blood with one firm strike of steel and flint. Flame spread hungrily across the fuel. Octavia checked Ted's reflective shielding once more. Unlike the other mirror shields which stood straight, the dragons' shields curved to protect the tops of their heads as well.

We're ready. Octavia took a breath. She swallowed a nervous flutter and waved to Grandfather.

He nodded and stepped behind his reflective mirror to join the chorus made up of himself, Argana and Maru. Their lack of numbers struck Octavia like a physical blow.

Madame Marcato's notes said that she used twelve singers and six junior masters in her chorus when she made her last *Hygeia paraphasis*. A grand master, head of another house, stood as head dragon. Three of Tulum's finest physicians voluntarily took part.

And what do we have in our chorus? A bitter tang filled her mouth. *An untutored flute player, an ailing grand master and a midwife. If only we faced a plague of birthings.*

"Are we ready?" Grandfather called from behind his shield. His mild bass snatched Octavia back to the present.

Focus.

"More than," Lorraine snapped.

"Yes," Phyllis said.

"Ready," Martin called.

"Yes. Let's get on with it." Frank gave his spectacles one last quick polish.

"Yes, Grandfather," Octavia said. "We're ready." *Mother Piasa, guide our voices.*

"Aye," Ted murmured, his voice catching in his throat.

"I am." Only the slightest quaver in Argana's voice betrayed her nervousness.

"And I," Maru's ever-cheerful tenor echoed.

"A last warning," Grandfather said in strong tones, "though no doubt unnecessary. Stay behind your reflective shielding until the mirror is bound, no matter what happens. The power of the mirror in its absorptive phase is impossible to resist. If you are taken, you will die. We will not hesitate to destroy the *Hygeia paraphasis* before it can become *mortolo*.

"Now, let us begin."

Grandfather called out the first notes and each person responded in their turn. There would be no turning back now, not until the *Hygeia paraphasis* stood before them, complete.

Or the *Hygeia mortolo* devoured them all. Octavia shivered. She would *not* let that happen.

Energy filled the room as Lorraine began the *making* chant. Very different than the melting tones, it involved a complicated six-part melody. Exactly eight people carried it. This included Argana, who as healer sang a basic four-note repeating counterpoint in a husky and not unpleasant second alto. Octavia felt a sense of relieved approval. The midwife might not be a physician but at least she could sing.

Under Ted's ministrations the melting fire flamed at just the right moment. Prepared this time, Octavia easily caught and channeled the flare of heat toward the base of the making box. Though she could see nothing more than the back and underside of her own reflective shielding she felt the obsidian ball's momentary resistance give way.

The power of song surrounded her on every side. Octavia marveled again at the strength of Grandfather's booming bass. He sang with every bit of his usual intensity, his voice untouched by the illness. The joy and self-awareness of Lorraine's clear tones inspired her as well. Caught up in awe of the moment, the sudden intensity of the mirror's desire all but knocked her off her feet.

The melting was complete. Absorption began.

Octavia's voice wavered enough to draw an anxious glance from Ted. His bright tenor, which coaxed and held the making fire to just the right temperature, never faltered. Octavia smarted from the beginner's error but didn't dare lose voice or energy to shame. She made herself smaller behind her reflective shield and allowed her song to expand. She felt the heat of the fire and the mirror's response to her voice. It felt as if the mirror breathed their very tones.

Is the Hygeia paraphasis self-aware? When this was over, she would ask Grandfather.

At this point, anything unattached or unprotected should fly without resistance into the mirror's orifice. The pages of the healing texts, the bits of precious substances and even the small plates that held those bits would be drawn in.

She could see dust from the floor rising. Even from behind the protection of the reflective shield, lint and loose hairs from Octavia's clothing floated after the dust. She could feel the very hairs on her arms and head struggling to answer that summons.

Even light bent toward that all-encompassing need. Time itself seemed caught in the mirror's pull.

Why doesn't Lorraine cast the binding? Is something wrong?

An unexpected noise made her turn toward Grandfather. This time she held to the iron discipline of her training and easily maintained her tones.

Grandfather, his voice silent, his eyes closed, his face slack and gray, toppled forward and out from behind his protective mirror. Octavia stepped out from under the making platform to catch him. She took his weight on her shoulder and pushed him back behind his reflective shield. Argana and Maru, nearly identical expressions of horror etched on their faces, caught Grandfather and eased him into a sitting position. Octavia breathed out in relief. Grandfather was safe.

I stopped singing, Octavia realized. *Grandfather is unconscious and I stopped singing. Will it affect the making?*

She turned to Lorraine for direction, but could not see the diminutive blonde. Instead, she found herself staring into a swirling cloud of glass. A tornado of molten obsidian pointed itself directly at her. She stood, Octavia realized, completely unprotected in front of the unbound mirror. Nothing could stop her from falling into it.

"Papa!" Halfnote ran to him. She snatched up her bag and pulled out the first piece of clothing she could find for bandage.

"In a moment. We can't stop here. They're still behind us. They'll see the light." Papa hurried them into the tunnel that led home, then stopped. "No. We can't go back to Verre House until they finish making the mirror."

"Come on." He led Halfnote and Robbie to another path. "We'll visit the pasture after all."

"Papa, you have to stop the bleeding." She pressed her makeshift bandage against his side as they hurried down the path. Pressure for cuts, cold water for burns, Alma said. Every apprentice learned that almost from their first moment in Verre House.

Papa took the cloth and held it against his side. He refused to stop until the path turned several times and he was certain their pursuers couldn't see their light. He sent Robbie back down the path a little ways to listen for the guard. Only then did he let Halfnote wrap her makeshift bandage tightly around him.

"It's not enough." Halfnote bit her lips. She'd managed to slow the bleeding but not stop it. She grabbed another piece of clothing out of the pack, one of her own dresses, and wound it around Papa as well. He waited impatiently as she tied it off with the long sleeves.

"It will have to do," he murmured. "We can't wait. Come on." He hissed at Robbie to join them, then hurried down the path. Robbie snuffed the candle out with his fingers.

Darkness enveloped them. At least this tunnel's walls were dry. Her fingers did not encounter anything that moved. She felt regular notches and shallows in the wall and wondered what the decorations might look like. Was it some kind of large lettering? Their path, smooth and not nearly as steep as the stairs, climbed on without mercy. They had not taken, Halfnote thought as her legs began to ache again, nearly enough of a rest.

A footfall sounded behind them; an iron boot cobble scraped loudly against stone. Papa's hand tightened painfully around Halfnote's. She froze, barely daring to breathe. Other steps echoed against the walls at the far end of the tunnel. Halfnote pressed against the wall, willing herself invisible. Fingers of light reached across the floor towards her.

The flickering torches cast as many shadows as they dispelled but Halfnote didn't think the guard could possibly miss the trail of damp footsteps they'd left behind. After an interminable pause the light retreated. An eternity passed before their pursuers' footsteps clattered away down another path. Papa held them frozen in place for another unending moment until he decided it was safe to move again. He didn't have to tell them to be quiet. Or to hurry.

The mirror calls

Halfnote had just started to breathe when the world changed.

"It's begun."

"What's begun?" Papa asked.

"The making. Can't you feel it?"

"Yes," Robbie said.

"No," Papa replied. Halfnote couldn't quite identify the undercurrents in his voice: not so much surprise or even disappointment but something that sounded a little sad and seemed to catch in the back of his throat.

"Why not, Papa?" It seemed strange that he couldn't detect the energy that seemed so obvious to her; as if she could feel the river currents while Papa, riding the same raft, could not. Papa understood the Khelana River better than anyone else she knew. How could he not feel the enormous force flowing past them now?

"It is not my gift." That same peculiar mix of emotion textured his voice.

Halfnote considered what must be happening in the creation room. In this absolute darkness she didn't even have to close her eyes to imagine it.

The singers would channel the fire and melt the purified orb of obsidian. Slowly, under the control of their notes, the hot liquid mass would rise, rotating faster and faster. Did it fight the notes? Grandpa called the obsidian wild, like fire itself. Any untamed creature would fight for its freedom.

Even so, she thought, the voices of the singers would be impossible to resist. Trapped and pushed by sound, the obsidian would widen and lengthen into a disc; become an ordinary mirror; then absorb all the elements necessary for its transformation into a *Hygeia paraphasis*. Lorraine would bind it with silver and they would have their tool for curing the plague. They had only to set it upright on a cooling frame and bring the first patient before it.

Under the circumstances it would probably be Grandpa.

And then Mama. I hope the second patient is Mama. In truth, she knew the next patient was likely to be one of the Samoyans. They were the sickest.

The hairs on her arms stood up. She felt a tingling all up and down her back. She stopped walking, filled by a sudden desire to run back down the path for home.

The absorbing phase had begun.

Halfnote stopped. She heard Robbie's heel turn on the rock path. Even Papa paused.

"Robbie, are you all right?" she asked quietly.

"Y…yes. It's strong, isn't it?"

"Is something wrong?" Papa's breath came in gasps.

"Papa, did they block the door behind us?"

"What do you mean?"

"They blocked the sick room door and put up a glass shield to reflect the mirror's call. But they didn't block our door, did they?"

"Our door is hidden." Papa sounded impatient.

"But we still feel the making. The creation energy is much stronger than usual. And now we can feel the absorption. It's even stronger. The mirror is calling us. Can't you hear that?"

"Put it out of your mind. We need to keep moving."

"But can you hear it, Papa?"

"What difference does it make?"

"What if the city guard hears it?"

Papa spat out a word of such amazing filthiness that both Halfnote and Robbie gasped aloud.

"Light your candle," Papa ordered Robbie. Robbie fumbled about and dropped his steel twice before the tiny flame finally sparked to life. Halfnote gasped at the horrible expression on Papa's face. She glanced at his bandage but it remained in place, with only a few bloodstains visible. Papa grabbed her arms, squeezing so tightly it hurt. She tried to pull free. His fingers dug painfully into her skin. He stared into her eyes with that same awful look in his own.

"Your grandfather said that the mirror would do anything, tell anyone anything, to lure them into it. How do you know this isn't the mirror lying to you?"

Robbie crept up behind Papa, his candle held high. He put one shaking hand on Papa's back.

"Trader Breydon? You're hurting Halfnote."

Papa released Halfnote as if she'd suddenly turned hot and burned his hands. He spun on his heel and grabbed Robbie by the collar. Robbie yelped and dropped his candle. It promptly died, leaving them in total darkness again.

"Papa?" Halfnote cried, too frightened to worry about the way her voice reverberated up and down the tunnel.

"How do you know this isn't the mirror's magic?" The tunnel walls caught and carried off Papa's voice as well.

"Papa!" Halfnote felt around with her hands until she caught his arm. He jerked free of her grasp and she stumbled back against the wall, cracking her head a little against the stone. Tears welled up in her eyes. What could she do? Was this the mirror at work?

If Papa couldn't feel the making, how could the absorption affect him? And shouldn't she and Robbie feel it even worse?

Almost without conscious decision, she began humming the calming tune. It worked on fire and fever. Would it help Papa? Her voice strengthened and after a moment Robbie joined in. Steel clicked against flint and a torch flamed to life. Papa held it up in one shaking hand. He looked considerably calmer but stricken with guilt.

"I'm so sorry. I don't know what came over me. I had such terrible thoughts. Melody ... Are you all right, Robbie?"

Robbie, his eyes wide, just nodded. He continued to hum the calming notes.

"Halfnote?"

"Yes, Papa," Halfnote all but whispered between notes.

"I'm sorry." Papa rubbed his jaw with a shaky hand. "You're right, Halfnote. We need to make sure the city guard can't get to Verre House. Come on!"

Papa dashed down the tunnel, with Robbie and Halfnote in hot pursuit. At least this time they could see the path.

"Keep singing," Robbie told Halfnote between breaths.

They stumbled into the crossroads surprisingly quickly.

"Papa!" Halfnote tried to call him back as they reached the circular cavern. They weren't the only ones running through the tunnels. She could hear other footfalls – many others, in boots made of thick leather and iron cobbles. The steps bounced and echoed off the walls in all directions, making it impossible to tell where the runners really were. The steps were getting louder, of that she was certain.

"I hear them," Papa gasped. "Hurry! This way."

They dashed down the tunnel that led back to Verre House. Halfnote panted, no longer able to draw enough breath to both run and chant. Her shadow flared out ahead of her in spite of Papa's torch and she nearly tripped.

"There they are," a man shouted. Halfnote looked back. No wonder she sprouted shadows. The city guard was behind them; at least six, all carrying torches.

Their shouts and pounding feet bounced off the walls, the echo redoubling the noise into a horrible cacophony.

We'll never escape. Halfnote sprinted down the tunnel behind Papa. She couldn't see Robbie anywhere. Was he behind her? And where were they running to? Even if they did reach Verre House, there was no safety there, not until the end of the making.

The guards were nearly upon her. Fingers clutched at her pack. Terror put wings to her feet. She raced forward, just out of reach. She even passed Papa as they darted under the archway decorated by that amazing sculpture of Mother Piasa bursting out of the rock.

She looked back in time to see Papa whirl and fling his torch into the faces of their pursuers. They fell back. One swore. Papa jumped to one side of the archway and then, did he punch the rock?

Halfnote, bent double and gasping for breath, stumbled to a stop. She couldn't make out what was happening through the flicker of light and shadow from the guards' torches.

Something crunched loudly. Something seemed to fall off the top of the arch. For a surreal moment she thought the sculpture of Mother Piasa might truly have taken flight. The floor rumbled beneath her feet and everything went black.

Inside the looking glass

Octavia turned back towards the safety of her reflective shield. She felt like an ant trying to swim through honey. She heard no singing, only a terrible roaring in her ears. Daylight still poured in through the round windows overhead but she could barely see. Everything blurred.

Where is Grandfather?

He fainted; the strain of the making too much for him. But

she'd pushed him back. She'd saved him, hadn't she?

At least the mirror no longer pulled at her with that terrible grasping need. Such a terrible hunger; impossible to ignore. But what had stopped it? Was it bound?

That must be it. She didn't remember Lorraine throwing the silver. She couldn't quite find her bearings.

Where was Grandfather? He fell and she caught him.

He should be right here. Is he all right? Why couldn't she see him? *Oh. Over there.*

He lay slumped against the wall behind his protective mirror. She realized that she looked down at him from above.

What? How could that be? Light flashed, blinding her. She fell back, confused. Why did it seem so difficult to move? Was it an effect of the *Hygeia paraphasis? Why isn't anyone singing?* Unless they were already finished …

She turned and saw, blurrily beneath her, the trio of shields on the making platform. Martin peered up at her from behind his shield, then ducked back. But...

How did I end up above the making platform?

She crouched down and peered through the blurry barrier under her feet. Just below she could make out the square form of the melting box, still bright red with heat. Just to the side, right where it ought to be, the cooling bath waited to catch the completed mirror. Realization struck like a sledgehammer.

I'm in the mirror. Grandfather fell but I'm inside the mirror.

She played the scene back in her mind. *Grandfather fell. I reached out to stop him. I pushed him back ...* And now …

Am I dead? Terror filled her veins. *I don't feel dead.*

Well, perhaps not yet, but it was only a matter of time. How often did Grandfather warn them? If anyone fell into the mirror – anyone – it would be destroyed. As quickly as possible. And she had agreed with the rest, certain that there could be no other solution.

But I'm not dead. Surely there must be a way out. If I can fall into the mirror, why can't I fall back out?

She felt around her container's floor. It was solid.

That's not right. It isn't finished. We haven't cooled it. Lorraine hasn't cast the glazing. This is a whirling ball of hot liquid. How can it feel so solid? Maybe that's what makes it so blurry. It's moving and only seems stable from inside. But it shouldn't be solid.

She slapped her hands against the surface in frustration. That only made her hands sting. The glass didn't feel hot. The heat of the globe ought to have cooked her through. Why didn't it?

Octavia peered through the blurry barrier that surrounded her. She hovered above the making platform, just below the trio of sunports set into the ceiling. She looked for Grandfather. One of his feet stuck out from behind his shield. As she watched, the foot moved, then drew back out of sight. At least he was conscious.

Looking at the mirror shields hurt. Light reflecting off the silvered surfaces seared her eyes. Octavia found Lorraine, at last, just beneath her. The newly promoted master hid behind her shield, but Octavia saw her blue eyes peering out.

"Lorraine!" Octavia shouted, or at least tried to. She pounded on the glass wall until her hands ached. "I'm in here. I'm all right. You don't have to destroy the mirror."

Lorraine jerked out of sight. Light reflected from the protective mirror burned Octavia's eyes. She blinked away pain and tears. Moving as if swimming – and movement did become easier with practice – she turned in her molten cocoon to look for Phyllis. She found only Phyllis' blinding shield and looked quickly away.

Martin. Maybe Martin can help me.

The smooth-cheeked singer peeked out from behind his shield. The making fire burned hot and bright between him and the *Hygeia paraphasis*. Still, the flames didn't burn her eyes as badly as the light reflected from the protective shields.

"Martin!" She waved frantically at him.

"I'm in here. I'm alive. Help me!"

For a moment it appeared that she'd succeeded. Martin leaned out, coming closer to her. Phyllis jerked him back behind his shield.

"No, no, it's all right!" Octavia smacked the glass in frustration. "It's me. I just need your help to get out."

Martin looked out from behind his shield again. He took a step toward her and then another. He started to push the mirror shield out of the way, so he could come closer.

"That's right. Come on." She shook with renewed hope. Martin would help. She was going to escape this cursed glass.

A high-pitched reverberation filled her container. Octavia fell to her knees, hands tight against her ears. Nothing she did blocked that terrible vibration. She thought her bones might shatter. The ball became a flat disk, stretching her in two directions. It dropped. Flat on her back, she felt it as if her own center was giving way. She pressed against the walls of the glass, desperate to steady herself.

Then the walls froze. Literally. She tore her hands free, leaving behind bits of skin. Cold burned through her dress and hair where she pressed against the glass. Her hands and fingers felt like solid bits of ice. She stuffed them under her arms for warmth, but this only chilled her further. Her teeth chattered horribly. Would she freeze solid herself?

A thin silver layer now covered the mirror rim, further obscuring Octavia's view. She could just make out the walls of the cooling tub around her. The mirror bobbed as it floated.

Octavia tried to regain her feet but that just unbalanced the mirror. It tipped in one direction, then the other, never quite capsizing. She rolled helplessly with it. Her sense of disorientation grew.

This is horrible. Her stomach churned. *I can't stand this.*

And, more chilling than even the mirror's frozen surface, she remembered Grandfather's dire warnings.

He wouldn't destroy the mirror with me inside, would he? Dread filled her. *I've got to get out of here.*

Robbie's trip

"Papa?" Halfnote managed when she got her breath back, "where's Robbie?" The darkness that surrounded her seemed so solid she was surprised to find she could still move. The insistent thought that she must return to Verre House throbbed in her veins.

Maybe Robbie was already on his way there.

"I'm here," Robbie called from somewhere further inside the cavern. "I lost my candle. What happened to the guards?"

To Halfnote's great relief, a light flared. Papa held up a torch and stared around, his face pale in its flickering glow. He stood in front of the archway, just under the sculpture of Mother Piasa. A smooth piece of granite, inset in the archway, blocked the tunnel. Halfnote could just hear the city guards shouting through the stone.

We stopped them. We can go home. She bit her lip hard enough to make it bleed. *No, we can't. That's the mirror talking.*

And were they truly safe from the guard?

"Is there a way to open it from the other side?"

A muscle in Papa's cheek twitched. "There is, but it isn't anywhere you'd think to look. They would have opened it by now, if they knew how. We can leave."

"Papa ..."

"Let's go." Robbie's voice was an agony of impatience.

"Alma needs us. Can't you hear her calling? Come on!" He started down the path toward Verre House.

"Robbie, get back here!" Papa snapped.

Halfnote began singing the calming notes again. It helped a little, but Robbie only stopped in place, he didn't back up. Halfnote sang louder and louder until the distant walls sent her song back to her. Robbie shivered and, after a moment, joined in.

"We can't stay here." Papa raised his voice to be heard over the singing. "And we can't return to Verre House until the making is done. What can we do, Halfnote? How do we avoid the mirror's call? I can't stand this. I keep hearing your mother ..." He broke off.

How would I know, Halfnote fretted, then angrily shoved that thought aside. Papa needed her help. What would Octavia do?

"In a normal making music forms a barrier. That's why the calming notes help, I think. But the absorption phase is too strong. That's why Grandpa said everybody had to have ..."

"W...we need a mirror," Robbie broke in, "to reflect the call b...back. So it can't reach us."

"A mirror? Of course, like a reflective shield. But where will we find a mirror down here? Does it have to be a mirror?" Papa started pacing. Each round of steps took him further up the path toward Verre House. "Or just anything that reflects?"

"Water reflects. There's a s...stream up this w...way."

"Excellent lad!" Papa hurried after Robbie. "Of course there is. Come on, Halfnote. There's no time to waste."

Halfnote tried to think why she didn't want to go that way, but her head hurt and her throat ached and she really did want a drink. Soon they were all dashing up the steps toward home, with little breath left for anything but climbing.

Mama.

"Alma," Robbie whispered. "I'm on my way."

Papa said nothing. He continued up the stairs, torch held high. He didn't care anymore whether they could keep up.

By the time they reached the little waterfall that slid down one smooth wall into a circular pool at the bottom of the first – or, in this direction, last – curving staircase, Halfnote had all but forgotten why she wanted to reach it. Nothing mattered anymore but getting to Verre House. Papa moved on past the pool. The light faded up the stairs after him. Robbie caught his foot against a step and tumbled head first into the pool. Water splashed everywhere; first when he fell in and then when he jumped out, exclaiming at how cold it felt.

"Robbie! Watch where you're going." Halfnote tried to push past but he caught her arm.

"Trader Breydon," Robbie called.

"Hurry up," Papa shouted back. "I can't waste any more time waiting on you two."

"Let go." Halfnote fought Robbie's grip.

"Take a drink." Robbie kept hold of her arm. He hummed a few calming notes. "You'll go faster if you do."

"Oh, all right." Halfnote knelt quickly by the pool, meaning only to grab a sip. She was a big girl now. She could handle a little thirst. Robbie grabbed the back of her neck and shoved her under the cold water. The cold shocked her overheated senses and cleared her head instantly. She pulled back out of the pool coughing.

"Papa," she shouted with her first breath, "Come back!"

Halfnote chanted the calming tune as loud as she could. Robbie jumped to his feet and shouted the notes. The curving rock walls caught up his voice and flung it back and forth between them. The multiplying echoes increased in volume until she thought they roared like a dragon.

Papa's dwindling torch rolled towards them. Robbie caught it up and coaxed it back to full light.

They found Papa just around the last curve as the final echoes of Robbie's shout faded. Papa sat on the top steps, his head in his hands. The tunnel just beyond Papa led back to the lift and Alma's kitchen. Halfnote wanted nothing more than to follow it home.

She called out the calming notes in a carrying voice. As the chant echoed she touched Papa's shoulder.

"We need to go back to the pool. I think it will help us."

Robbie took up the chant before it faded away. To her great relief, Papa stood up.

As he did, she felt the world tilt. She took a breath but couldn't get any air. The relentless call of the mirror stopped for a moment. Then it resumed, worse than ever.

Something was terribly wrong.

"Octavia's in trouble," Halfnote said. "Something's wrong. She needs us."

The Dragon's Cry

Octavia pounded desperately against the walls of her mirror prison. Ted and Martin positioned their reflective shields around the cooling bath where the mirror floated.

What are they doing?

She ducked to avoid the searing light they reflected. When she dared to look again reflective shields surrounded her. The focused illumination burned her eyes. She buried her face in her knees.

Why are they doing this? I just need a way out. Why are they making it worse? They know I'm in here.

If she could just tip the mirror out of the cooling bath, it might smash when it fell against the stone floor. She rolled back and forth. The mirror wobbled but didn't go anywhere. She didn't have any way to steer her craft.

Her plan probably wouldn't work anyway. *Of course it won't break. It's Verre House glass.*

She remembered saying those very words to Mischa on the night of her celebration. How long ago had that been? Two weeks? It seemed an eternity.

If she could just get someone's attention. If she could get the mirror to fall, even if it didn't break, might the others realize that she still lived inside? She made slits of her eyes and used her hands to block out as much of the glare as possible. Through a gap in the hastily positioned mirrors she could just make out the blurry heads of Grandfather and Lorraine as they spoke to each other. The diminutive blonde waved her arms in apparent excitement while Grandfather, his shoulders slumped, simply kept shaking his head.

"Grandfather!" Octavia pounded on the glass again. "I'm all right. Look at me. I'm here. I'm not dead."

He glanced in her direction, then looked away. Lorraine reached out to him but he turned abruptly from her.

"Come on, Grandfather. You'll think of something. You know you always do," Octavia said.

Stay positive. If I were Grandfather, what would I do now? She shivered, remembering his warnings. If he didn't think he could help her, she would just have to help herself. But how?

First, understand the substance you work with, she thought, falling back on her earliest training. *This is glass. I'm a glass singer. If I understand anything, it's how to work with glass.*

Something moved outside the mirror and she looked up. Light from the shields burned across her vision. She covered her eyes, impatiently blinking away tears of pain.

Focus, Octavia. You can't reach them. This is glass. I'm a glass singer. What about the melting chant? Shouldn't it also melt glass from the inside?

She had no fuel. No spark. No way to start or maintain a fire. And this was obsidian.

"Oh shut up," Octavia growled aloud to her doubts. She squirmed around into the best position she could manage for singing. She kept her eyes tightly shut against the burning glare from outside.

All right. Melting. Melting begins with fire, heat, stirred energy. She just needed a spark, a way to begin.

Can I use the light? This is a mirror. It reflects. It is already reflecting. Light without heat. That won't help. I need heat. The vibration of the song generates heat. Just not enough. But that's outside. What happens on the inside?

"Mother Piasa," she cried out. "I sing the Dragon's Cry."

Trapped

"Octavia's in trouble," Halfnote told Robbie again. He continued to chant the calming notes.

"It's the mirror lying to you." He kept up the chanting.

Papa, sitting next to her on the top step of the curving staircase, nodded. "I keep hearing your mother."

"Let's go to that pool," Robbie said. "It helped, before."

Papa stood up and took Halfnote's hand. "Yes," he said in too firm a voice. "This will end soon. As your grandfather explained, the absorption phase is the last part of the making. Next they will glaze the mirror and this will stop."

No it won't. She reluctantly took a step, then another.

"Sing," Robbie said in between his own notes. "It helps."

Halfnote took up the chant. Her heart slowed and her breath evened out. The conviction in the pit of her stomach that Octavia needed help grew. She could no longer tell the difference between the mirror's voice and Octavia's call.

Halfnote stopped dead on the stairs.

"Don't stop." Papa pulled on her hand. "We need to keep moving away from the mirror."

"The mirror has Octavia. I can feel it."

"Don't say such things. You know it's just the mirror talking. Octavia is with Master Verre. She's safer than we are. Now please come on while we still have our wits about us."

"No." Halfnote stamped her foot. The mirror's thrumming surrounded them, filling her mind. It did make thinking terribly difficult. "Listen, Robbie. Before, the mirror had a different voice; Its own. Now when the mirror calls, it calls with Octavia's voice. Can't you hear the difference?"

Papa began to pant again. He took up the calming chant. His chanting did little to ease their fears. Papa sang in a clear, pleasant baritone, but he lacked power. He knew how to sing but he didn't know how to use the music.

Robbie paused to *listen*. His eyes clouded and the torch wobbled in his hands. He turned toward the head of the stairs.

"Wait, Robbie," Halfnote called. He didn't.

"Robbie! No!" Papa shouted. He took one step after another up the stairs, carrying the light with him.

Octavia. What would Octavia do? Octavia always said the way to solve any problem was to break it down into little pieces. Then solve each piece one at a time.

How could she protect Robbie and Papa?

How could she block the way to Verre House?

How could she help Octavia?

How could she keep her mind clear of the mirror's demands? Could she keep her mind clear?

What can I do? I barely know anything.

The thrumming and Octavia's cry for help grew more insistent. Halfnote turned, twisting free of Papa's tight grip.

He grabbed for her but she darted out of his reach. Robbie, his eyes vacant, his lips moving silently, barely noticed as she snatched the torch from him. Papa pounded up the steps after her.

She almost made it to the supply lift. She could see it in the flickering torchlight. Papa caught her around the waist and threw her back down the tunnel.

He grabbed the hoist's oiled ropes and jerked down as hard as he could. The wooden platform flew out of sight. Papa's knife flashed in the light of the dropped torch.

"No, Papa!" His blade sliced through the lift's leather straps. The pieces vanished into the crevice below. Now they had no way of returning to Verre House.

And Halfnote had lost her chance to help Octavia.

"No, Papa, no." She pounded on him with her fists. "Octavia needs us. She's been taken by the mirror. She'll die, Papa, if we don't get her out. Grandfather said so."

Papa caught her hands. He sheathed his knife and, still holding her at bay, picked up the rapidly diminishing torch. Sweat glinted on his face in the flickering light.

"Papa, we've lost Octavia."

"I can't say if we have or not." Papa led her back to the curving staircase. He sounded much calmer. "If the mirror speaks truly then we've lost Melody as well; and no doubt Madame Verre and all the rest. But at least I have saved you and Robbie."

Octavia sang the Dragon's Cry. She felt her power surge.

She saw golden sparks gushing out of her mouth and fingertips. She sang the alpha notes. They were said to be the very first tones that Falafel, Piasa's son, taught Melinda, the very first glass singer. Energy burned without pain. It poured out of her body even after she stopped singing.

The energy rebounded against the top of her prison and poured down like water. It pooled on the floor then rose, too quickly. Had she outsmarted herself? She couldn't move out of the fluid's way and she couldn't stop it.

Call the completion notes, she thought too late. The fluid filled her mouth even as she drew breath to sing. Would she choke to death? Would she drown?

Apparently not.

The temperature rose considerably within the fluid of her music. Her hands and feet felt warm and supple again.

The energy swirled and sped up. The glowing flow cheered her but seemed to have no effect on the mirror. The substance circled now as if it had a life of its own. The temperature continued to rise and became uncomfortable.

She tried the damping notes but the fluid snatched these from her mouth incomplete. The horrid sense of disorientation returned as the walls of her chamber liquefied and oozed around her. Molten glass bubbled up and dribbled down. It seared her skin and bones.

"Stop!" she shouted in her strongest command tones.

Energy exploded in all directions.

After a few moments, Octavia dared to open her eyes again. She lay on her side. The molten glass and burning pain were gone. She expected to see charred skin, but her arms and hands were whole and healthy. So was the rest of her.

Images of comfrey glowed in the glass walls. *Of course. Comfrey poultices ease burns.* This was a healing mirror, after all.

The images faded. Octavia realized that her chamber was larger. She could stand and take a few steps in each direction.

Light from outside didn't bother her. She peered cautiously through the silver-coated wall and saw the reflective shields shattered on the floor.

Did I do that?

If her energy could affect events outside the mirror, why couldn't she use it to break out?

Perhaps I could, if I don't mind burning to death in the process. She squatted inside her glass chamber and considered her options. The floor felt cold again, perhaps a little warmer than before but still too cold to sit on comfortably.

As far as she could tell the creation room stood empty.

How might she reach Grandfather and the others? Her stomach turned; when they returned it would be to destroy the mirror. Grandfather had been all too clear about that.

I've got to get out of here.

The door to the creation room opened. Lorraine and Phyllis entered. After a moment, Martin stumbled over to the fire pit. Octavia sucked in her cheeks.

They have no protection. I knocked the shields away. Can I use my chanting to knock them away as well? Can I strike out at my friends? Do I want to die?

She felt cold all over in a way that had nothing to do with her surroundings.

If only I could talk to Lorraine. She would know what to do. If I got Lorraine in here, I'm sure together we could find a way out.

Flames shot up out of the fire pit.

They mean to melt the mirror. Grandfather said we must.

There couldn't be much mountain's blood left. But they might also try fast-burning pine pitch. And coal. Would that create a fire hot enough to melt purified obsidian?

Lorraine picked up the net and came forward. Behind her Martin and Phyllis chanted. Octavia couldn't hear their voices, but she could see their mouths moving. How strange that they didn't seem concerned about their lost shielding.

Come on, Lorraine. You want to help me, don't you? You won't leave me in here to die.

Something gold and sparkly, like dust motes thick in bright sunlight, spiraled toward her from the singers' mouths. A golden wall enveloped Lorraine, blocking Octavia's view.

"No!" Octavia slammed her hands against the mirror's surface. "We're friends, Lorraine."

"We've known each other all our lives. Don't do this."

They'd met when Octavia was five years old and Lorraine eight, in fact. The mirror slid into the net and bobbed along toward the fire pit. The rocking knocked her off her feet.

"How can you? How dare you?" she screamed, weeping. Why had she waited so long? She didn't want to hurt her friends, but *some friends these!* They meant to kill her.

She began the melting chant more quickly this time. She let the energy build as fast as possible. If she could knock away the reflecting shields what could she do to three frail people? So what if she burned? The mirror would heal her.

A feeling

Halfnote sat on a step beside the small pool, Papa on one side, Robbie on the other. No one sang or spoke. It was pitch black again. Their torch had finally given out despite Robbie's best coaxing. He was right about the pool, though. Or perhaps it was the music of the tiny waterfall that fed it. She could hear the mirror's voice still, but it did not draw her – or Papa or Robbie – as it had before. It did reach for them, but could not quite touch them as long as they kept the pool and waterfall between them and the way to Verre House.

She could not explain how she *saw* the mirror's essence, in that darkness. Perhaps the image was only a creation of her mind, built from the burble of the waterfall and the entity's hissing whispers. Still, she did see it. The energy slithered and rolled down the curving staircase like a great snake made of gray cloud. It held Octavia's voice within it. The mirror had not yet absorbed her sister. Not completely.

But it was surely only a matter of time.

Halfnote hummed the maintaining notes, directing them against various curls and eddies of the mirror's essence. To her surprise, the barrier created by the stream did not stop the energy of her voice. Of course, she wasn't a mirror.

At first she learned only what she already knew:

Here shimmered the force of the mirror; there Octavia's potent spirit vibrated within. Both continued to expand in verve and vitality. For the moment they still ran along their separate courses, but …

Halfnote sucked in her breath … here and there they began to combine. How long before the two streams became one? That joining, she somehow knew, was what she had to stop at all costs.

She heard tiny feet scampering up the stone staircase. The mirror was growing stronger. She could feel it. Octavia was growing more desperate. She felt that too.

Different channels of energy spiraled out of Verre House like various currents caught and directed by rocks in a river.

The mirror generated one large channel of energy; within it Octavia's desire to escape created a smaller swirling force.

The other singers would melt the mirror with Octavia still in it, as horrid as that sounded. They had little choice. They would melt the mirror because if they didn't it would draw in every life within its reach. At first the *Hygeia paraphasis* – now *mortolo* – would take mice, birds, moths and fleas and other vermin. Like the tiny animals now scurrying up the stone staircase. But as the *mortolo* grew in strength, and she could feel it growing even now, it would take larger lives. Soon it would call even the strongest singers like Lorraine and Grandpa. By then it would be strong enough to draw in people from the houses next to Verre House.

Eventually it would eat everything in Albermarle. Even Gajah the elephant would answer its call, Grandpa said. What if he got loose now? The singers had to destroy the *Hygeia mortolo* before it got any worse. She understood that.

Octavia is still alive. I can feel it. She isn't part of the mirror yet. There's a difference in the energy. I can feel that too. Why can't Grandpa feel it?

Maybe he could. Maybe he thought it didn't matter. Grandpa had said all along that they would destroy the mirror if it took someone. No matter who that might be.

Halfnote half closed her eyes. She felt Papa on one side, his energy a sharp stab of grief. She took his hand. He started, then clasped hers tightly. His energy lightened a little. On her other side she felt Robbie's concern. He was an annoying prickle, like a fly that won't go away. She pushed that feeling aside as much as she could.

She focused only on the energies in front of her. Octavia's energy turned red, spiky. It burned painfully, like real fire. The mirror's outpourings began to reflect the jagged edges of Octavia's spirit. The two courses of energy intertwined more and more. Once they merged completely it would be too late.

Something flared on the edge of her awareness. The mirror's energy visibly shied from it, like a frightened horse. Heat. The melting fire. Lorraine's sparkling tones swirled around the mirror's energy and surrounded it's essence with intense heat. Frank, Ted, Martin and Phyllis added their vibrations to the mix. The mirror's spirit, and Octavia's, blazed against that strengthening barrier of sound. The potency of the singers' music faltered, then renewed.

Octavia's still separate essence raged against them with her own determined tones.

She must stop that. It just brings her and the mirror closer together. If they completely merge there will be no separating them.

It's like the Khelana, just below the point where a stream enters the river. For a time the smaller current might manage to carry itself intact among the mightier waters. Soon however, the greater river inevitably engulfs the lesser flow.

How could she keep Octavia's energy from losing itself inside the mightier mirror?

When Papa needed to push the raft through the turbulent confluence of two or more currents, he just poled harder. That moved the raft but didn't stop the waters from merging. Halfnote sighed and drew another concerned prickle from Robbie. Papa squeezed her hand. She took a breath and remembered how Octavia held her concentration even as the glasses screamed during the test.

Focus.

How could she keep the energies separate? When the villagers at Palidoro decided they wanted to build a port, they dumped huge boulders in a curved line out into the Khelana. The wall diverted the fierce river current. It created a large backwater, perfect for harboring rafts and boats. Papa said it took three years of constant labor by nearly a thousand people to build that wall. Now Palidoro hosted a weekly market attended by hundreds of traders.

Would something like that work here? What kind of barrier could she build between Octavia and the mirror? And what good would it do, so long as Octavia remained trapped inside the glass? She would still die in the melting fire.

Halfnote knew how to damp fire. She'd learned the basic tones from Mama before she learned to walk. But dampening the fire would only leave the mirror intact and Octavia trapped. She needed a way to encircle her sister's energy, something to separate Octavia from the mirror and protect her from the fire. What would do that?

She could feel how the singers' tones captured the mirror. She could do the same for Octavia with cooling energy, couldn't she? But where could she find air cool enough to withstand the intense heat of the melting fire?

"Halfnote," Robbie said.

She shook her head. She needed to concentrate. She watched how the energy of Lorraine's song rubbed against the mirror's energy. The new master's tones focused the heat of the melting fire along the edges of the glass. Little flecks of mirror sparked and vaporized as the heat intensified. The mirror spirit grew more frantic as the temperature increased. The rising temperature and the mirror's frenzy only increased Octavia's absorption. Halfnote couldn't wait. The water in the little waterfall was cold; was it cold enough?

"Halfnote," Robbie said, louder this time. She frowned and patted his leg. *Not now.* Humming, she gathered the tumbling cold of the waterfall and inserted it *there*. The energy sliced quickly between Octavia's bright essence and the fierce red heat of the mirror.

It's working.

At least, it worked for a moment. Then the stream reddened and boiled away. The freshet did leave a clear boundary between Octavia and the mirror. For about three heartbeats. Then the line crumbled under the unrelenting attack of the singers' melting chant. It wasn't enough to insert coolness there. She had to find a way to keep it cool.

No hope

Octavia fought for balance as Lorraine, Frank, Martin, Ted and Phyllis flung their melting tones against her container. The heat grew worse. The mirror's exterior bubbled and dribble away. Octavia chanted and focused and swore, but nothing she did had any affect.

Curse my soft heart for holding back earlier. The singers' chant created a protective barrier that saved them both from the heat of the melting and thwarted Octavia's efforts to stop them.

She fell against the wall. Heat seared her arm. She jerked away. The burning and the charred flesh it caused vanished.

As the mirror dissipated it released more than energy. Octavia found herself racked by various diseases, then healed of them. Pox, congestion, thrush, twenty different poisons, heart spasms, arthritis, gout, even labor pains attacked her body, then vanished; all the while more and more of the outer mirror vaporized into smoke.

For a moment the pain disappeared and she felt a wonderful sense of refreshment.

Is that Halfnote's voice?

That vanished too and the review of illnesses continued.

I'm dying. No! Not now, not yet!

At Halfnote's age, or only a little older, she'd planned out her whole life: A brilliant singer of glass, naturally; a teacher of other brilliant singers; mother to several and grandmother to more. She had planned on dying old and wrinkled after a long career as Grand Mistress of Verre House. She imagined having a large flock of children and grandchildren gathered at her bedside to say goodbye.

I've never accepted failure. Dying now seemed like the ultimate betrayal: of herself, of Grandfather and the other singers; of Halfnote's trust; of all the ill.

Lorraine will never forgive me. How will she save Gregory and protect her unborn child?

Without the mirror the plague would rage unchecked.

No hope for Mother and Grandmother. No hope for the Samoyans and their prince; for Grandfather; for Falchion's family and the rest of Albermarle. All because she lost focus at one crucial moment. One mistake and she'd doomed the most important making she'd ever taken part in.

Oh Grandfather, I am so sorry.

And what of Halfnote and Father? Cadie and cousin Mischa? Little Robbie? Would the illness find them as well?

Octavia remembered her last moment of triumph, when she successfully completed the counter clockwise swirl in front of everyone, in spite of the glass' screaming. Would she trade the joy of that moment for one more instant of life?

Halfnote sings

Her head ached. She forced herself to focus. Sweat dripped off her chin and into her eyes. She barely dared notice it enough to wipe it away. Heat radiated from her skin as if she were consumed by the worst sort of fever.

"Halfnote," Papa whispered, clearly concerned. She twitched at this disturbance like a horse from the bite of a fly.

A memory surfaced: Octavia at her test, triumphantly completing the counter clockwise swirl even as the glass screamed. The double vibrato of Octavia's voice turned energy against energy, smoothly separating two smaller balls of liquid glass from the original molten globe. She rubbed away the sweat that teetered perilously at the end of her nose.

If she could apply the swirl to the current she sent to surround Octavia; if she could just push the current to roll counter to the mirror's energy it might keep the mirror's rising heat from affecting the temperature of her cooling current.

That's what the counter swirl did, after all. It separated things. Could she do it?

I know how Octavia did it. I see it in my mind. Can I do it?

I have *to do it to save Octavia.*

I will *do it.*

Halfnote stood up. She thrust aside the obvious worry rolling off Papa and Robbie.

Her mouth was half open, every fiber of her being focused on the image of Octavia at her test, in triumph, calling out the tones of the counter clockwise swirl.

She focused on the energies from the mirror and called out, in her strongest, clearest voice, the tones of the swirl.

"Halfnote." Robbie grabbed her arm but she refused to notice. "Listen to me. What are you doing?"

"She's gone mad." Papa's voice broke. "It's the strain. It's too much for her."

She ignored them. She drew a current of cold energy from the pool and sent it swirling toward the rapidly fading boundary between the energies of the melting mirror and Octavia's fiery spirit. The energies separated. The mirror's glowing heat touched but did not change the relative coolness of her protective current.

"Halfnote, please," Papa begged. "Sit down, at least."

Minute after agonizing minute Halfnote held her tones.

The mirror's energy vanished. Octavia's did not.

Now, at the end

Octavia heard Halfnote's voice again. This time her sister chanted the tones for the counter clockwise swirl.

Now I'm hearing things. By all the dragons, let this end soon.

The temperature in her quickly dissolving chamber became more bearable. Something soft and silver, like a cloud of mist, gathered around her. It thickened. She felt refreshed.

Halfnote's chanting grew louder. Octavia heard a subtle error in her sister's tones and instinctively added her own correcting voice to the notes.

With a sudden crackling, the mirror crumbled away. The protective fog dissipated. The golden wall of musical heat disappeared. Octavia stood on the making platform beside the melting box in the main creation room of Verre House.

Is this real or a last illusion?

Lorraine stood head back, palms toward the ceiling as she cried out the last melting tones. When she saw Octavia, the new master gasped and stumbled backwards. Frank and Ted gawped. Frank jerked his spectacles off, then put them back on again. Phyllis, behind her and so out of sight, screamed. Bald Martin hurried out from under the platform. His mouth fell open. Octavia, holding her head in her hands, sank to her knees in relief.

I'm alive. I'm really alive and free of the mirror.

"Octavia?" Lorraine asked. "Is it you? Are you all right?"

"Yes." The word stuck in her dry throat and she coughed to clear it. "Yes," she said again, looking around the making room to make sure it was actually true. "I am alive."

"How?" The petite blonde half turned, as if about to flee.

"I heard Halfnote singing." Octavia felt dizzy. "She used the counter clockwise swirl to protect me while you melted the mirror."

"*Halfnote* did that?"

"It was her voice. I couldn't mistake it for any other."

"And I thought you were gifted," Lorraine said, her voice husky. "But quickly now, go to your grandfather and show him that you're all right. He's in the sickroom, distraught at your loss."

Octavia found balance enough to regain her feet.

"Wait," Phyllis, still behind Octavia, shrieked. "How do we know … how do we know … anything? Is she truly Octavia? Is she a ghost? Is she a demon? Does she carry the *mortolo* within? This is sorcery, this is. I mean ..."

"Be silent!" Lorraine barked in her most vibrant command tones. Phyllis closed her mouth.

Glaring fiercely at Phyllis, the master singer walked over to Octavia, took a deep breath and grabbed her hand.

They locked eyes for a moment and then Lorraine clutched Octavia in a tight embrace. Thick tears covered Lorraine's face when she finally released her.

"Now, go to your grandfather. We'll clean up here."

Blinking back her own tears, Octavia hurried out.

"But what of the plague?" she heard Martin ask. "We still don't have a cure."

"I don't know," Lorraine said, her despair clear. "I don't know what we can do. But at least we are not murderers."

Halfnote felt the silence like a blow. Light-headed she stumbled back against the rock wall behind her. It felt warm.

"It's done. The mirror's gone."

"Yes it is," Robbie agreed, relief clear in his voice. "I don't hear it anymore either."

Halfnote laughed. It had worked, somehow. She had done it. Octavia lived!

"Stop it, Halfnote," Papa snapped. "Please stop it."

"It's all right, Papa. Octavia lives. Do you still hear the mirror talking in your head?"

"No. What does it mean?"

Destroyed

Octavia all but danced down the basement steps.

I'm alive. Alive and free, thanks be, thanks be.

The heavy mirror shield was still in place in front of the sick room. It took all of her strength to wrestle it aside, but the outer bolts on the door slid easily under her excited touch.

She pulled the door open.

Maru, flute in hand, stood in the entrance. He took a step back. His other hand dropped to his knife hilt.

Octavia just folded her arms and glared at him.

Maru paled. "Are you a ghost?"

"No more than you. I am alive and free of the mirror and glad of it. And if you'll excuse me, I need to see my family."

"Of course." Maru stepped back out of her way, returning to his usual courteous manner. And softly, so that Octavia only just heard him, the elephant keeper added, "I am so very glad that you have returned to us."

"Where's Grandfather? Where's Master Verre?"

"Over here, child." Alma sat in a corner lit only by one of the herb-burning braziers. "Thank the dragons you're all right. They said you'd been taken by the mirror."

"You're alive," gasped Argana before Octavia could answer. The midwife stood so quickly that she knocked over her stool. It clattered loudly against the stone floor. Intan Negarawan, who lay in a cot next to her, stirred and moaned.

"What happened to the mirror?"

"Destroyed." Argana's expression turned bleak. She found her discarded stool and sat again next to the Intan.

"Where is Grandfather?" Octavia demanded.

"Just here, child." Alma wiped tears from her eyes and grabbed Octavia in a fierce hug. "Master Verre was overwrought, believing you lost and him ill already with the sickness. I gave him some valerian, to make him sleep."

Grandfather lay under a woolen blanket on a wooden cot built so recently that Octavia could still smell the cedar boughs that made it. The skin of his face looked slack and gray. Octavia's heart tightened at the sight. She never imagined her grandfather could look so helpless.

"Speak to him," Alma said. "Your voice is better medicine than anything I have."

"Grandfather. It's me. I'm all right."

He did not respond. He lay silent except for the awful whistling breaths brought on by the illness. Grandmother and Mother lay still nearby. But ...

"Where is Halfnote?" Octavia looked around. "Didn't she stay here with you?"

"Master Verre sent them away with your father; Robbie and Halfnote, that is. He didn't think it safe for them to stay."

"He was right about that. But the quarantine ..."

"Won't stop your father," Alma said with a faint smile.

"If there is a way out why didn't he send them sooner?"

"There were risks either way, I think, given the quarantine. They are surely safe now, though."

Octavia frowned. "I ... I don't know about that. My heart says otherwise. I keep seeing ... When I was in the mirror ... and now ... I keep seeing Halfnote. It's like she's lost in the dark. Somewhere in the heart of the mountain. Almost directly beneath us, if that's possible. Whatever Father intended, I fear something's gone wrong."

Alma sat back, her eyes dark with alarm. "How could you know that?" Then she shrugged. "Might as well ask why the glasses scream their warning, or how a mirror can see a cure. I'll send the boys to check the tunnels. You stay here with Master Verre. Talk to him. Hold his hand. I feared your loss would be the death of him. He needs to know you're all right. It'll be a relief to get out of this stuffy room, in any case."

The cook pushed herself to her feet and dabbed at her brow with a corner of her linen apron. The air in the room did feel very hot and still. It stank of burnt herbs and the sweat of fever. Octavia thought again of Artemisia. She could see it clearly in her mind: the herb grew in the back garden. The wild kind, the one that grew next to the stone wall.

"Wait, Alma. I think I know how to cure the illness."

"You think ..." Alma frowned at her.

"Try an infusion of Artemisia."

"The cooking herb?"

"No. The weed. Common wormwood. It grows ..."

"I know where it grows," Alma snorted. "Can't get rid of the stuff, no matter how often I pull it up. I thought that elephant would eat it all, but no, it keeps growing back. An infusion of wormwood? Are you serious?"

"Quite serious. Tea from the leaves is best. The darker green the better. One cup a day for those still healthy until all danger is past. Three cups a day for the ill; five if they resist recovery." Octavia put a hand to her mouth.

What? Where had that come from?

Alma gave her a sharp look, then shrugged again. "Why not? We've tried everything else."

"And Grandfather needs some Hawthorn tea."

"That's a blood tonic."

"Yes, but it's also a restorative for the heart. His heart ... I think it could use some restoring."

The guard, Hugo, jumped up from his seat by the door.

Oh no.

"I'll help you gather the plants." Hugo bounced around the portly cook like a puppy begging to be petted. The young guardsman was all elbows and knees and eager to please. "I know what they look like. My mother's an herbalist."

"And you waited this long to say so?" Alma pretended to fuss. "You shouldn't hide your talents like that, young man. People will think you're afraid of a little work. Come on then."

The guard grinned and followed her out. Octavia, relieved, smoothed the blanket covering Grandfather. She looked up in time to catch Alma's sharp glance before the cook left the basement.

No, I can't explain it. Perhaps I am also overwrought and imagining things.

"Grandfather?" Octavia spoke quietly to avoid disturbing the other patients.

What a job it will be, to carry all of the ill out of this dank basement. Still, it had to be done. They needed fresh air, warmth and light, and soon. A knot formed in her stomach. At least Grandfather still breathed. His wheezing left no doubt of that. She squeezed his hand and was surprised when he squeezed back.

"Can you hear me? It's me, Octavia."

His grip tightened painfully. His eyes fluttered open, shut, then opened and fixed on her face. He took a deep, shuddering breath and clutched her hand to his chest.

"How do you feel?" Octavia put her other hand on his forehead. His skin felt hot and dry, not a good sign. An image of the garden weed Artemisia came to mind again.

He shoved himself up into a sitting position and put a trembling hand on her arm, then reached up to her face.

"Is it really you? But how? I saw the mirror take you. I saw you peeking out from it, just as Devin did. Was it truly just a nightmare?"

"Shhh. I'm safe now. You're the one we're worried about. You've taken ill. You're in the sick room with Mother and Grandmother. You must rest."

He fell into a sudden fit of coughing.v Octavia hummed the calming tune for him. His eyelids flickered shut and he let out a long breathe. Octavia sat back with her own sigh of relief. Suddenly, Grandfather started up, his eyes wide.

"Octavia! The mirror!"

"Shhh. I'm here. I'm safe. The mirror is destroyed. Now you must sleep."

"But ..."

She pressed his hand against her cheek. "I'm right here."

Eternity, or no time at all

Later, Halfnote would remember their time in the tunnel as an eternity or as almost no time at all. The darkness pressed against her from every direction. At least the tiny waterfall continued to burble cheerily along, easing their spirits. After a while, even Papa agreed that the singers must be finished. Still, he hesitated.

"We can't go back to town. Not with the guard on the other side of the door. I expect they will be especially unhappy to see us at the moment. We'll have to find a way to get Verre House's attention. I wonder how long it will take Alma to notice the lift is damaged."

"Not long," Robbie said in an unusually confident voice. "She uses it a lot. And I think it's almost time for lunch."

Halfnote's stomach growled in agreement.

"Well," Papa said, "at least we won't get thirsty."

They sat in the dark listening to the waterfall's music until they all fell asleep. Halfnote dozed with her head against Papa's shoulder. Robbie lay next to her, curled close for warmth. Papa sat with his head back against the wall, his arm around Halfnote.

"Halloo," a cheery and familiar voice shouted down the tunnel. "Is anyone there?" Papa banged his head against the wall as they all three started awake.

"Halloooo!"

"Hello!" Papa shouted back. "We're here! Who is it?"

It was Ted and Martin, carrying ropes and a wonderful amount of light in the form of two blazing torches.

"You shaved," Halfnote exclaimed. Martin blushed and put a hand on his bare cheek.

"I couldn't stand it any longer. Beards itch."

"Well," Papa asked. "How did it go? Do we have a mirror? Do we have a cure?"

Ted and Martin exchanged uneasy glances.

"Well, Trader, things didn't go quite as planned," Martin said. "We had to destroy the mirror." Papa blew out a breath.

"But we may have a cure."

"And don't worry, sir," Ted chimed in, "Octavia's fine."

"That's right." Martin agreed. "Octavia's just fine."

Papa frowned. Martin and Ted exchanged another uneasy glance. Ted looked down as if sorry he'd spoken. Papa opened his mouth, looked at Halfnote and Robbie and bit back his first words.

Halfnote did her best to look unconcerned. She knew what had happened. Octavia *was* fine. And did Papa really think she wouldn't hear the fear in Ted and Martin's voices?

"I'm glad to hear that Octavia is all right." Papa's face cleared a little. "A cure? Did you say we have a cure?"

"Well ..." Martin shrugged, "Alma says it will take a few days to know for certain."

"But she's optimistic," Ted supplied.

Papa considered the two nervous young men before him.

"Alma's always optimistic. Now, let's get out of here."

I heard your voice

Halfnote took in lungfuls of the wonderful scent of baking bread as they entered the kitchen. Alma gave each of them an enormous hug. She instantly sat Robbie down so that she could clean and bandage his bloody knees.

"And you get over here as well, Paul," she ordered Papa. "I need a look at that cut in your side."

"Wow, I had no idea those tunnels existed," Martin said.

"Now don't you boys go getting any ideas," Alma told Martin and Ted with a wink and a grin at Papa. "Those tunnels are a sacred Verre House secret. Don't start thinking you can use them to go visit your sweeties on the sly."

Papa threw back his head and laughed. At this moment, Halfnote thought, Papa's laughter was the most wonderful sound in the world.

"What's so funny?" Robbie asked her. She just grinned and shrugged. She didn't know and she didn't care. Martin and Ted looked equally bemused but they smiled all the same.

Loud voices carried in through the door to the front garden. Halfnote looked out to see Lorraine going toe-to-toe with Falchion, trading shouts. For all that the top of her head barely grazed the top of the metal worker's shoulder the diminutive blonde seemed to have the upper hand in the argument. Maru stood at attention to one side of Lorraine, his hand on his knife hilt.

Some city guards, including the red-headed woman, stood on the other side. Though they were next to Falchion, Halfnote couldn't decide if they were with him or against him. What did that mean?

"Looks like Lorraine could use some help," Alma said.

"Looks to me like she's handling things just fine," Papa said, still grinning. Martin and Ted headed outside, in case.

"Hold still, Paul," Alma fussed. "I need to wash this cut and bandage it. Halfnote, we need comfrey and linen strips. If there's any honey left, bring that as well."

"Um, Alma," Robbie said, "could get some lunch?"

"And I really need to talk to Octavia," Halfnote said.

"Yes you do," Octavia agreed as she entered the kitchen.

Halfnote flung herself into her laughing sister's arms. They clung to each other for long moments before either could speak.

"You saved me," Octavia said, laughing and crying at the same time. She hugged Halfnote so tightly the younger girl could hardly breathe. She didn't mind at all.

"I heard your voice when I was in the mirror," Octavia said. "However did you do it?"

"It was the counter clockwise swirl. I remembered how you did it at your test. I watched you practice it so often; I just knew, somehow, what to do."

"Oh my. What a singer you'll make. Even I couldn't do it that well until a few months ago."

Halfnote blushed. "I just wanted you to be all right." She hugged Octavia again.

Drinking the bitter worm

Grandfather slept through the next three days, stirring only when Octavia left his side. He barely noticed when Maru and Hugo carried his cot back up the stairs and put him in his own bed in the master suite. He woke with a start about mid-day, and then relaxed when he saw Octavia dozing in a chair beside his bed.

Octavia sat up and smiled.

"It's about time you woke up, Grandfather. We thought you were going to sleep the rest of the summer away. How do you feel?"

"Well enough. Just seeing you here is a tonic. I had the most awful dream about the mirror. What happened to it?"

"The mirror is destroyed. Melted away into nothingness. And the sickness is defeated, thanks to the cure it gave us. All those who took ill here in the glassworks are recovering.

"Grandmother and Mother are now up, helping to tend those few still abed. You are the toast of Albermarle. The council unanimously declared you a 'Son of Piasa' yesterday. I'm sorry you weren't there. Even Falchion has been forced to sing your praises."

Grandfather frowned and put a shaky hand to his head.

"Was it really all a dream then? I don't remember completing the mirror. I only remember seeing you fall into it. And ... and ordering its destruction. Your destruction."

Octavia took his hand in hers. "Those things did happen, Grandfather, but it's all right. You did what you had to do. We all did. Things worked out. Now messengers travel in every direction with the news: Fortis Verre dared the forbidden and so saved us all."

"I think this praise is misplaced."

"We have the cure, Grandfather. That's what matters."

"What is the cure?"

Octavia's smile turned wry. "Artemisia."

"Artemisia? Do you mean tarragon? The cooking herb?"

Octavia laughed. "No. Its poor cousin, the weed that the Khelani call 'the bitter worm.' We had some right in our own back garden the whole time."

"Huh." Grandfather lay back. "No wonder the doctors couldn't solve it. Artemisia. I wouldn't have considered it."

Halfnote heard the welcome sound of Grandpa and Octavia talking and paused with her tray just outside the door. Should she just go on in? She really couldn't wait long. Alma had given her a day's worth of chores, all to be done before the next meal. Besides helping with meals, she and Robbie had to collect and dry more herbs from the back wood.

She heard footsteps behind her and turned to see Maru. He smiled and bowed.

"I come to pay my respects to Master Verre and offer our goodbyes. My lord prince is on his way to the great lifts."

"And Gajah?" Halfnote asked.

"He travels always with the prince. The Intan is a trained *mahout* from his earliest childhood. The elephant is the symbol of his house, after all."

Maru bowed deeply to both Grandpa and Octavia while Halfnote set the tray on a bedside table. Octavia curtseyed in return. Halfnote thought Maru's eyes glowed when he looked at her sister. The younger girl offered him a cup of tea but the elephant keeper declined.

"Alas, I have only a moment to speak. My lord the Intan sends his greatest respects. He declares that the people of Samoya owe Verre House an unpayable debt. He begs that you nevertheless accept these few baubles as a token of our esteem." Maru handed Octavia a round leather bag tied off at the top with a red velvet ribbon. Her arms sagged under the weight of it. She quickly set the bag down on the table.

"It's very heavy." She glanced at Grandpa.

"Among our people," Maru added quickly, "to refuse the Intan's largesse would be an unforgivable insult. Such misunderstandings have caused more than one civil war."

"Certainly we have no desire to insult the Intan or the people of Samoya," Grandpa said gravely. His mouth quirked. "Give Intan Negarawan our thanks for his thoughtful gift. If you think it appropriate, please tell him that we," Grandpa paused, "tell him that the glass singers of Albermarle do not blame him for recent events. His people were dying. It was his duty to seek a cure."

Maru bowed low. "I know the Intan will appreciate your kind understanding. And again, on his behalf, I do thank you for the hospitality of your house. I must leave now to join him before he takes the lifts down to Kerguelen."

He offered a parting smile to Halfnote. She grinned and waved in return. He bowed again to Oct aviation. His eyes lingered a moment on her before he left.

Grandpa accepted the cup of tea Halfnote offered.

"Well," he said after a long sip. "I, for one, will be glad when I can put aside drinking this 'bitter worm'."

Halfnote giggled. The Khelani words sounded funny when spoken in the accent of Albermarle. Grandpa smiled.

"Halfnote, please tell Alma that I am ready for some porridge. And an egg. Poached, if she insists. I need my strength. There is much to do here in the House of Verre."

End

Author's Note

Dear Reader,

I hope you enjoy the stories of Halfnote, Octavia and the other glass singers of Verre House. It is your support and enthusiasm that continues to inspire the writing of these tales.
You can, if you like, leave a review to let others know how much you enjoyed the book.

Visit **www.facebook.com/halfnotesong** to find out what's new. And now, read on for a preview of *Octavia's Journey*, book two in the Glass Singers series …

Lynette Hill

Octavia's Journey

By Lynette Hill

Octavia looks into the mirror

Octavia pulled her mass of dark braids into a tight bun with quick, practiced hands. She glanced at the mirror to make sure all was in order. Her eyes flinched instantly away from the round glass' silver surface. Taking a calming breath she forced herself to look back at her reflection; and to keep looking at it until her heart's pounding slowed to normal.

Only the image of her own black eyes returned her determined gaze.

"I am Octavia Breydon, a singer of Verre House." Alone in her own room in the early morning no one else would hear. "I survived the monstrous mirror; perhaps not by my own voice, but still. I survived." She took another breath.

"As a result, I have a new gift to share."

Octavia smiled. Her double smiled back. See, her mirror image seemed to say, all is well. All will be well.

"Octavia?" Sylvia called. "Are you awake?"

Master Verre's Concern

Halfnote, youngest apprentice in the House of Verre, put the heavy tray on the table outside her grandparents' rooms. Both Grand Master and Madame Verre had recently recovered from the plague and so chose to breakfast in their own chambers.

She raised a hand to knock. She paused at the sound of

voices inside. Of course, she shouldn't listen. Of course, she couldn't help overhearing anyway.

"Fortis, you look nearly as ill as when you suffered from plague. Shall we bring Octavia in to diagnose this new ailment?" Grandma asked. Grandpa's voice rumbled in response, but Halfnote could not make out the words.

"Honestly, Fortis. Must you worry? Surely this new ability of Octavia's is a blessing and not a curse. She is well. Thanks to her we are all alive and well."

"This apparent gift ... I'm afraid it means the tainted mirror's influence on her has not ended," Grandpa said.

Oh no! Halfnote sucked in her breath. From the sound of it, so did Grandma.

"Will Octavia become *mortolo* after all?"

"Not a monster, no. I believe that danger is past."

"But ..." Grandma prompted.

"I don't know," Grandpa admitted. "I just don't know what will happen next. That is what concerns me. I have read every scroll in our library. I am writing to all of the most learned scholars. As far I can find out, no one else has ever survived the monstrous glass.

"That's why I asked Physician Cornelius to observe Octavia as she makes her diagnoses. If anything unusual happens perhaps he will know what to do. Perhaps you are right and I worry unnecessarily. Perhaps all will be well."

"But," Grandma prompted again. "You must have some reason for your concern."

"But ... there are rumors, stories from ancient times of glass walkers; people who deliberately entered living glass and returned."

"Alive?"

"Ye...es, though not always unchanged."

"Octavia appears ... better for her experience."

"I hope so. But she will now certainly be of interest to anyone who dabbles in the dark arts. I have already received some enquiries which give me reason for concern. If there is anyone out there still foolish enough to try creating living glass, they will most certainly have an interest in Octavia."

Halfnote considered her own encounter with the tainted mirror. Would it affect her as well? She didn't feel any different. She wanted to ask Grandpa but now didn't seem like the right time.

A Queen Watches

"Sandrigal, I do not understand. Explain what is happening in Albermarle. How could anyone survive the *mortolo*?" Bhima Suresha Niliya Anula, the Queen Mother of Samoya demanded. She stood in one of the outer rooms of her tower chambers, peering out the great window at the clear blue of the morning sky.

Queen's Companion Clara stood straight-backed beside the drawn curtain, hands clasped, attentive to whatever her mistress might require.

"I do beg your pardon, Brightest Star," Sandrigal, the Queen's Scryer replied. Light glinted off the intricate, interwoven dragons that made up his frame. "I can add little to what you already know. So far as I can tell, your great-grandson's report was correct in every detail."

"So this singer, Octavia, was truly devoured by the unformed healing mirror?"

"She was indeed, my Queen. Grand Master Verre was already ill with plague when they attempted to make the mirror. He fainted at a critical point and the singer naturally moved to protect her grandfather. She saved him but was taken herself."

"And yet she survived though the mirror was destroyed."

"As the Intan reported."

"Was the *mortolo* truly destroyed?"

"Yes, Illumined One. Completely destroyed."

"And yet, Verre House discovered and disseminated the cure to a plague no one else could stop. What of Octavia? My agents say she is now diagnosing the sick. Not only has she brought back the cure for the plague, but apparently for all other ailments as well."

"Indeed, my Queen. It does appear that Octavia absorbed the unformed mirror's healing properties. She now spends her hours observing the ill and providing remedies, as a mirror would."

"A human *Hygeia Potencia*," Queen Anula murmured in an awed voice. "In all your days, Sandrigal, have you ever heard of such a thing?"

"I have not. There is no precedent that I know of."

"Has she become a true creature of the mirror? I wonder ... I have heard stories of others who walked through living mirrors. Not through *mortolo*, of course, but formed and settled mirrors such as yourself. Having entered a mirror and returned once, do you think Octavia could do so again?"

A moment passed. Sandrigal replied, "It seems likely."

"Yes. Excellent. You will bring her to me. You can bring her to me, can't you?"

Sandrigal's silver surface rippled. Clara thought the mirror seemed agitated, if that were possible of a solid object.

"Sandrigal. Answer. Can you bring her to me?"

"Gracious Lady ... the matter is complex. Much depends on Melampus. Perhaps with his help ... at the peak of the full moon ... we are not yet certain she has changed ... "

"How can we know that?"

"Further observations ..."

"Pah. The time for watching is done. Now is the time to act. If we wait too long someone else will seek to use her. We will know for certain if she can do what I require when she enters the mirror."

"Apologies, Beautiful Queen, but I must recommend caution. If she has not already been changed Octavia might still be brought to us by Melampus' magic; however, once in the mirror she will not leave it. To waste such a talent ..."

"Inside the mirror, changed or not, will she do as I require?"

"If she survives the entry, oh Bright Star, I believe so. However, I do not believe she could live through such a thing unless she has truly changed."

"Surely this healing ability she now manifests is a sign of transformation."

"Not ... necessarily."

"Enough, Sandrigal. You grow as cautious as the girl's cowardly grandfather. It is time to put theory into practice. Clara, call Melampus. Our preparations begin immediately."

~~~

From *Octavia's Journey* by Lynette Hill.

Available soon on Kindle and in print from Amazon.

About the author

Lynette Hill is an American writer who lives in middle England with Ruth, her partner, and Badger, their cat.

As a print journalist in she watched elephant races and delved into the secrets of professional magicians.

On the web she covered amateur sports and recreation as a 'Going Out Guru' for the Washingtonpost.com's Entertainment Guide in Washington D.C.

As a freelance writer she explained whale hunts and the mechanics of flying squirrels for the Washington Post newspaper, among others.

When not writing she enjoys hiking, music and live theater. She is taking advantage of her time in England to explore places made famous through folklore and mythology.

She has climbed the coastline around King Arthur's castle Tintagel in Cornwall and visited his apparent burial place in the magical town of Glastonbury.

She knows where to buy a magic wand in London and has made a wish inside Oxfordshire's Uffington White Horse.

Her adventures and the *Glass Singers'* series continue.

Halfnote's Song is her first novel.

Octavia's Journey will be her second.

Printed in Great Britain
by Amazon